THE
CRANE
WIFE

Also by Patrick Ness

THE
CRANE
WIFE

PATRICK NESS

CANONGATE
Edinburgh · London

Published in Great Britain in 2013 by Canongate Books Ltd,
14 High Street, Edinburgh EH1 1TE

1

www.canongate.tv

British Library Cataloguing-in-Publication Data
A catalogue record for this book is available on
request from the British Library

ISBN 978 0 85786 871 8
Export ISBN 978 0 85786 872 5

Typeset in Sabon and Mrs Eaves by Palimpsest Book Production Ltd,
Falkirk, Stirlingshire

Printed and bound in Great Britain by CPI Group (UK) Ltd,
Croydon CR0 4YY

This book is printed on FSC certified paper

For Marc

*And all the stars were crashing round
As I laid eyes on what I'd found.*

The Decemberists

In her dreams, she flies.

I.

What actually woke him was the unearthly sound itself – a mournful shatter of frozen midnight falling to earth to pierce his heart and lodge there forever, never to move, never to melt – but he, being who he was, assumed it was his bladder.

He huddled under the covers, sending out mental feelers to see how urgent the call was. Urgent enough. He sighed. Forty-eight still seemed too young to be having to get up in the night so often to relieve what was patently an old man's need, but there would clearly be no getting back to sleep until the matter was addressed. Maybe if he was quick about it he wouldn't even really need to wake all the way up. Yes. All right, then. Here we go. Upright, down the hall.

He gasped as he stepped onto the bathroom floor, cruelly cold against his bare feet. The room had no radiator, just a mysterious flat pad-type thing on the wall – he could never describe it adequately to other people – that, when turned on, grew too hot to touch while also managing to not even vaguely warm the surrounding air. He'd been meaning to remedy the problem since he'd moved here after the divorce, but a ninth year had just passed, a tenth begun, and here he was, still freezing his toes and the surprisingly soft skin of his arches as he stood, naked, at the toilet.

'Cold,' he murmured, using the glow of moonlight through the window to more-or-less aim into the bowl, guiding the rest by sound once he'd got a stream started.

The winter had been strange and contradictory, as if it were battling with itself. Mild days, even sometimes gloriously sunny, but nights that were particularly bitter, the damp of the house making them seem even more so. A huge city allegedly thrummed and dazzled just metres from the man's doorstep, yet inside might as well have been draped in the chill fog of a hundred years past. At her last visit, his daughter Amanda had stopped halfway through taking off her coat and asked if he was expecting a plague cart.

He finished urinating, shook off the last few drops, then tore a square of toilet paper to gently dab away the excess from the tip of his penis, a habitual action that his ex-wife had inexplicably regarded with enormous affection. 'Like pretty eyelashes on a bear,' she'd said.

She'd still divorced him, though.

He dropped the square of paper into the bowl, leaned forward to flush, and in that ignominious moment the sound came again, heard consciously for the first time.

He froze, hand mid-way to the flush handle.

The bathroom window faced his small back garden, a narrow one that elongated back in perfect mirror of the two on either side, and the sound had clearly come from there, somewhere beyond the marbled glass.

But what on earth was it? It matched nothing in the hurried catalogue of plausible things it might be at this time of night in this particular neighbourhood: not the

6

unnerving scream of a mating fox, not the neighbour's cat trapped in his garage (again), not thieves because what thief would make a sound like that?

He jumped as it came yet again, slicing through the night, clear in a way that only very cold things are.

A word sprang to his groggy, shivering mind. It had sounded like a *keen*. Something was *keening* and it welled him up with entirely unexpected, in fact, frankly *astonishing* tears. It tore at his heart like a dream gone wrong, a wordless cry for help that almost instantly made him feel inadequate to the task, helpless to save whatever was in danger, pointless to even try.

A sound which, later on, when he remembered this night forever and always, thwarted all sense. Because when he found the bird, the bird made no sound at all.

He rushed to his bedroom to dress: trousers without underwear, shoes without socks, jacket without shirt. He didn't look out of any of his windows as he did so, the one logical action, simply checking on what the sound might be, left bafflingly undone. Instead, he moved with instinct, feeling somehow that if he hesitated, it – whatever it might be – would somehow slip away, dissipate like a forgotten love. He merely moved, and quickly.

He bungled down the stairs, fiddling his keys out of his trouser pocket. He stepped through the cluttered sitting room and into the kitchen, angering himself at how loudly the keys banged against the back door lock (and who had a key lock on the *inside* of a house? If there was a fire, then *whoof*, you were gone, banging on a door that would never open. He'd meant to fix that as well, but ten years later . . .).

He opened the door, swinging it out into the freezing

night, knowing that whatever had made that noise *must* be gone, surely, in all the racket he was making from his clumsy door-openings and key-clatterings. It would have fled, it would have flown, it would have run–

But there it stood. Alone in the middle of the modest stretch of grass that made up the modest back garden of his modest detached home.

A great white bird, as tall as he was, taller, willowy as a reed.

A reed made of stars, he thought.

Then, 'A reed made of stars'? *Where the hell did that come from?*

The bird was illuminated only by the moon in the cold, clear winter sky, shades of white, grey and dark against the shadows of his lawn standing there regarding him, its eye a small, golden glint of blinking wet, level with his own, its body as long as he'd been when he was at his teenage gangliest. It looked somehow, he stupidly thought, as if it was on the verge of speaking, as if it would open its pointed, clipped bill and tell him something of vital importance that could only be learnt in a dream and forgotten on the instant of waking.

But he felt too cold under his one layer of clothes for this to be a dream, and the bird, of course, remained silent, not even a repeat of the keening that could only have come from it.

It was magnificent. Not just in its unexpectedness, its utter incongruity in the backyard of a London suburb celebrated for its blandness, a place from where native-born artists were noted for moving away. But even in a zoo, even to a non-bird lover, this bird would have caught the eye. The staggering whiteness, even in the dark, of its breast and neck, a whiteness that seemed as much a part

8

of the cold as the frost on the grass behind it. The whiteness flowed down into its wings, the one on the side facing him dipping almost low enough to brush the grass.

Triangles of black pulled away from its bill on either side, and a startling cap of red crowned its head, distinguishable even in this low light, like a military insignia for somewhere impossibly foreign. Its stare was commanding, unyielding in that way of birds. It knew he was there, it met his eye, and yet it didn't start or fly away or show any fear.

Or rather, he thought, the fear it showed wasn't of *him*.

He shook his head. These thoughts weren't helpful. The cold, far from waking him, was so ferocious it was actually making him sleepier, and he thought for a moment that this must be how people die in snowstorms, this lethargy which felt warm against all available evidence. He rubbed his arms, then stopped should the action startle the bird away.

But the bird remained.

A heron? he thought. *A stork?* But it was nothing at all like those hunched, purplish grey birds he sometimes saw skulking around the city like unwashed old gentlemen.

Then, for the second time that evening, the word came to him. Who knew if he was right, who knew such things any more, the right words for birds, the right words for anything, who bothered to remember them in an age when knowledge was for putting into a cloud and forgetting, then forgetting again that you ever needed to remember it? But the name came to him, and regardless of where it might have come from or how it might be right, it *was* right. He knew it, and speaking made it more so.

'A crane,' he said, softly. 'You're a crane.'

The crane turned, as if in answer to his naming of it,

its eye still on his, and he could see that the wing the bird had kept behind it wasn't folded down like the nearside one. It was outstretched, awkwardly.

Because it was shot through with an arrow.

'Oh, shit,' the man whispered, the words appearing before his lips in a fruitless puff of steam. 'Oh, no.'

The arrow was long, extraordinarily so, at least four feet, and the more it resolved in the man's vision, the more he could see that it was some kind of terrifyingly *proper* arrow, too, with crisply cut feathers fletched up in three evenly spaced rows around one end and a glinting, shiny arrowhead easily the width of two of his fingers at the other. There was something weirdly ancient about it as well, something that hinted at its carving from authentically expensive wood, not balsa or bamboo or whatever chopsticks were made of, and it was a whole world more serious than the business-like rods you saw fired on the Olympics coverage of smaller nations.

This was an arrow for killing. An arrow for killing men, even. An arrow over which a medieval archer might have prayed that the grace of God would bless its arc and send it straight into the rancid heart of the infidel. The man could see, too, now that he was looking for it, the dark stain at the crane's feet where its blood had dripped from the arrow's tip onto the frosted grass.

Who in the world would fire such a thing these days? And *where*? And, for God's sake, *why*?

He moved forward to help the crane, not knowing what he might do, feeling certain he would fail, but he was so surprised when it didn't back away from him that he stopped. He waited another moment, then found himself addressing it directly.

'Where have you come from?' he asked. 'You lost thing.'

The crane remained silent. The man remembered again the keening he'd heard, felt an echo of the mournful pressure of it in his chest, but no sound came now from the bird. No sound came from anywhere. The two of them could have been standing in a dream – though the cold that shifted through his shoes and bit at his fingers suggested otherwise, and the quotidian leaking of a stray drop, despite his best efforts, onto the crotch of his underwear-less trousers told him definitively this was still real life, with all its disappointments.

But if it wasn't a dream, it was one of those special corners of what's real, one of those moments, only a handful of which he could recall throughout his lifetime, where the world dwindled down to almost no one, where it seemed to pause just for him, so that he could, for a moment, be seized into life. Like when he lost his virginity to the girl with the eczema in his Honours English Class and it had been so intensely brief, so briefly intense, that it felt like both of them had left normal existence for an unleashed physical instant. Or that time on holiday in New Caledonia when he'd surfaced from snorkelling and for an oddly peaceful moment or two he'd been unable, due to the swells of the ocean, to even see the boat from which the divers had leapt, and then the angry voice of his wife had shouted 'There he is!' and he'd been sucked back into reality. Or not the birth of his daughter, which had been a panting, red tumult, but the first night after, when his exhausted wife had fallen asleep and it was just him and the little, little being and she opened her eyes at him, astonished to find him there, astonished to find *herself* there, and perhaps a little outraged, too, a state which, he was forced to admit, hadn't changed much for Amanda.

But *this*, this moment here, this moment was like those, and more so. The gravely injured bird and him in a frozen back garden that could have been the borders of the known universe for all he knew. It was in places like this that eternity happened.

And as he watched, the crane took a single step to the side, and stumbled.

He leapt forward to catch it, and like that, it was in his arms, the surprising weight of its upper body and its reaching neck (so like a swan's but so different, too), its good wing flapping and out.

And the smell! Of panic and shit. Of blood and fear. Of the impossible labour of flight that seeps through every atom of a bird. The smell, more than anything, convinced the man this wasn't a dream. Even in his worry about hurting the crane, even in the sudden calamity of flapping wings and flying feathers and the stabbing of a beak that looked as if it might well be able to go straight through his chest and into his heart, he knew that his brain – likeable though it was – was incapable of conjuring a scent this crowded, this peopled by so many different spices.

'Whoa, there,' he said, the bird twisting, fighting, perhaps realising too late that a separate, possibly predatory creature now had it in its grasp. The beak poked again, notching his cheek, drawing blood. 'Dammit!' he said. 'I'm trying to help you.'

At which the crane leaned back its neck, its head reaching to the sky, and it opened its beak to call.

But it didn't call. It gaped silently at the moon, as if breathing it out.

The crane's full weight suddenly pressed against the man's chest. That long neck fell forward like a ballerina's arm accepting applause, and it wrapped around him, its head hanging down his back, as if embracing him. Only the heaving of its narrow breast told the man that the bird was still alive, that in its exhaustion it had given itself into his keeping, that it would hand over its life to the man if that was what was required.

'Don't die,' the man whispered, urgently. 'Please don't die.'

He knelt down into the grass, the frost instantly wetting his knees, and with one arm still around the body of the crane, he used his free hand to gently grasp the arrow-pierced wing and unfurl it.

The span of a bird's wing is mostly feather; the meat of the muscle that regularly performs the casual miracle of self-activated flight is entirely in a long, narrow arm above the spray of feathers below. The arrow had pierced this length of sinew on the underside, catching quite a lot of white feather but still hitting more than enough muscle to have lodged, seemingly irrevocably, through the crane's wing.

The man wondered if he should call someone who'd be about eight million times more qualified to help than he was. But who? The RSPB? A vet? At this time of night? And what would they do? Would they 'put it down'? A crane so gravely injured?

'No,' whispered the man, though he was unaware of doing so. 'No.'

'I'll help you,' he said, more loudly. 'I'll try. But you have to hold still for me, okay?'

Foolishly, he found himself waiting for the bird's response. All it did was continue its desperate breathing against his neck. The arrow had to come out, and the man had no idea how he was going to do that, but that's what needed to be done and he could feel himself already manoeuvring the crane to do so.

'All righty then,' the man said, and then he said it again. 'All righty then.'

He cradled the bird's weight away from him, and with no small amount of awkwardness, he worked his way out of his jacket, gently moving the crane's head and neck to slip the cheap fabric from underneath. One-handed, he stretched the jacket out on the frost and laid the crane down onto it, folding its good wing beneath it. The crane acquiesced with an ease that terrified him, but he could still see it breathing, its chest rising and falling, more rapidly than seemed right but at least still alive.

The man was now naked from the waist up, kneeling in frozen grass, on a clear night in a cold season that could very well kill him if he stayed. He worked as quickly as he could, keeping the crane's injured wing unfurled in a vertical from the ground. He – along with conceivably everyone else in the entire world – had only ever seen arrow injuries in the movies. The rescuers always broke the arrow and pulled it out the other side. Was this even the right thing to do?

'Okay,' the man whispered, taking hold of the arrow's end in one hand and slowly letting go of the injured wing with the other, so that all that was holding up the crane's wing was the arrow itself, now in both his hands.

It felt shocking against his fingertips, even though they were quickly numbing in the cold. The wood was surprisingly light, as it would have to be for an arrow, but still

14

signifying strength with every inch. He looked for a weak spot, found none, and felt increasingly sure of his inability to break it, certainly of his inability to break it without having to try several times and cause the creature unthinkable agony.

'Oh, no,' the man mumbled to himself again, starting to shiver uncontrollably now. 'Oh, shit.'

He glanced down. It looked back at him with that golden eye, unblinking, its neck curved against his coat like a question mark.

There was no solution then. It was too cold. *He* was too cold. The arrow obviously too thick and strong. It might as well have been made of iron. The crane was going to die. This reed made of stars was going to die right here, in his sad little back garden.

A tidal wave of failure washed over him. Was there another way? Was there any other way at all? He turned back to the door to his kitchen, still open, letting out every bit of meagre warmth from the house. Could he carry the crane back inside? Could he lift it and get it there without hurting it further?

The crane, for its part, seemed to have already given up on him, to have already judged him, as so many others had, as a pleasant enough man, but lacking that certain something, that extra little ingredient to be truly worth investing in. It was a mistake women often seemed to make. He had more female friends, including his ex-wife, than any straight man he knew. The trouble was they'd all started out as lovers, before realising that he was too amiable to take quite seriously. 'You're about sixty-five per cent,' his ex-wife had said, as she left him. 'And I think seventy is probably my minimum.' The trouble was, seventy per cent seemed to be *every* woman's minimum.

15

Seventy seemed to be the crane's minimum, too. It had made the same mistake as all the others, seeing a man when, upon closer inspection, he was only really a *guy*.

'I'm sorry,' he said to the crane, tears coming again. 'I'm so sorry.'

The arrow moved unexpectedly in his hands. The crane, seemingly in an involuntary shudder, nudged its wing forward and the arrow slid through the man's fingers.

And stopped.

The man felt something. A small crack in the wood of the arrow. He looked closer. It was hard to see in such dim light, but yes, definitely a crack, one big enough to follow even with frozen fingertips. It spliced through the shaft, no doubt broken there by the struggles of the crane's great wing. The man could even feel that the arrow was at slightly different angles on either side of it.

He looked back down at the crane. It regarded him, thinking who knew what.

An accident, surely. Absurd to think that the animal would have led his fingers to it.

But also absurd that a crane with an arrow through its wing had landed in his back garden.

He said, 'I'll try.'

He gripped the side of the arrow closest to the pierced wing and held it as steadily as he could. He took the other end in his fist near the crack. The cold was so fierce now that he was feeling actual pain in his hands. It would have to be now. It would have to be right now.

'Please,' the man whispered. 'Please.'

He broke the arrow.

* * *

A massive sound rent the air, not from the breaking arrow but as of an enormous flag slapping in a gale. The crane surged to its feet, flinging wide both its wings, and the man fell back in surprise onto the concrete slabs at the edge of his lawn. He threw up an arm to protect himself as the pointed end of the arrow flew free, bouncing harmlessly off his arm and leaving a smear of the crane's blood across it, the other half disappearing into darkness. He would never find either, always firmly believing that the blood had been too tempting for a starving winter fox not to carry them off.

The bird stood above him now, reaching its head up into the night and calling silently again at the moon. Its wings, fully unfurled, were wider than the man was tall. The crane flapped them in long, slow, powerful movements. It shook the damaged wing once, then once more. The man could still see blood staining the feathers from the wound, but the crane seemed satisfied with its performance.

It stilled itself, its wings reaching out as far as they could go.

It turned its head to regard him with that unblinking eye, a shock of gold under its dark, red crown. The man wondered for a fanciful moment if it was going to reach down and scoop him up in those wings, as if this was some kind of test that he'd passed, one that, had he failed, he would never have remembered taking.

Then he found himself saying something stupid, something that made no sense at all.

'My name,' he said, 'is George.'

He said it to the crane.

As if in answer, the crane bowed its long, long neck low towards the ground, keeping its shoulders up and wings out. It began flapping them in a different way, one that caused it to almost fall forward onto the man. He scooted back some more, and when the crane left the ground its burning white breast soared an inch from the man's upturned nose. He looked back to watch it veer sharply upwards to avoid running into his house, carrying on up to the peak of his roof and alighting there for a moment. The moon was bright behind it, cutting it into a frozen silhouette.

It ducked its head once more, unfurled its wings, and swooped down over the back garden, its thin black legs trailing behind it, then up and up and up and up and up, until it was nothing more than one star among many in the night sky and soon not even that.

The man, George, rose slowly from the icy ground, a worrying ache starting to curl through his bare torso. He was shivering so badly now it was all he could do to stand, and he wondered if he was falling into shock. He would need a warm bath, and he'd need it soon, though he was already wondering if he'd have the strength to make it back inside—

A jolt ran through his body as he heard it, one more time. The *keening*, the mournful call that had brought him out here in the first place. It echoed through the frosty, clear air, as if it was the night itself calling out to him. The crane was saying its goodbye, its thank you, its—

And then he realised that the call hadn't come from an impossible bird vanishing from his garden and life and out of the whole world for all he knew. The keen had been set free from his own body, cried out from icy blue lips, torn from a chest that suddenly seemed to hold his irreparably broken yet still beating heart.

'**B**ut this says *Patty*.'
    'Yes, that's what it says here on the order form, too.'

'Do I look like a Patty to you?'

'I suppose they could have thought it was for your wife.'

'My wife is called Colleen.'

'Well, then, Patty would have clearly been wrong for *her*–'

'I saw the man type it in myself. Pea, ay, double dee, why. Paddy. And yet, follow along with my finger here as I underline the letters, this very, very unambiguously says *Patty*.'

'Which is what it says here on the order form.'

'But which is not what I saw the man type.'

'I'm guessing maybe they looked at the vest and thought that since it was so *pink*–'

'They? Who are they?'

'The printers.'

'This isn't a printers?'

19

'Not *that* kind of printers. We're more of a flyer, poster-design kind of–'

'So you're a printing shop that doesn't do its own printing.'

'Not at all, as I say, we're more of a flyer–'

'Regardless, for printing onto running vests–'

'And t-shirts.'

'What's that?'

'It's not just running vests we send out. T-shirts, too. Hen nights, stag dos, that kind of–'

'You send them out.'

'We send them out.'

'With specific orders that someone in this shop types into a form on your screen there.'

'Yes.'

'So when I saw the man, quite a bit older than you, which is to say a grown-up, he typed in, before my very own eyes, Pea, ah, double dee, why–'

'That would have been the specific orders to the outside printing company, yes.'

'Which they didn't follow.'

'According to you, anyway, but it clearly says *Patty* on the order form–'

'DO I LOOK LIKE A PATTY TO YOU?'

'There's no need for the shouting. We're just trying to solve a problem, two reasonable men–'

'Neither of whom are called *Patty*.'

'I'm from Turkey. We don't have Paddy versus Patty, okay? So how am I to know? Like I said, they probably saw the colour of the vest–'

'That's the colour of the charity. Pink is the colour of the charity. Breast Cancer. Pink. Because it affects women. Mostly women do the fundraising, but some men do, too.

We run, we raise money. It's the colour of the *charity*. It has nothing to do with the gender of the vest.'

'Well, now, see, that's interesting. Would you say vests *had* genders?'

'Yes, I *would* say that. Men's extra large. It's right there on the tag. Men's. Extra. Large. Really, am I being filmed? Is that what this is? Ah, *here's* the guy–'

'What's going on, Mehmet?'

'Customer here not happy with his order, Mr Duncan.'

'Do I look like a Patty to you?'

'I couldn't really say without knowing you better, but I'm guessing no.'

'Then why does this say–'

'Obviously an error. I very clearly remember typing in Paddy with two dees.'

'*Thank* you.'

'We'll get that fixed for you overnight.'

'The race is on Sunday.'

'And overnight will be Friday. It'll be fine.'

'I'm just saying there's no room for error. Any *more* error.'

'Don't you worry. You've got my personal guarantee.'

'You hear that? George Duncan's personal guarantee.'

'Which means exactly what?'

'It'll be here tomorrow, Paddy, I promise you. If I have to drive to St Ives–'

'Your printer's in *St Ives*?'

'If I have to drive to St Ives and pick it up myself.'

'That's a twelve-hour round trip.'

'You've done it? I've found the A30 not too bad if you–'

'Just . . . By tomorrow, please. Spelled properly.'

'You have my word.'

'. . .'

'. . .'

'. . . Well, *he* was a grouchy one.'

'Stop winding up the customers, Mehmet. There's a recession on.'

'Ah, see, another good point. *With the recession on, Patty, does the misspelling of one's name really amount to so very, very much—*'

'What do I keep saying? Customer service. It's not something I've just made up to punish you.'

'They only do that stuff in America, George. Can I Help You, Sir. You Look Fabulous In That, Sir. Can I Get You Some More Iced Tea, Sir.'

'. . . so you've never *been* to America then.'

'Television. Exactly the same thing.'

'Please, just call St Ives, tell them we have an urgent correction. And while you're at it, ask them where the Brookman Stag Do t-shirts are. The boys are leaving for Riga tonight and they should have been here by—'

'Brookman?'

'. . . Oh, what's that look, Mehmet? I don't like that look. Please tell me—'

'The Brookman ones have already gone out. He came by when you were at lunch.'

'Oh, no. No, no, no. I checked the order myself and all that had come in were—'

'The light blue ones with the kittens on the front.'

'Those were the O'Riley Hen Night! Why on earth would light blue kittens be for a stag do? They even *said* Hen Night—'

'We don't have hen nights in Turkey! How am I supposed to know the difference?'

'You moved here when you were *three*!'

22

'What's the big deal? They'll all be so drunk, who's going to notice?'

'I suspect ten soldiers from Her Majesty's Coldstream Guards might notice that a light blue cartoon kitten with a hand over its genitals isn't quite–'

'Paw.'

'What?'

'If it was a kitten, it'd be a paw. And what's it supposed to be doing, anyway? Pleasuring itself? Because how is that a theme for a hen night?'

'. . .'

'What?'

'Call Brookman, Mehmet. He obviously hasn't opened his box of t-shirts yet for whatever reason–'

'Yeah, he did seem in a bit of a hurry. Not even enough time to look at them.'

'. . . You're smiling.'

'I'm not.'

'You are. You did it on purpose.'

'I did not!'

'Mehmet!'

'You accuse me of everything! It's racist!'

'Call him. Now.'

'I don't see why I have to do all the crappy jobs around here. All you do is moon around in the back making your precious little *cuttings*. Like what's that one even supposed to be?'

'What one?'

'The one you've been carrying this whole time. The one you just hid behind your back.'

'This? This is nothing. This is–'

'Looks like a goose.'

'It's not a goose. It's a crane.'

'A crane.'

'A crane.'

'. . . like the kind that builds buildings? 'Cause, George, I hate to break it to you–'

'Go. Now. Now, now, now, now, now–'

'I'm *going*. *God*. Slavery was abolished two hundred years ago, you know.'

'Yes, I know, by William Wilberforce.'

'And you wonder why no one asks you out. I really don't think women get turned on by William Wilberforce references. Not that I'd *know*, I'll admit–'

'I have had no problems with girlfriends, Mehmet.'

'You mean like the last one? The secret girlfriend no one ever saw who didn't have a name? Did she live in Canada, George? Was she called Alberta?'

'I don't even begin to understand those sentences.'

'Musical theatre reference. Like a foreign language to you. Which reminds me, I've got an audition–'

'Yes, fine, whatever, just put it in the schedule and *make the call*. And don't spend a half hour twittering before you do.'

'*Twittering*. Was the world in colour yet when you were born, George? And gravity all the time?'

'Do you honestly think you're a quality enough employee for me not to fire you?'

'Oh, here we go. "It's *my* shop. *I* own it–"'

'I *do*.'

'Fine. I'll leave you here alone with your goose.'

'Crane.'

'Well, I hope you're gonna label it, because no one is ever going to think "crane" when they see that.'

'It's not for everyone. It's . . .'

'It's what?'

24

'Nothing.'

'No, you've gone all bashful. You're even *blushing*!'

'No, stop, what? Nothing, no. I just. Saw a crane. Last night.'

'. . . by "crane", do you mean "prostitute"?'

'No! Jesus Christ, if you must know, a crane landed in my garden.'

'. . . And?'

'And nothing, go make the calls!'

'Fine, watch me walking.'

'And quit sighing like that.'

'Customer, Mr Duncan.'

'What?'

'I said, *customer*, George. Behind you.'

'I didn't hear the door–'

'. . .'

'. . .'

'. . .'

'Can I . . . ?'

'My name,' she said, 'is Kumiko.'

People were always surprised to find out that George was American, or at least that he had started life that way. They told him he didn't 'seem' American. When asked what exactly this entailed, they would look uncertain – not uncertain about what 'seeming' American might mean but uncertain about how badly they wanted to offend him.

These people, friends even, many of them highly educated, many who had visited America several times, were surprisingly difficult to budge from their assumption that, George aside (of course, of course), his 300 million compatriots were all of them passport-less, irony-hating Jesus-praisers who voted for apparently insane politicians, all the while complaining that their outrageously cheap petrol wasn't nearly cheap enough. 'America is,' they would say, and so confidently, without fear of contradiction or rebuttal to anything that followed.

'*The New Yorker*,' he would reply. 'Jazz. Meryl *Streep*.'

This usually just prompted them to try out their approximation of an American accent, all wheedling brightness and too much blinking. At least it had morphed over the years; for a full decade after he'd moved to England, people would dive ecstatically into J.R. Ewing's worst twang. 'I'm from Tacoma,' he would say.

No one wanted to hear that people other than themselves might be complicated, that no one was ever just one thing, no history ever just one version. It was oddly hard for them to accept that, though American, he was neither from the Deep South or the East Coast, that his upbringing was in the Pacific Northwest, where the accents were mild and nearly Canadian, and even though his parents had ticked a stereotypical box by being regular church-attenders – which, all right, it *was* difficult to find American Protestants who weren't – they'd been slightly *laissez-faire* about it, as if it were a duty, like vaccinations. His father had been a secret smoker, for example, even though the church was of an evangelical strain and frowned on such things. George also knew from a startling, never-to-be-discussed accidental sighting that his parents occasionally rented pornography on VHS from the gas station down the road. 'People are legion,' he would insist, 'even when it's inconvenient to a worldview.'

Take his one anomalous school year. Even *that* wasn't a simple story, as if there were any such things. He had sailed through kindergarten (though who doesn't sail through kindergarten? he thought. Wasn't it basically just showing up and not choking on things?) and performed above his level through first and second grades – indeed, occasionally being sent up to fourth grade reading groups just to keep the boredom from setting in. The teachers loved him, loved his big blue eyes, loved a compliance that bordered on the slavish, loved a complexion that looked like he was about to grow a beard, aged six.

'Sensitive', they called him in Parent/Teacher Conferences. 'Dreamy, but in a good way.' 'Always with his hand in the air.' 'Such a special, tender little guy.'

'Not special at all,' said Miss Jones, in the first Parent/Teacher Conference of third grade, a scant two weeks after he'd started. 'And far too much of a smarty-pants. No one likes a know-it-all. Not the other students and certainly not *me*.'

George's parents had sat there in polite astonishment, his mother clutching her handbag as if it were a dachshund about to leap down and soil the carpet. His mother and father exchanged a look, his mother's face especially retreating into that shocked expression she always got when unexpectedly confronted by life. Which essentially was every time she left the house.

George knew all this because 1) they were the kind of parents who would go to every Parent/Teacher Conference (he thought it might be the 'only child' thing; they didn't want to miss even a moment, lest they irreparably screw something up) and 2) they'd been unable to get a sitter that night, despite the vast squadron of teenage girls usually on offer at the church, so he quietly drew with coloured pencils at a spare desk while his mother and father crouched, comically low, in the plastic children's seats before Miss Jones's desk.

But Miss Jones was only getting warmed up. 'I just cannot tell you how tired I am,' she said, lifting her eyes to Heaven as if praying for an answer to her tiredness, 'of *every* single parent coming in here and telling me how their little Timmy or Stephanie or *Frederico*' – she said the name so scornfully even George knew she was talking about Freddie Gomez, the only other boy who'd gone up to higher-grade reading groups with him and who smelled eye-wateringly of soap – 'is special and talented and God's gift to third grade knowledge.'

His father cleared his throat. 'We're not the ones saying it, though,' he said. 'The *school*–'

'Oh, the *school*, is it?' Miss Jones leaned forward, coming nearly all the way across her desk. 'Let me tell you something, *Mister* Duncan,' she said. 'These boys and girls are six and seven and eight years old. What do they know about anything except how to tie their shoes and not wet themselves when the bell goes? And not that all of them are so great at *that*, I can tell you.'

'Well, what does that have to do with the price of milk?' his mother said, in a tense, strangled tone that made George's ears prick. She was a nervous lady, his mother. She'd clearly been thrown off balance by Miss Jones's forthrightness, her volume, her – let's face it – blackness, and already he could see that things weren't going to go well. He went back to colouring every quadrant of Snoopy the same shade of green.

It was just this moment when Miss Jones made her mistake. 'Now, you listen to me, Mrs Duncan,' she said, and she stuck out her finger and shook it in George's mother's face. 'Just because your boy doesn't eat paste doesn't mean he's gifted.'

George's mother's eyes never left the end of the dark brown finger wagging so close to her nose, following it as it bobbed up and down in righteous instruction, invading George's mother's space in a way that even George found obscurely upsetting, and just as George's father said, 'Now, you listen here,' in his authoritative, construction foreman voice-of-doom, George's mother leaned forward and bit the end of Miss Jones's finger, snapping it hard between her teeth and hanging on for a surprising second or two before all the screaming started.

Now this story, when George told it, always made him nervous in that it gave slightly the wrong impression of his mother. Biting an obnoxious teacher's finger – though not drawing blood and not quite so painfully that Miss Jones couldn't be talked out of an assault charge by a principal who acted for all the world as if this wasn't the first biting-of-Miss-Jones incident to come across his desk – could easily be read as a heroic action. His mother was the star of this story, and why shouldn't she be? As family anecdotes went, it was a corker, retold with gales of laughter and at frequent request.

'And I thought,' his mother would say, blushing with horror and delight that every eye in the room was on her, 'someone's gonna bite that finger one of these days. So why not today?'

But George knew, really knew in his heart, that the biting wasn't the act of someone mastering a situation and bringing it to a close with the perfect outrageous resolution. His mother had *actually* bitten Miss Jones because of a certain detachment from reality, a certain panicky falling-away from things. She was anxious to the point of brittle, like a champagne flute – when, age nineteen, George finally saw his first champagne flute – that needed wrapping and packing away. His father performed this function, taking care of every emergency, handling every possible crisis. His love of his wife – and George was quite certain that he loved her – took the form of ongoing protection that perhaps, in the end, did her more harm than good.

When Miss Jones waggled the finger, George was pretty sure his mother hadn't felt insulted, she'd felt *attacked*, as if the world was tipping beneath her, and she'd bitten Miss Jones not as an act of triumphant assertion, but because she was trying to *hold on*. By her literal teeth. Life was unravelling under the threat of a single, terrible finger, looming as large as a coming apocalypse from which there would be no mercy, no forgiveness, just everlasting despair. Who wouldn't lash out in the face of such a terrible affront?

That his mother had gotten it accidentally exactly right, well, that seemed to be just one of those things, and a part of him was pleased for her that, for once, she had. But the story that was told and the story *underneath* that story were different things, and perhaps irreconcilable.

The immediate result, anyway, was that George was airlifted out of Miss Jones's third grade class at Henry Bozeman Elementary School and sent to the O Come O Come Emmanuel & Ransom Captive Israel Self-Directed Learning and Holiness Academy, which despite having 'Israel' in its name was wholly staffed by people who might never have actually met anyone Jewish in their entire lives. (Growing up in Tacoma, George knew any number of other evangelicals, plus a packet of Mormons, a few Catholics, and even practising Buddhists from the largest integrated Asian community in the country. Jewish people, not so much. He would only actually meet two Jewish people in his life before going to college in New York. Where he met several more.)

O Come O Come – loosely affiliated with his parents' church, if perhaps only by good intentions – had a student body of a mere forty-eight pupils, kindergarten through twelfth grade, with learning done from self-read (and often self-marked) booklets, plus a half-day on Wednesday when the O Come O Come visiting minister held a church service in lieu of afternoon classes. This involved songs and sermons and a once-weekly change from the school uniform of yellow shirt with green tie and trousers to *white* shirt with green tie and trousers.

George was eight, and at eight the definition of normal is whatever is happening in front of you. He glossed over the differences from public school – starting with the comprehensively pale ethnicity of his new classmates – and got on with it, doing his usual ingratiation with the two elderly bachelorettes who ran the school: Miss Kelly with her red hair pulled back so tight she looked permanently surprised and Miss Aldershot with her kindly eyes, hairy chin and vicious way with a ruler.

George enjoyed himself there, on the whole, though his standards weren't perhaps wildly high. He wasn't a fan of the school-wide dodgeball, which was about all the elderly bachelorettes could come up with by way of physical education, aside from the occasional round of jumping jacks and running in place (all done for brief, sweaty spates without ever involving the removal of a tie), but he liked their library, though even 'darn' and 'gosh' had been blacked out of the school's dog-eared copy of *The Incredible Journey*.

The boy closest to him in age there was Roy, an old-fashioned name even then, if not in quite the same way as 'George'. Roy was a year older, a year taller, a year wiser, all of which was proved by the fact that he had a bike.

'It's from the War,' he'd said to George when they first met. 'My dad brought it back. He stole it from the Japs after we bombed them.'

This was the seventies and Roy's dad was undoubtedly

not much more than an infant during Nagasaki, but George swallowed every word like God's Own Truth.

'Wow,' he said.

'That's why it's so heavy,' Roy said, tipping it up with some effort in his nine-year-old hands. 'To survive the grenade attacks when you ride behind enemy lines.'

'Wow.'

'When I get older, I'm riding it all the way to Vietnam and throw grenades at the Japs.'

'Can I try it?'

'No.'

The school was on 35th Street. Roy lived on 56th and George lived on 60th in a house no one in the family would remember fondly. Usually his mother, who didn't work, would pick him up at school and drive him home, but occasionally, when she was busy, he'd walk, going part of the way with Roy, who'd push the bike between them, its green metal bulk as steadfast and calm as a cow.

On this particular day, a spring one, the sun held court in the sky, with a few supplicant clouds criss-crossed by the vapour trails of jets from the nearby Air Force Base. Just the kind of lovely day when God liked to test you, Miss Kelly often said.

'So then you find out the whole ship is a gun, right?' George was saying, excitedly. 'The *whole* ship! And it shoots this huge blast of light out the end and BOOM! They destroy the Gamilon home world!'

Roy's family didn't have a television because TV was where the Devil did his best recruiting (George had decided not to mention this problem to his own parents, though in retrospect it seemed unlikely they would have agreed, given the porn), so George would often fill their walk home with what Roy was missing.

33

'Except it's not a whole planet?' Roy asked.

'No!' George shouted with amazement. 'That's the most incredible thing ever! It's *half* a planet and it's floating in space and there are cities on the top half and it's all rocky and round on the bottom. Except it isn't any more, because the Starblazers blew it up.'

'Sweet,' Roy said, with due respect.

'No kidding, it's sweet,' George agreed seriously.

They reached 53rd, the busiest street between O Come O Come and their respective homes. They walked past the supermarket on the corner, its parking lot filled with slightly sluttier versions of their own mothers, along with kids smaller than Roy or George who tended to stare at their uniforms. Across the street was a gas station, filled with much the same.

Roy and George waited at the crosswalk for the light to change.

'Except I think some Gamilons escaped or something,' George said, 'because no one seemed very happy. And there was also a lot of shouting and stuff I didn't understand.' He smiled again. 'But the whole ship was a gun all along!'

The light turned green, and the 'Walk' signal came on. They entered the crossing, Roy pushing his bike along, George caught up in the unfathomable mysteries of Japanese animation.

'I'm going to turn this bike into a gun,' Roy said. 'I'll take it to Vietnam when I turn sixteen.'

George said, 'That'd be.'

And the car hit them both.

When George told this part of the story, he invariably found himself saying 'This actually happened' and 'I'm not

34

making this up' because it seemed too cruel that the car that had run the red light and knocked into Roy and the bike and him should have been driven by an eighty-three-year-old lady who could barely see over the steering wheel.

Sadly, it was the truth. If George had ever learned her name, he'd long forgotten it, but he'd remembered that she was eighty-three, that she was barely taller than him or Roy, and that the words she kept repeating afterwards were, 'Please don't sue me. Please don't sue me.' For the dignity of old ladies everywhere, George often wished this part of the story hadn't happened, but there you were, sometimes life didn't oblige with appropriate variation.

She wasn't going especially fast, but the impact was so shockingly irresistible, so bluntly unstoppable, that both George and Roy cried out simultaneous, surprised 'Ohs!' as she drove into them.

And didn't stop.

There were theories about this afterwards, most of them unsurprising: that the impact had taken a short while to filter through her diminished-by-age capabilities; that it had shocked her so much that she had simply frozen, her foot remaining on the accelerator rather than moving to the brake; or that the disbelief at what was occurring in front of her was so strong that, for a few terrible moments, she simply expected someone *else* to act. Whatever the reason, she hit them, and on she drove.

Roy had seen her coming at the very last second and had taken a step back, though not nearly far enough. The car hit his knees, spinning him around and throwing him to the pavement, out of the way, as she ploughed on through George and the bike.

George saw the impact, of course, but he couldn't remember feeling it. Roy had been thrown out of his line of vision, and suddenly here was this massive, unstoppable block of metal filling it, knocking the wind out of him as he flattened his stomach across the bike seat and onto the hood of the car.

It didn't stop. It kept coming. There was nowhere for George to put his feet, nowhere he could stand that made sense as the ground was dragged away from underneath him, and he fell, still so surprised it was happening it seemed as if only his eyes were working, that each of his other senses – ears to hear it with, feeling to register pain – had been shut off.

He fell with the bike, its handlebars catching the front bumper, and as the old lady *still* drove on, ten, twenty, thirty feet past the crosswalk, George slipped all the way to the ground, the body of the bike pushing him along the road in front of the car. He remembered the sensation vividly, more vividly than any other detail of the accident. It felt like sliding on his back across snow, any feeling of pain from the scraping still just a future possibility. He was helpless to stop it anyway, his arms refusing to grasp anything, his legs refusing to push him out of the way, his head refusing to even look around for help.

What he remembered most was that it was, paradoxically, a moment of tremendous calm. All he saw was the sky above, its serene and soothing vastness, looking impassively down on him as he bumped and scraped along the pavement, pushed by a massive car and a fallen bicycle. It was a moment like when he found the crane, or the crane found him, a moment of stopped time, a moment to live in forever. He stared back up at the sky with a kind of ecstatic disbelief and was only able to ever remember a single coherent thought, 'This is really happening.'

'This really happened,' George would say as he told the story. 'It sounds like I'm making it up, but I'm really, really not.'

The handlebars dislodged from the bumper of the car, and the bike fell, but somehow – luckily? miraculously? improbably? impossibly? – did so in a way that the old lady's car pushed it to one side and George along with it. Instead of being crushed flat by the tires, George had a close-up view of them as they drove past, inches from his face as the car trundled down the road.

And then there was only silence. Utter silence. George, still on his back, glanced up the street and saw Roy. Such a little amount of time had passed that Roy was still lying on the road, too, struggling to get up. George did the same, and he and Roy discovered at the same moment that neither of them could walk. Both lurched forward and fell in exactly the same way.

Which made them laugh.

Nearly forty years later, George could still remember the feeling of that laugh, the sincerity of it, the *truthfulness* of it. In their mutual, eight- and nine-year-old shock, before the inevitable pain that hovered seconds away came rushing in, before the acceptance or even knowledge that they had just survived a possibly fatal calamity dawned, they had, for an instant, *laughed*.

But the world would no longer wait. What was probably not more than a dozen adults but what felt like *thousands* came running in a flood from the forecourt of the gas station and out the glass doors of the supermarket, unthinkable terror written so clearly on their faces that all at once the pain showed up, too, and George began, suddenly, to cry.

They put their hands on him and Roy, lifted them from

the pavement and out of the road, while some of them also went racing angrily after the car of the old lady, who was only just now coming to a stop a good hundred feet past the point where she'd hit them. These people called the ambulances that came, and a fire truck, too, that even in his bewildered pain, George thought was a bit much. He didn't remember giving anyone his phone number, but he must have because one woman said to another behind him – he remembered this part so clearly he could still hear the precise words to this day – 'Well, I called the mothers. One of them's fine, the other's hysterical.'

George's shoulders slumped, like a deflating ball.

Sure enough, his mother arrived in tears as unstoppable as the old lady's car, and the first words out of her mouth were – and George remembered this clearly, too – 'Why didn't you call me to pick you up?'

Now, the rarer times when he told this later part of the story, the part where his mother came off so badly, he would remind his listener that she had just heard the news that her eight-year-old son had been run over by a car, so she certainly had cause to be overwhelmed. But still, George found himself wanting to apologise to all the kind strangers who'd helped him for how his mother was acting, for how she was needing to be calmed by the ambulance driver herself, for how she was eagerly accepting an oxygen mask from a paramedic. This same woman who had so (ostensibly) heroically bitten Miss Jones's finger, now hogging the spotlight at her own son's car accident.

They lived. Of course, they lived. They hadn't even been that badly injured. No bones were broken, though Roy had torn ligaments in both his knees. George, though in by far the worst danger from the actual impact, came out of it better. Two huge bruises across both thighs that prevented him from walking for a week and a host of bloody scrapes across the back of his head and arms from being pushed across tarmac, but a breathtakingly minor haul of injuries from something that could have been so much worse. George, in fact, didn't even get an ambulance ride. It had driven off with Roy in the back, sirens wailing, and George was left with his own mother to take him to the hospital, weeping all the way, to the point where *he* had started comforting *her*.

She was so upset, in fact, that he never told her or his father what he realised even in his eight-year-old brain, which was that if Roy's bike hadn't been there, if it hadn't fallen in such a flukey way, first catching on the bumper to hold him in place, then coming dislodged at precisely the right moment to guide him clear, the old lady would have run right over him. The tires he could see turning through the frame of the bike – like dragons behind a cage, seconds away from eating him – would have driven over his head and neck.

But the unlikeliness of it all also meant that he wouldn't have had that moment of staring up into the sky, a moment where he had been the only person who had ever lived in all of glorious creation.

George had no idea of the fate of the old lady. Perhaps even more strangely, he had no other memories of Roy either. He couldn't even remember his last name or how well or badly he had recovered from his injuries. Nor could he place him back at O Come O Come, so perhaps he never even returned, his parents having who-knew-what reaction to the near death of their son. George did know that his own parents had given him $100 of the insurance

39

settlement to spend – he bought books – and then used the rest to re-carpet the house. But as for everything else? Well, he lived, and what could have been a tragedy became instead a minor story, to be told now and then by his mother, exclusively in the context of how upsetting it had been for her.

Time passed. The fourth grade teacher at the public school turned out to be a wonderful woman called Mrs Underhill, and for reasons unknown – probably financial, his parents not being people who could really afford even a heavily church-sponsored private school; though possibly also because it was, frankly, a bit of a weird place and there *were* limits, after all, for sensible people – George left O Come O Come and returned to Henry Bozeman the following year. He performed well, well enough that both the town and his parents started to seem increasingly parochial, until he won a scholarship to a university on the whole other coast.

Once in New York, Miss Jones was finally proved prophet. Whatever small scholastic flair George had shown seemed to throttle back towards average. He managed to scrape a post-grad scholarship that took him to England just in time for him to stop really caring about a degree altogether. It didn't matter. He met Clare at a party and rarely went home again, save for the funerals of first his father, from an on-site accident, then his mother, ostensibly from a heart attack but more likely from putting too much of her vital self into the keeping of her husband. Which happens. George settled in and had now lived in England longer than he had lived in the United States, which seemed like it should mean something important, but never actually quite did.

This story, though, had really happened, every detail,

despite all its improbabilities. When he talked about it now, he realised as the years passed that he was telling it less and less as an emblem of his own history, as a single strand that told part of his life.

Because all those people, yes?

All those people who ran from the gas station and the grocery store, those were the people George began to think about more as he got older, especially as he became first a father to Amanda, then a grandfather to JP. All those people, strangers whose names he never knew, whose faces he would never remember, all those random individuals who had seen two very small boys get run over by an old lady in a massive car.

Did *they* ever tell this story, he wondered? Even though Roy and George had fully recovered, there were those unbearable few seconds where their fate was in flux, where all that was knowable was that two boys were probably on their way to death and there was nothing, not one single thing, that any adult watching could do about it, something that George only fully understood one afternoon when Amanda, fifteen steps ahead of him on a pavement and still struggling with this whole new walking lark, had suddenly lurched sideways and fallen off a curb between two parked cars, momentarily disappearing from sight. She'd actually stopped crying when she saw how upset her own father was and how fiercely he held her to his chest.

George felt connected, *was* connected to those nameless, anonymous witnesses who were now unfindable, even in this unstoppably networked age. Their lives had intersected with his for a moment, something that real life did in various ways at every instant of every day for every person everywhere, of course, but it only ever really mattered when it was you, didn't it?

What was true, though, and what he thought about often, was that although he was the hero of his version of the story, naturally, he was also a supporting player in this same story when told by someone else. How did these people tell it, because it seemed likely they might? 'You won't *believe* what happened to me one day. I was at the supermarket, and I remember clear as anything, I'd bought a carton of cigarettes for Del and two bottles of grape juice. Don't know why I remember it was two, but then I just happened to look up . . .'

And what of the old lady? What story did she tell, if at all, in her presumably few remaining years? And what about the ambulance drivers who can only have quickly forgotten an incident where two boys were mildly injured?

For that matter, what would Miss Jones's version be like of the story where the crazy white woman bit her finger? Would it be any less true than his own? Than his mother's? Which between them were different enough already.

Did it matter? George thought perhaps it did, and not in terms of finding the truth or of any hope of discovering what *really* happened at any given moment. There were as many truths – overlapping, stewed together – as there were tellers. The truth mattered less than the story's *life*. A story forgotten died. A story remembered not only lived, but *grew*.

Whenever he finished telling someone his version of this story – his surprising American-ness explained, his late parents cast in their various thumbnails, the finger-biting that somehow led to a car accident – and the conversation then diverted itself down another track as someone else told their own story, he would often sit back a little, not listen very closely, temporarily retreating into his memory.

He would picture himself there, decades and an ocean and a continent away, under a beautiful blue sky, in the impossible silence of being pushed along a road on his back, under the watchful, terrified eyes of dozens of co-tellers, and because he could see it, and because *they* could, too, in all their different versions, as their lives crossed each other and bound together in what George could only describe as a mutual embrace, that moment still happened. It was *always* still happening.

And for that eternally repeated instant, pain was at bay, fear was held off, and everything was astonishment and wonder.

Things started to go wrong for Amanda this time when, of all the stupid places on this whole green earth, she and Rachel and Mei drove past the Animals In War Memorial.

'What a fucking disgrace,' Amanda said, alone in the back, despite being taller than Mei by almost half a foot and therefore a plainly more logical choice for the passenger seat. It reminded her, unavoidably, of trips as a child with her parents where she was expected to sleep her way to Cornwall across the back seat while George drove in his hummingly distracted fashion and her mother tried to catch up on legal briefs. It had already put a damper on Amanda's mood for today's picnic, but different arrangements were, it seemed, impossible. Mei always sat up front, and Rachel always drove, even though Mei and Amanda both had cars.

Those were the rules, among so many others. Amanda tried to follow them, but tended to fail on an ever-downward curve.

'What, *that*?' Rachel asked. Without lifting a manicured

hand from the steering wheel, she pointed at the huge wall of curved marble plonked on a stretch of extraordinarily expensive real estate in the middle of Mayfair. It was approached, humbly, by statues of a horse, a dog and possibly a carrier pigeon, though Amanda had never ventured close enough to be sure. Why would she? Why would anyone?

'Yes, *that*,' Amanda said, even though a part of her brain was already screaming warning signals. '*They Had No Choice*,' she read, intoning the motto of the Memorial in what she felt was a pretty fair approximation of Huw Edwards. 'Of course they had no choice! They were animals! It's an insult to the actual men and woman, actual fathers and sons and mothers and daughters who died in war to equate them with a fucking *Labrador*.'

There was a silence, as Rachel and Mei exchanged a look in the front seat, and Amanda knew then that she was lost, that this might not be the last time she was invited to cram into Rachel's car for a let's-*carpe*-the unexpectedly-sunny-*diem*-and-have-an-impromptu-picnic/endurance-session in the park with her and Mei, but the list of invitations had definitely become finite.

Even saying 'fucking' (twice) had been a bit of a risk, but she'd thought she was the friend among the three of them who swore, the friend who knew how to roll a joint if required (it had not yet been required), and the friend who'd chewed through her marriage with a lack of decorum bordering on the hyena-like. Rachel and Mei were both divorced, too, though not quite so young and not quite so vigorously. It was the role they'd given her, one she'd done her best to fill.

Oh, well, sighed the voice in Amanda's head. *Fuck 'em.* Even after eight months, Amanda was still the new girl.

She was a transport consultant, as were Rachel and Mei. They were three of nine women in a company of seventy-four, which *had* to be illegal. It wasn't that transport was such a non-woman sort of industry necessarily (though it was a little), it's that this particular company – Umbrello Flattery and Unwin – had a Head of Personnel (Felicity Hartford, unquestionably woman number one out of nine) who hated other women. She'd informed Amanda at her interview that Amanda was 'at best' the eighth most qualified applicant (of eight), but that even the elderly Umbrello Senior had begun to wonder why his newly-retired secretary had been replaced by a fashionable young man with what looked like a 'shaft of metal, Mrs Hartford' pierced through the skin under the back of his shirt collar. Before Mrs Hartford was 'bored into her grave by yet another lawsuit', Amanda would have to do.

Amanda worked in Rachel and Mei's unit – Mrs Hartford liking to keep the women in as few groups as possible, which made it easier to fire the worst one should she wake up in the morning with the inclination to do so – and they'd taken her under their wing as a fellow young divorcee. They invited Amanda out to lunch her first day, and in those forty-five minutes Amanda had learned not only that Rachel had put the naked pictures she'd found of her ex-husband's mistress on the memorial website of said mistress's late mother and that Mei struggled with thrush, but also that Rachel had survived – and possibly started – a house fire in college that had killed two of her roommates and that Mei had three separate, eye-watering anecdotes about circumcised men. 'Were they brothers?' Amanda had laughed, a deep, gravelly, dirty laugh she might have said was her best feature, had anyone ever asked.

No one had laughed back. It had been a long eight months.

'Can you get the picnic basket?' Rachel asked, as she pulled her Mini into a space.

'Sure,' Amanda said. She always got the picnic basket.

Mei got out of the passenger side, face concentrating hard on her phone. She was tracking her infant daughter on GPS during a visitation weekend with the baby's father. 'That's unbelievable,' said Mei, who didn't believe anything. 'He's taken her to *Nando's*.'

'What the fuck is in here?' Amanda asked, gracelessly dragging the unreasonably heavy basket out of the Mini. She felt like a rhinoceros backing out of a display cabinet.

'You know, you're twenty-five?' Rachel said. 'Which is younger than us, okay, I get that, but still too old to talk like you're on *Skins*?'

'Sorry,' Amanda grunted, as she finally got the picnic basket out of the car. Where it promptly plummeted to the ground. A puddle of wine bubbled out the basket's bottom like a particularly expensive spring.

Rachel sighed. 'That was like our only bottle of red?'

'Sorry,' Amanda said again.

Rachel said nothing, just let an awkward moment of silence pass while she waited for Mei to notice Amanda standing in the puddle of Pinot.

'Ooooooh,' Mei whispered, finally seeing. 'I don't believe it.'

Amanda always *started* well with friends. In primary and secondary school, in college, at the different jobs she'd had since graduating, plus of course the gang of friends that had hung around Henri. They all liked her when they first met her. Really, they *did*.

Things that might have been threatening in a man – her slight tallness, her slightly broad shoulders, her deep, commanding voice – were conversely disarming in a woman. Men would look at her and think 'woman' but also somehow 'rugby' and find themselves buying her a pint while asking her whether she thought that hot Dutch girl reading Economics would give them the time of day. Gay men rather liked her, which had its benefits but was also a bit like being spayed, while women seemed to cherish her at first as someone around whom they could *finally* be themselves, speak their minds, not feel so bound up in girly competitiveness. She was a proper *mate*, she was.

In this, apparently, they were mistaken.

'Oh, look!' said (to select one among many) her newest best friend in college, Karen, who also read Geography and also didn't see the point of Bristol and also thought that the failure of each and every political philosophy throughout history could be boiled down to the simple, basic truth that People Are Dumb. '*The Wizard of Oz* is on!'

'Really?' Amanda said, flopping down on the couch beside her. They'd had a hot night out. Her best clubbing clothes were stuck to her from the evening's sweat, her feet were killing her in these shoes – women this calcium-dense were not natural matches for high heels – and though she and Karen had danced and drunk and laughed and smoked all night, neither of them had managed to pull or even catch a boy's eye. To be fair, Karen had a nose issue. And an eyebrow issue. And, well, a limp, but you could hardly see it while they were dancing. Still, they'd had fun. It was all very promising.

With some help from her mother and stepdad Hank
– her father was paying the tuition fees and she knew he
could barely afford those, so she always lied when he
asked if she ever needed anything more – Amanda had
just about enough to rent half a two-bedroom near the
university for her final year. Karen had responded to
Amanda's notice on the college room exchange site. They'd
had coffee, they'd hit it off, they'd moved in. Two weeks
and no problems so far.

'I didn't even think they bothered showing this on TV
any more,' Karen said enthusiastically, tucking her uneven
feet beneath her on the couch. She inhaled deeply, readying
herself to join in on the next chorus of 'We're Off To See–'

'I *hate* this fucking movie,' Amanda said.

Karen choked on what could only have been the air
she just breathed in. 'You *what*?' she coughed, looking
like Amanda had just punched her. Actually *punched* her.

Amanda ploughed on, oblivious. 'None of it's real, even
in terms of the story. In order for the plot to work at all,
everyone has to act like a complete moron, and then they
get to the end and not only is there no magic, the wizard
is just some show-off loser who's tricked everyone into
following him, and before they can try his ass before the
International Courts of Justice, he escapes in a balloon.
He's practically Milošević.'

She stopped briefly, because she could see the whites
around every part of Karen's eyes, but she hoped it was
from the dodgy tablets they'd bought from the overweight
boy by the toilets, who'd said they were Ecstasy he'd
found in his older brother's old bedroom, so they could
have been up to twenty years expired and were probably,
in the end, Panadol.

'You're joking, right?' Karen said.

'And then she goes back home,' Amanda sailed right on, thinking, somehow, that this was encouragement, 'and we're supposed to be *happy* that she's returned to her old, small, black-and-white horizons? That dreams are all well and good, but don't forget that you're actually trapped on the farm forever? Same reason I hate the Chronicles of fucking Narnia. Oh, God, and don't get me started on *him*.' The Cowardly Lion minced onscreen. 'The stuff of nightmares.'

Karen looked incredulous. Or rather, *more* incredulous. 'The Cowardly Lion?'

'Oh, come on. *Look* at him and tell me you don't see every paedophile you'd warn your daughter away from. I always think he's about to whip it out and lay down on top of Dorothy.' She put on a frankly hideous version of the Cowardly Lion's voice. '*Come on, little Dorothy, sit on your Uncle Lion's lap and he'll show you* why *he's king of the jungle, uh-huh, uh-huh.* And then he pushes her to the ground and pulls her panties right on down to those ruby—'

Amanda stopped because the look on Karen's face was, at last, unmistakeable. Panadol never made anyone look that way.

'Well, don't *cry* about it,' Amanda said, but it was too late.

Karen, it turned out, had been 'fiddled with' – Karen's own horrible, multiply-repeated phrase – by her grandfather from ages five to fourteen. It only stopped when he'd died. Not only that, when she'd told her parents, they'd thrown her briefly out of the house, allowing her back to do A-levels only when she'd completely recanted.

'You don't know,' she'd sobbed into Amanda's arms in the long, long hours that followed. 'You just don't know.'

'I'm sorry,' Amanda said, awkwardly patting Karen's head. 'No, I don't.'

It might have brought them closer together. It probably *should* have, but instead, Karen started bringing friends over with whom she'd abruptly stop talking whenever Amanda entered the room. And that, once more, was that.

The baffling thing was that she had no idea *why*. Her childhood had been perfectly normal, from what she could tell. She was still close to both George and Clare, despite the divorce, and there'd never been any undue worry about money or security. It just felt like she'd been born with a small flaw, right at the centre of herself, a flaw somehow too shameful to be shown to anyone else, so she'd spent her life building a carapace around it to keep it hidden. Inevitably, the carapace *became* her true self, a fact she could never quite see, a fact that might have offered relief. Because all *she* knew was the truth deep inside of her, the little something wrong no one else could ever, ever know. And if that wasn't the real her, then what was? At her core, she was broken, and life was just one long attempt to distract people from noticing.

'Are you having a good time, sweetheart?' her father would ask in his every-other-day call.

'Yes, Dad, *Jesus*,' she would say to keep from crying.

'Because everyone says your college years are your best years, but I have to confess, I found them sort of awkward and . . . Well, awkward actually about covers it.'

'You find everything awkward, George,' she'd said, bending at the waist to stop the sob rising in her throat.

He'd laughed. 'I suppose so.' Which was so upsetting somehow – his kindness, the pointlessness of it – that when he'd asked, 'Are you sure you don't need any more money?', she'd had to hang up on him.

*   *   *

Rachel and Mei sat down, taking up five-sixths of the picnic blanket between them. It wasn't quite warm enough for a picnic, really, but Rachel liked these sorts of gruelling challenges, wanting to see, Amanda thought, how much she could get her friends to put up with. If you complained, you lost.

'So who's looking after JP?' Rachel asked, not taking off her coat.

'My dad,' Amanda said, looking through the basket and failing to find anything she liked to eat. She settled on a plastic tub of salad. 'Is there dressing?'

Another pause, then another quiet, shared laugh between Mei and Rachel. Amanda ignored it and found, at least, a small, very expensive-looking bottle of olive oil. She poured it sparingly over the greens and the other greens and the various other greens besides those. She screwed the cap on too vigorously and felt it snap under her fingers. It now spun fruitlessly and refused to stay on. She carefully put it back into the picnic basket, setting the cap on it in a way that at least made it *look* closed, checking to be sure that neither Rachel nor Mei had seen.

'My dad would never babysit,' Rachel said, pouring a mug of coffee from an outrageously sleek thermos. 'Never changed a nappy in his life? Didn't bother learning our names until we were five?'

'Oh, please,' Mei said, surprising both Amanda and, it seemed, herself, before quickly re-shaping her face into one of cheerful acquiescence. Amanda didn't dare hope for solidarity here; it was probably just how much Rachel liked to play up the Australian-ness of her father until he was practically roping cattle with his teeth while surfing and drinking a beer. *Does he have that weird Australian pug nose?* Amanda had never asked. *Or the omnipresent layer of Australian male baby-fat?* she'd never queried. *Or a ponytail out of an inbred '70s jug-band?* she'd never wondered aloud. She checked herself internally. She was being grossly unfair. But wasn't grossly unfair sometimes *thrilling?*

'Dad's great with JP,' she said. 'He's very kind, is my father. Gentle.'

'Mmm,' Rachel didn't quite say, looking across the field they'd chosen to some youths also taking advantage of the weather to kick around a football. 'Jake Gyllenhaal's younger brother, three o'clock.'

Mei blinked. 'You know, I never know what you mean by that. You say "three o'clock" like it's a direction.'

'It *is* a direction?' Rachel said, pointing. 'Twelve, one, two, *three* o'clock? Not that difficult?'

They turned and looked at Mr Three O'Clock who, Amanda would never admit out loud, was indeed handsome, if a bit too young even for her, though possibly not for the six-years-older Rachel. His hair was as thick and luscious as a milkshake, and there was no way he didn't know it. Even at this distance, he gave off self-regard like the Queen gave off forbearance.

'He looks like he cries when he comes,' Amanda said, not realising she'd said it out loud until she heard Mei snort with laughter. She turned, but Mei was already retreating again under Rachel's glare. Mei quickly picked up her phone to keep tracking her daughter. 'Still in Nando's,' she said.

'Well, at least Marco takes an interest?' Rachel said. 'At least he's not off with some hot new girlfriend in another country? Forgetting every bit of his duty?'

Amanda's fork stopped halfway between the last bite

53

of the salad and her mouth, momentarily so stung that swift tears filled her eyes. Blunt willpower alone kept them from spreading down her cheeks.

Because it wasn't like that. Well, it *was*, but it also wasn't. Henri *was* back in France and living with Claudine now but Amanda had basically forced him to go, booting him out of her and JP's life with a force and constancy that had surprised even her. He called JP every week, though, even if JP's four-year-old phone skills were barely rudimentary. Henri said he just wanted his son to hear real French, wanted him to hear his name (Jean-Pierre) pronounced properly, wanted him to hear the lullabies his own grandmother had sung to him.

If Amanda's heart hadn't ripped freshly in two every time she heard Henri's voice, it might have even been sweet.

They'd met her last year at university, seeing each other first in a shared tutorial, then overlapping at the same parties. He was stocky, and manly to the point of bull-headed. His hair was going saltily grey even at twenty, and out of every girl in the tutorial, *she* was the one he sat by, seeing – he eventually told her – a kind of kindred intensity, like she'd not only be able to kill an enemy, but eat him, too.

For her part, she got so giddy every time he was in the same room that she began to live in a state of almost permanent fury. She'd refused to even tell her parents about him for months, lest there be any hint of laughter at her falling so hard, though they would of course have been the last people to do so.

She took most of it out on Henri. 'You've got *fire*,' he

said, and though it sounded ludicrous even in a French accent, they'd each been so turned on it hardly mattered. It was like a hurricane courting a scorpion. Objects thrown, unbelievable sex, months lived in a kind of constant, shivering fever. It had all felt so young! It had all felt so French! She'd been swept away, but in hindsight only in the sense that a landslide brings down a highway: unstoppable catastrophe, followed by rubble. They'd even argued at their wedding. During the ceremony.

One month into their marriage, she discovered she was three months pregnant and immediately began finding even more fault with him. He didn't separate the knives into steak versus regular. He piled his fag ends in the potted camellia she'd hung out on their new balcony in a flat he never finished renovating like he promised. And then, one night, during still-rather-amazing seven-months-pregnant make-up sex, he had looked so angry that she'd spontaneously slapped him across the face, hard enough for her wedding ring to cut his cheek, an action that shocked her so deeply she'd stayed at her father's that night, frightened of what she was capable of doing next.

Henri left the next day. 'It is not the slap,' he said, maddeningly calm. 'A Frenchman can take a slap, Lord knows. It is how your face looked when you did it.' He took her arm with a gentleness that told her it was over more brutally than any fight ever could have. 'You fight your hatred for yourself, anyone can see, and you do your best, taking it out on people who you think will be strong enough to handle it. I understand this. I am the same. It is hard but it is bearable if your love for me is bigger than your hate. But it has tipped somewhere along the way, and there is no recovery from that, I do not think. For either of us.'

The pain of this made her anger blaze anew, and she'd swept him away in a torrent of vengeful promises that he'd never see his son, that if he didn't disappear, she'd tell a judge *he* slapped *her* – and what English judge wasn't prepared to believe that about a Frenchman? – so he'd better leave the country altogether or she'd have him arrested.

He finally believed her. And left.

Yet when their son was born, she named him after Henri's beloved late uncle, like they'd once discussed. She'd immediately shortened it to JP, but still. Even now, she spoke French to him as much as English to make sure he stayed fluent and could talk freely to his father.

Henri had been the love of her life, and she'd never be able to forgive him for it. Or herself, it seemed.

In the meantime, he called, and the sound of his voice made her sad enough to turn up the telly while he spoke, haltingly, to JP, who answered everything into the receiver with a very cautious, '*Oui*?'

'Look,' Amanda said, shoving her fork back into the salad container and swallowing the tears. 'I'm sorry for what I said about the Animals In War thing. I'm sorry for swearing. I'm sorry for fucking *everything*, all right? There's no need to dole out more punishment.'

Mei's eyes seemed to genuinely fill with surprised concern, but Rachel stormed in first. 'It's not the Memorial?' she said. 'It's more like your overall *vehemence*?'

Amanda, who'd expected – foolishly, it now seemed – to be greeted with fast assurances that she had nothing to apologise for, got irritated all over again. 'My grandpa Joe lost a leg in Vietnam,' she said. 'And then got spat on by peaceniks when he came back in his wheelchair. So forgive me if I think a monument to a *carrier pigeon* is in bad taste.'

'*Whoa*,' Mei whispered. 'Your grandfather fought in Vietnam?'

'That can't possibly be true,' Rachel said, her voice growing harder.

Amanda froze. It wasn't actually true. Grandpa Joe had never been drafted and had died on a worksite when a digger accidentally severed an artery in his thigh. She could just feel the bad karma piling up for pretending otherwise even for a moment. But needs must.

'Did he kill any Vietnamese?' Mei asked, suddenly serious in the way she always was when anyone within hearing distance might have been disrespecting any Asian of any kind.

Rachel tutted scornfully. 'British soldiers didn't actually *fight* in Vietnam? Australians bloody well did, though. My father–'

'My grandfather was *American*,' Amanda said, because that part was true.

Mei looked at Rachel. 'Was he?'

'On your mum's side?' Rachel said, looking perplexed, in a way that was perplexing to Amanda.

'No, my dad,' she said. 'My dad's American.'

'No, he isn't,' Rachel laughed. 'Your dad's British? I've met him? Like more than once? You're such a little liar, Amanda. It isn't clever? And it isn't funny?'

'Excuse me,' Amanda said. 'I think I know the nationality of my own father.'

'Whatever you say,' Rachel said, taking a sip of her coffee.

'Maybe you're thinking of your *step*father,' Mei said, obviously worried they were being too unkind.

'My stepfather is also American,' Amanda frowned. 'My mother clearly has a type.' This wasn't true either. Hank was American, yes, but he was big, strapping and black. He couldn't have been more different from George if George had been a woman. 'My mother is British, but my father is definitely American.'

Rachel just raised her eyebrows and carried on looking at Mr Three O'Clock.

'Ask his new girlfriend, if you don't believe me,' Amanda said, but quietly, because she'd given up.

'New girlfriend?' Rachel asked, surprisingly sharply.

'He's dating?' Mei said, mouth open. 'At his age?'

'He's forty-eight,' Amanda said. 'Hardly even out of range for either of you.'

'Eew?' Rachel said. 'Don't be gross?' She flicked another olive out of her pasta. 'So what's she like then? Your new stepmother-to-be?'

Amanda wondered that herself. George had been even more unfocused this week than usual. He'd first called her with a story she couldn't quite follow about a bird landing in his back garden and then flying away, a story she'd eventually convinced him must have been a dream, before suddenly announcing this morning that he'd been seeing a new woman who'd wandered into his shop. He'd sounded so open and vulnerable that the worry about what would inevitably happen – this was George, after all – made her a little bit sick.

'Hardly a new stepmum,' Amanda said. 'It's only been a few dates, and I haven't even met her. All I know is she's called Kumiko and–'

'Kumiko?' Rachel said. 'What kind of name is that?'

'Japanese,' Mei said, eyes laser-like. 'Very common name.'

'I'm not sure about that, but from what he says, she seems really nice.'

'If she puts up with your allegedly American father, she must be?' Rachel said, draining the last of her wine.

'What's *that* supposed to mean?' Amanda asked, but only got to 'What's *that*–' when the football thumped her in the back of the head so hard she practically went face down into the picnic basket.

'Sorry,' said Mr Three O'Clock, leaning in dynamically to retrieve the ball.

'What the *fuck*?' Amanda said, hand on the back of her head, but she stopped when she saw Rachel laughing in her most attractive way, boobs pushed up like an offering.

'Don't worry about it?' Rachel said. 'She deserved it for telling porky pies?'

Mr Three O'Clock laughed and brushed a lock of hair out of his eyes. 'Is this picnic ladies-only or can any riff-raff join?'

'Riffraff would be an improvement?' Rachel said. 'Have some calamari? It's Marks & Spencer's?'

'Don't mind if I do,' he said, sitting down roughly next to Amanda, knocking her Diet Coke into the grass. He didn't apologise. Rachel was already dishing up a napkin of calamari for him.

Amanda was still holding the back of her head. 'Olive oil?' she asked, her voice flat.

'*Love* some,' he said, not even looking her in the face.

She carefully grabbed the bottle of oil and handed it to him, looking as innocent as she could manage. 'Make sure you shake it first.'

He did.

'I don't *believe* it,' Mei said.

To take his blade and cut into the pages of a book felt like such a taboo, such a transgression against everything he held dear, George still half-expected them to bleed every time he did it.

He loved physical books with the same avidity other people loved horses or wine or prog rock. He'd never really warmed to ebooks because they seemed to reduce a book to a computer file, and computer files were disposable things, things you never really owned. He had no emails from ten years ago but still owned every book he bought that year. Besides, what was more perfect an object than a book? The different rags of paper, smooth or rough under your fingers. The edge of the page pressed into your thumbprint as you turned a new chapter. The way your bookmark – fancy, modest, scrap paper, candy wrapper – moved through the width of it, marking your progress, a little further each time you folded it shut.

And how they looked on the walls! Lined up according to whatever whim. George's whim was simple – by author, chronological within name – but over the years he'd also done it by size, subject matter, types of binding. All of them there on his shelves, too many, not enough, their stories raging within regardless of a reader: Dorothea Brooke forever making her confounding choice of husband, the rain of flowers forever marking Jose Arcadio Buendia's funeral, Hal Incandenza forever playing Eschaton on the tennis courts of Enfield.

He had seen a story once about sand mandalas made by Tibetan Buddhist monks. *Unbelievably* gorgeous creations, sometimes just a metre across, sometimes big as a room. Different colours of sand, painstakingly blown in symmetrical patterns by monks using straw-like tubes, building layer upon layer, over the course of weeks, until it was finished. At which point, in keeping with Buddhist feelings about materialism, the mandala was destroyed, but George tended to ignore that part.

What was interesting to him was that the mandala was meant to be – unless he'd vastly misunderstood, which was also possible – a reflection of the internal state of the monk. The monk's inner being, hopefully a peaceful one, laid out in beautiful, fragile form. The soul as a painting.

The books on George's walls were his sand mandala. When they were all in their place, when he could run his hands over their spines, taking one off the shelf to read or re-read, they were the most serene reflection of his internal state. Or if perhaps not quite his internal state, then at least the internal state he would like to have had. Which was maybe all it was for the monks, too, come to think of it.

And so when he made his very first incision into the pages of a book, when he cut into an old paperback he'd found lying near the rubbish bins behind the shop, it felt like a blundering step into his mandala. A blasphemy. A desecration of the divine. Or, perhaps, a releasing of it.

Either way, it felt . . . *interesting*.

He'd never considered himself an artist, certainly didn't consider himself one *now*, but he'd always been a half-decent drawer of things. He could sketch a face with some skill – less so the hands, but who besides John Singer Sargent could ever do hands? – and he'd even, for a period in college, made nude charcoal rubbings of Clare, lounging over a pillow or failing to hold steady the feathered head-dress she'd found God knew where. These were usually precursors to sex, of course, though none the worse for that, and perhaps an emblem of their eventual marriage, as she misunderstood the sort of person he essentially was.

'That's really not half-bad,' Clare would say, looking over the sketchpad as she pulled his shirt out of his trousers. And what followed was always relaxed and amused and full of the right sort of joy.

He hadn't stopped sketching and drawing when they married, even when he started the business and she began moving up the civil service solicitor ladder – she'd be a judge some day, they were both sure of it – but he'd never really *progressed* in the way Clare kept (nicely, encouragingly, full of hope) thinking he would. He remained a sketcher, and the nude charcoals grew fewer and farther between, the headdresses never found again, the languorous afternoons turning slowly, prematurely, into middle-aged naps.

Clare's new husband, Hank, managed an enormous hotel for an American conglomerate. George had no idea if he drew.

After the divorce, George still sketched, sometimes nothing more than doodling while on the phone, sometimes taking sheets of the posher paper out of stock at the shop and trying his hand at a tree through sunlight or a rainy park bench or a heroically ugly pair of shoes Mehmet had once left behind after a failed audition for *The Lion King*. Nothing more than that, though. Nothing past lines of pencil, sometimes ink, never charcoal these days.

Until he found the book. He could easily have missed it. It had fallen behind the bins, and he only spotted it when he was gathering up the remains of a thrown-out lunch a lucky pigeon had dragged over half the alley. The book was a John Updike he'd never read (he'd never read any John Updike) called *In the Beauty of the Lilies*. He had taken it inside, in all its damaged state, and flipped through the ruined pages. Many of the edges were stuck together after having survived rainfall, but there was maybe half a workable book inside.

He was struck by an impulse to draw something on a page. The book's life was over, it was effectively unreadable, but still, drawing on it seemed both tantalisingly vandalous but maybe also – and this felt increasingly right – a way to lay it to rest, give it a decent burial, like sewing pennies in its eyes. But as he lowered his pencil onto one of the emptier pages, he stopped.

A cutting blade would be better.

Not thinking too hard on the why of this, he dug into his desk and found the blade he used for trimming and splicing when a job needed actual physical assemblage – far rarer these days in the age of computer design, which he did *not* resist, as it was faster and left him free time to doodle and dawdle and dream. He turned back to the book on his worktable.

It was a Saturday morning. He needed to open the shop any moment now, but instead, he placed the blade on the page. He let out a little gasp as he cut, half-expecting the book to gasp as well. It didn't, but he still paused after that first cut, looking at what he had done.

And then he did it again.

He cut and cut, small strips, larger ones, curved ones, angled ones, some tearing, *many* tearing, actually, until he got used to the paper's particular give. More were just not quite the right shape, so he kept cutting, deep into the words of John Updike (he read snippets when he rested, the paragraphs with their astonishing numbers of semi-colons and not especially much happening).

At some point, he'd opened the shop and left the customers to Mehmet's mercy while he focused with surprising force on the cuttings, the hours melting together in a way they rarely did. He was unsure what shapes he was really making, but by late afternoon, when Mehmet was getting itchy feet to go home and get ready for a Saturday evening out, he assembled the most smoothly cut shapes on a square of black paper, cajoling them together in the shape he'd begun seeing in his mind's eye. He didn't stack them or allow them to reach out into three-dimensions, just laid them flat on the page, not even always touching, urging them towards the shape that felt right, the scattered words and parts of words looking back at him, as if through small, curved windows onto the world built inside the book.

'Lily,' Mehmet said, brushing past him to get his coat.

'What?' George said, blinking in surprise, having almost forgotten where he was.

'Looks like a lily,' Mehmet said slowly, as if talking to a coma patient. 'My mother's favourite flower. Which tells you a whole lot about her, if you ask me. Fragrant and likely to stain.'

Mehmet shrugged on his coat and left, but George sat there for a long while, looking at the cuttings.

A lily. Clearly, a lily. From a book called *In the Beauty of the Lilies*.

He gave an irritated laugh at his own obviousness, precisely the shallowness of vision that had always prevented him from becoming a proper artist, he felt, and he reached to brush it all into the rubbish bin.

But he stopped. It really was a rather *good* lily.

And so it began. He started haunting the £1 bins of second-hand bookstores, taking only the most damaged, unloved and unlovable books. He never exactly *tried* to make themed cuttings – hoping to avoid a repeat of the unsubtle lily – but sometimes a line would strike his fancy from the pages of a sixty-year-old, half-mouldy Agatha Christie, and he'd cut the shapes of a paragraphed hand dangling a multi-claused cigarette. Or a lettered horizon with three haiku-looking moons from the pages of a sci-fi novel he'd never heard of. Or a solitary figure carrying a small child, marked only by a single '1' from the 'Part 1' of a history of the siege of Leningrad.

He only ever showed the final outcomes to Amanda – Mehmet saw all of them, since he worked at the shop, but that was a different thing than 'showing' – and she was courteous about them, which was disheartening, yes, but still he kept on. Experimenting with glues to find the best way to secure them against a background, testing them under glass or not, in frames or not, bordered, unbordered, small or large. He would some-times try to make a silhouette from a single cutting, managing once a near-perfect rose (from, as an homage to his lily, a falling-apart copy of Iris Murdoch's *An Accidental Rose*), but more often getting results akin to the very goose-like crane that Mehmet had accidentally seen.

He had no ambition about them, would never have even considered they were good enough for public view, but they passed the time. They let his hands work, often detached slightly from his mind, and always headed towards something, a mystery only revealed, sometimes even to him, at the moment of assembling the pieces on a flat background. He finished them in various ways and kept them in a corner of the storeroom that Mehmet, graciously, never rummaged through.

They were a bit of fun, sometimes a bit more than that, but usually nothing much, he'd be the first to say, although he would also insist that they were *his* nothing much.

Until the day Kumiko had arrived. And changed everything.

She was carrying a suitcase, a small one, such as you'd see – his mind went to the image so quickly it distracted him – on the arm of a forties film heroine at a train station: the case barely more than a small box, clearly empty so the actress wouldn't be distressed, and hanging from a white-gloved hand that showed no dirt. Yet also clearly a suitcase and not a briefcase or handbag.

She was smaller than average without actually being *small*, long dark hair cascading down to her shoulders, pale brown eyes watching him, unblinkingly. He couldn't have put a finger on her nationality just then if you'd asked him. She wore a simple white dress, the same colour as the coat draped over her non-suitcase carrying arm, also like a train-bound forties heroine. Finally, she wore a small red hat perched on the top of her head, an anachronism that somehow fit with all the rest.

Her age was as difficult to fix as her origins. She looked younger than him, possibly thirty-five? But as he stared at her, his speech momentarily having left him, something about her stance, something about the *exact* simplicity of her dress, about the steady eyes still watching him, seemed suddenly from a figure out of time: a lady of vast estates and influence during an ancient Scottish war, a dauphine dispatched to marry in the wilds of South America, the patient handmaiden to a particularly difficult goddess . . .

He blinked, and she was a woman again. A woman in a simple white dress. With a hat that looked both ninety years out of date and a harbinger of the latest thing.

'Can I . . . ?' he finally managed to say.

'My name,' she said, 'is Kumiko.'

No one in the twenty-one year history of the print shop had opened an order this way. George said, 'I'm George.'

'George,' she said. 'Yes. George.'

'Is there something we can help you with?' George said, very, very much not wanting her to leave.

'I was wondering, please,' she said, lifting her small case up to the counter, 'if you could possibly offer advice on how best to print facsimiles of these.'

On closer inspection, the suitcase looked both as if it was made out of paper and as if it was the most expensive piece of luggage George had ever seen. She opened it, undoing small leather straps, and pulled out a stack of large card tiles, each roughly A5-sized and each one black, similar to some of the ones George used for his own book-cut creations.

She set five of them down, one by one, in front of George.

They were pictures, evidently her own work from the way she regarded them, that odd artist's combination of shy and bold, so expectant of a reaction, good or bad. On one level, they were nothing more than pictures of beautiful things placed against the background of a card. But on further viewing, on a deeper look . . .

Good Lord.

One was a watermill, but nothing nearly so twee as 'watermill' suggested. A watermill that seemed to be almost turning from the brook that ran through it, a watermill that existed not in fancy but somewhere specific in the world, a real watermill, a *true* watermill, near which the great and terrible tragedies of life might have recently happened. And yet also merely a watermill, too, and pretty with it.

There was a dragon in the next one, partially Chinese in style but with the wings of European myth, caught in mid-flight, its eye staring back at the viewer in malevolent mischief. Like the watermill, it was on the border of kitsch, of the sort of tourist tat you could buy for next to nothing from a street vendor. But it didn't cross that border. This dragon was the one those fake dragons dreamed of being, the meaty, heavy, living, breathing animal behind the myth. This dragon might bite you. This dragon might *eat* you.

The others were the same, so near easy vulgarity, yet so clearly not. A phoenix rising from the bud of a flower. A stampede of horses cascading down a hill. The cheek and neck of a woman looking away from the artist.

They should have looked cheap. They should have looked tacky and home-made. They should have looked like the worst kind of car boot sale rubbish, the work of a plump, hopeless woman with no other options than an early death by drink.

But these. These were breathtaking.

And what tumbled George's heart, what made his stomach feel as if he'd swallowed a fluttering balloon, was that they weren't drawings or carvings or paintings or watercolours.

They were cuttings. Each was made with what looked like slices of an impossible array of feathers.

'These are . . .' George said, unable to think of exactly what to say, so he simply said it again. 'These are . . .'

'They are not quite there yet, I know,' Kumiko said. 'They lack something. But they are mine.'

She seemed to hesitate in the face of George's intense consideration of the pictures. He looked at them as if he were a kidnap victim and they were his long-sought ransom. He felt as if he was losing his balance, as if vertigo had given his ears a thump, and he raised his hands to steady himself on the counter.

'Oh!' Kumiko said, and he saw her smiling down at his left hand.

There was his own cutting, utterly dismal, painfully amateur in comparison, still gripped in the hand that had tried to hide it from Mehmet. He moved to hide it again, but her eyes were already on it, and they weren't scornful, weren't mocking.

They were delighted.

'You've made a crane,' she said.

She was from 'all over', she said when he asked her over dinner that night, and had been a sort of teacher. Overseas. In developing countries.

'It sounds noble,' she said. 'I do not want it to sound like that. Like some great woman offering her services to poor, adoring unfortunates. Not at all. It was not like that. It was like . . .'

She trailed off, looking into the dark wood panelling that overpowered the ceilings and the walls. For reasons he couldn't fathom, George had taken her to a self-consciously old-fashioned 'English' restaurant, such as men in morning suits might have eaten at anywhere from 1780 to 1965. A small sign above the door read 'Est 1997'. He'd been surprised she'd accepted his invitation, surprised she'd been free at no notice whatsoever, but she said she was new to this place and not, at the moment, overflowing with friends.

She'd used that word. Overflowing.

'The teaching,' she said, furrowing her brow, 'the *interaction*, I should say, was like a hello and a goodbye, all at once, every day. Do you know what I mean?'

'Not even a little,' George said. She spoke in an accent he couldn't place. French? French/Russian? Spanish/Maltese? South African/Nepalese/Canadian? But also English, and possibly Japanese like her name but also neither or any, as if every place she may have travelled hadn't wanted her to leave and insinuated itself into her voice as a way of forcing her to take it along. He could understand the feeling.

She laughed at him, but nicely. 'I do not like talking of myself so much. Let it be enough that I have lived and changed and been changed. Just like everyone else.'

'I can't ever imagine you'd need changing.'

She pushed some roast beef around her plate without eating it. 'I believe you mean what you say, George.'

'That was too much. I'm sorry.'

'And I believe that, too.'

She'd had a relationship, perhaps even a marriage, that

had ended at some point, though it didn't seem amicably so, like his had with Clare. She didn't want to talk about that either. 'The past is always filled with both joy and pain, which are private and perhaps not first date conversation.'

He'd been so pleased she'd called it a 'first date' that he missed several of her next sentences.

'But you, now, George,' she said. 'You are not from here, are you?'

'No,' he said, surprised. 'I'm–'

'American.' She leant back in her chair. 'So you perhaps do not quite belong either, do you?'

She said she'd taken up the cuttings on her travels. Paints and brushes were too hard and too expensive to truck around from place to place, so she'd first started using local fabrics – batiks or weaves or whatever was to hand – and had moved, more or less by chance, to feathers, after coming across a market stall in Paramaribo or Vientiane or Quito or Shangri-La perhaps, that sold every colour of feather you could imagine and beyond, some concoctions so unlikely they hardly seemed to have come from an animal at all.

'And looking back on it,' she said, 'what an impossible market stall to find. Feathers are difficult to source, and expensive. Yet here they were, pinned to the walls of a poor market seller in melting heat. I was bewitched. I bought as much as my arms could carry, and when I went back the next day, the stall was gone.'

She took a sip of mint tea, an odd thing to have with roast beef, but she'd declined all offers of the red wine George was desperately trying not to drink too quickly.

'Your pictures are . . .' George started, and faltered.

'And again, the sentence you cannot finish.'

'No, I was going to say, they're . . .' Still the word failed him. 'They're . . .' Her face was smiling, a little shy at an incoming critique of her work, but beautiful, so beautiful, so beautiful and kind and somehow looking right back at George that to hell with it, in he went, 'They're like looking at a piece of my soul.'

She widened her eyes a bit.

But she didn't laugh at him.

'You are very kind, George,' she said. 'But you are wrong. They are like looking at a piece of *my* soul.' She sighed. 'My as yet incomplete soul. They lack something. They are nearly there, but they . . . lack.'

She looked into her cup of tea as if what she lacked might be there.

She was impossible. Impossibly beautiful, impossibly talking to him, but also impossibly *present*, so much so that what else could she be but a dream? The soles of her feet must be hovering a centimetre above the ground. Her skin would turn out to be made of glass that would shatter if touched. Her hands, on closer inspection, would be translucent at the least, clear enough to read through.

He reached forward impulsively and took her hand in his. She let him, and he examined it front and back. There was nothing unusual about it at all, of course, just a hand (but *her* hand, *hers*) and, embarrassed, he set it back down. She didn't let him go, though. She examined his hand the same, looking at his rough skin, at the hair that gathered so unattractively across the backs of his fingers, at the nails chewed too short for too many decades to be little more than buried tombstones at his fingertips.

'I'm sorry,' he said.

She gently let him go and reached into the small suit-case, placed down by her chair. She took out the small

72

cutting of George's crane, which she had asked if she could have at the shop. She held it in the palm of her hand.

'I wonder if I might perform an impertinence,' she said.

The following day was a nightmare. Retrieving the kitten t-shirts from the Brookman party had proven surprisingly difficult as they'd taken an equally surprising liking to them.

'What's funnier than ten army officers wearing way-too-tight light blue t-shirts with a wanking kitten on the front?' Brookman had said on the phone.

George could think of any number of things. 'It's just that the O'Riley Hen Party were sort of *counting* on them. They're personalised to each member's—'

'We know! We've already divvied up the names. The Best Man is *definitely* Boobs.'

George had ended up having an in-town t-shirt printer do a rush job at his own exorbitant expense to reproduce another batch for the hen party and hoped to God they hadn't found any sudden EasyJet bargains to Riga as well. Mehmet, meanwhile, was feigning stomach illness to try and leave early, which he regularly did on Friday afternoons, and George had also spent the entire day toiling over the almost literally incredible news that Kumiko had yet to acquire a mobile phone that worked in this country, so he had no way of calling or texting her, or obsessing over calling or texting her, or obsessing over *not* calling or texting her and had reached a point of near-implosion about having nothing but her word that he'd ever see her again.

When, of course, in she walked.

'My impertinence,' she said, laying the suitcase on the front counter.

She removed her feathered tile of the dragon: white, tightly woven strands of feather and stalk on the plain black background.

And beside the dragon, she'd affixed his cutting of the crane.

'Holy shit,' Mehmet said, seriously, peering over George's shoulder. 'That's amazing.'

George said nothing, because if he spoke, he would weep.

'It's a picnic,' Amanda said the next morning, handing JP over to George in a pile of biscuit-smelling flesh.

'*Grand-père!*' JP shouted.

'Bit cold for a picnic, isn't it?' George asked, after he'd kissed JP and taken him inside. Amanda followed him in but didn't sit down.

He saw her glancing at the papers and clothes and books galore that made his sitting room not the most obviously child-friendly place in the world. It didn't matter. JP adored George, and George adored his grandson. They could have been stuck in prison and made a day of it.

'Not for Rachel and Mei,' Amanda said.

'Rachel?' George asked.

'You remember,' she said. 'The girl from work who came to my birthday a few months back. Mei, too. Both pretty, both vaguely evil-seeming. Rachel more so.'

'Yes,' George said, bouncing a giggling JP up and down in his arms. 'I think I remember them.'

'We sit in the sun. We look at boys. We drink wine.'

'Sounds nice.'

'They hate me. And I think I hate them.'

'I met someone,' he said, so quickly it must have been obvious he'd been holding it in. 'She's called Kumiko.'

Amanda's face froze for a minute. 'All right.'

'Came into the shop. We've gone out the last two nights. And again tonight.'

'Three nights in a row? Are you teenagers?'

'I know, I know, it's a lot all at once, but . . .' He set JP down on the sofa, burying him in dusty, old cushions so that he'd have to escape, a game JP *loved*.

'But?' Amanda asked.

'Nothing,' George shrugged. 'Nothing. I'm just saying I met a nice lady.'

'All right,' Amanda said again, carefully. 'I'll pick him up before four.'

'Good, because–'

'Because you've got a date, gotcha.'

But George wasn't embarrassed, felt too full of sunshine to even be bashful. 'And wait,' he said, 'just wait until I show you the dragon and the crane.'

He kissed Kumiko that night. For a moment, she was definitely the one being kissed, but then she did kiss him back.

His heart sang.

'I don't understand it,' he said to her some time later, after they lay together under sheets he hadn't even bothered changing, never imagining for a moment that anything like *this* was going to happen. 'Who *are* you?'

'Kumiko,' she said. 'And who are you?'

'I'll be honest,' George said. 'I haven't the foggiest idea.'

'Then I will tell you.' She turned to him, taking his

75

hand as if bestowing a blessing. 'You are kind, George. The sort of man who would forgive.'

'Forgive what?' he asked.

But she kissed him for an answer and the question was lost, lost, lost.

She is born a breath of cloud.

She sees neither her mother nor her father – her mother has died during the birth and not hung around; her father is the cloud itself, silent, weeping, consumed with grief – and so she stands alone, on legs unfamiliar.

'Where have I come from?' she asks.

There is no answer.

'Where am I to go?'

There is no answer, even from the cloud, though he knows.

'May I ask, at least, what I am called?'

After a hesitant moment, the cloud whispers into her ear. She nods her head and understands.

2 of 32

She takes flight.

The world below her is young, too young to have quite grown together. It exists in islands of floating earth, some connected by rope bridges or bamboo walkways, others reached across expanses of sky by rowing boats made of paper, others to which she can only fly.

She lands on an island that is mostly meadow, the grass bowing to her in the breeze. She pinches it between her fingertips and says, 'Yes. Just so.'

In the meadow, there is a lake. She goes to it, following the sand along its shores, until she reaches the river that flows from it. She stands on tiptoes and sees that the river empties over the edge of the island and into space in an outrage of angry water.

Why does the water do so? she thinks.

There is a fisherman on the far shore. She calls to him. 'Why does the water do so? Will it not spend itself completely and leave only empty earth?'

'This lake is sourced from the tears of children who have lost their parents, my lady,' the fisherman replies. 'As you see.'

'Ah,' she says, looking down to see tears falling from her own golden eyes into the water, sending out ringlets across the lake's surface.

'It makes the fish tender,' the fisherman says, reeling in a specimen with shiny golden scales. 'Though they do taste of sorrow.'

'I am hungry,' she says. 'I have yet to eat anything at all.'

'Come over to the fire, my lady,' the fisherman says. 'I will feed you your fill of grief.' He tosses the golden-scaled fish into his basket, its gills gasping fruitlessly in the air. 'And perhaps after,' he says, almost shyly, but only almost, 'you will lie with me to show your gratitude.'

He smiles at her. It is full of ugly hope.

5 of 32

She bows her head in reply and flies to him, her fingers delicately skating across the surface of the lake, pulling two long watery arrowheads behind her. She lands next to the fisherman and places her hands on the sides of his head, kissing him gently on the lips.

It is a new sensation. Wetter than she expects.

'You wish to trap me,' she says to him. 'Your thoughts are clear. You will take the spear you have lying next to your basket of fish, and if I do not agree to lie with you, you will use it to force me. You are perhaps not even a bad man, perhaps just one twisted by loneliness. I could not say. But what I do know is that you do not really ask for my body. You ask for my forgiveness.'

The man's face has become a curl of sadness. He begins to weep. 'Yes, my lady. I am sorry, my lady.'

'I believe you,' she says. 'You have my forgiveness.'

6 of 32

Quickly, mercifully, she bites out both of the fisherman's eyes and plunges two sharp fingers through his heart. He slumps to the muddy shore.

'You have killed me, my lady,' he says, regarding his body, squelching in the mud between them. 'You have set me free.'

'This I do gladly,' she says.

'I thank you, my lady,' says the fisherman. 'I thank you.'

A wind whirls around them, scattering the fisherman's spirit, which thanks her until it can thank her no more.

7 of 32

She feeds on his basket of fish. They do taste of sorrow, which is bitter but not unpleasantly so. After she has sated her appetite, she takes the fish that remain and places them back in the water, holding them between her hands until they wriggle back into life and swim off. When this is finished, she rolls the body of the fisherman into the lake, too, bidding him farewell when he catches the current, making his final journey as the angry water hurls him out into the space between the islands.

She looks at her hands, turns them this way and that, as if in curiosity of what she has done with them. She washes them in the river and dries them on the material of her dress.

Then, once again, she takes flight.

II.

'**I** want to ask her to move in with me.'

'Yeah, and I meant to see if you could take JP on Saturday again? I've got queue counting to do in Romford, if you can believe it. On a *Saturday*. Some kind of sporting event, I don't know–'

'Did you hear what I said?'

'Yes. Hiring a cleaner. Blah blah blah. I'd have to drop him off criminally early, like before six, but he'll easily sleep till eight, so really, it's just–'

'Did you hear the *reason* I'm hiring a cleaner?'

'The reason? I don't know. To have a clean house? What kind of question–?

'I think I'm going to ask Kumiko to move in with me.'

'. . .'

'. . .'

'Move *in* with you?'

'Well. I want to.'

'MOVE IN WITH YOU!?'

'I know it's a bit sudden.'

'*A BIT SUDDEN*? You've known her for *two weeks*! If that! What are you, mayflies?'

'Amanda–'

'Dad, you're talking crazy. You barely know her.'

'That's the thing. I *want* to know her. I almost feel greedy about it.'

'And this is how you want to find out? Look, you're smitten, and I'm happy about you being smitten, but it also makes me worry, George. You break. You love and it's too big and they can never love you back enough and you clearly can't ask her to move in with you now, she'll run a mile. And why wouldn't she? Any woman would.'

'She's not just any woman.'

'That's as maybe, but unless she's an alien–'

'There's a thought.'

'–she's going to think you're a crazy person.'

'You wouldn't say that if you'd met her. It just seems so natural already, so *easy*–'

'See, this is how much too soon it is for you two to move in together. I haven't even met her.'

'Why don't you come out with us for dinner on Saturday?'

'Because I'm in *Romford*, and I need to bring JP over–'

'Come after, when you pick him up.'

'I can't. Henri's got his call with JP that night and I–'

'I just want you to meet–'

'Why should I? Why should I even remember her name just before she never speaks to you again for asking her to move in with you after two weeks?'

'You know, Amanda, I sometimes wonder why you think it's okay to talk to me like this.'

'I . . .'

'. . .'

'. . .'

'Amanda?'

'. . .'

'Oh, don't *cry*, sweetheart, I didn't mean to–'

'No, no, I know you didn't, and that's why I'm crying. You tell me off and you do it so kindly and you're right and I don't know what's wrong with me and I'm just such an evil shit–'

'You're not an evil–'

'I am! Even this! How can we be sure I'm not bursting into tears so you'll rush in and tell me how not-evil I am?'

'Are you?'

'I don't know!'

'Sweetheart, what's the matter?'

'. . .'

'A sigh that long is never a good indicator of–'

'I think I've fucked it up with the girls at the office.'

'Oh, *Amanda*–'

'I *know*, you don't need to tell me.'

'Which girls?'

'What?'

'Which girls at the office?'

'The same ones. Mei and Rachel.'

'Rachel. The one who talks in questions.'

'And Mei is the one whose boobs aren't fake but look like they are. See? It's things like that. I *think* them and then I just *say* them–'

'What happened?'

'The usual. I opened my big, fat, fucking mouth–'

'I wish you wouldn't–'

'Not the time to be shaming me for my language, Dad.'

'Sorry.'

'I just, I don't *get* it. How do people do it? How do people talk so easily to one another? How do they just,

85

I don't know, *fall* into it and relax and there's repartee and banter and, whatever, *ease*, and I just sit there and I think, *Okay, what are we talking about? And what should I say? And what* shouldn't *I say? And how should I or shouldn't I say it?* And by the time I do fucking say something, we're three topics on.'

'You couldn't introduce topics yourself?'

'That gets me into *more* trouble. I mean, this all really started to go downhill at that godawful picnic when I said how much I hated that monstrosity on Mayfair—'

'Which monstrosity?'

'The Animals In War Memorial.'

'That? You don't like that?'

'. . .'

'Oh, sweetheart, I don't even know *why* you're crying now, but please—'

'Because I don't understand how people talk to each other, Dad. I try, but I just blunder on in and knock over the china and spit in the soup and break all these rules that no one will even *tell* me—'

'Ah, that's an English thing. They do like their unknowable rules.'

'Yeah, but I *am* English. I *am* they.'

'I don't think you're the only one who feels left out, is all I'm saying.'

'But that's just it. Feeling left out. It was supposed to stop when I grew up but . . .'

'Smart people often feel left out, love.'

'I'm not *that* smart. I mean, I'm smarter than Rachel. And probably Mei, too, though that's a well of many mysteries. So, I don't know, maybe. But what good is being smart when you speak words and no one hears the ones you mean?'

'I'm sorry, darling. Maybe they weren't good friends for you to begin with–'

'Well, *someone* has to be! I'm nearly twenty-six and I can't even point to a best friend. Do you know how freakish that is for a girl? Girls are all *about* best friends, even when you hate each other.'

'Boys have best friends, too.'

'Really not the point. For me, it's been two and a half decades of false starts, of sitting outside the glass, wondering how you get in. How you *stay* in.'

'Could be worse. Could be nearly five decades.'

'You've never had a problem getting inside the glass, George.'

'I've had a problem getting other people to stay in there with me, though. Same thing, different angle.'

'Mum stayed.'

'For a while.'

'For a long while. She's still your friend.'

'A friend is different than a wife, Amanda.'

'Yeah, I know. I know. I'm having . . . It's just been tough at work. And at home. Henri calls and talks to JP and he's *polite* to me. Friendly and polite and fucking *courteous*. And it tears three pieces out of my heart every single time . . .'

'Okay, I'm going to stop telling you to stop crying. Maybe it's a healing thing.'

'Not *these*. These are angry tears. Don't *laugh*.'

'Well, sweetheart, if it helps, *I'm* your friend.'

'Oh, Dad. You know that doesn't count.'

S he wouldn't let him see her working on the tiles.

    'I cannot, George,' she'd say, looking unexpectedly bashful (and how he couldn't not touch her when she blushed, how he couldn't not run his fingers across the line of her cheekbone, down to her jaw, under her chin, at which point he couldn't not kiss her, apologising at every step). 'It is too private, I am sorry.'

    'Even for me?' he asked.

    'Especially for you. You *see* me, clearly, with love–'

    'Kumiko–'

    'I know. You have not said the word, but it is there.' He tensed, but her creamy brown eyes were warm and kind. 'Your observation is exactly what I would want,' she went on, 'but it changes my work. It has to begin with just my own eyes. If you are there to see it, it is already shared, and if it is already shared, then I will not be able to give it to you or to anyone, do you see?'

    'No,' he said. 'I mean, yes, I do see, but that's not what I was going to say.'

    'What were you going to say?'

'That I do see you with love. That's how I see you.'

'I know,' she said, but she said it in such a way that 'I know' became every type of love he ever wanted to hear.

'Will you move in with me?'

And like every other time he'd asked that question, she just laughed.

On its own, her art was beautiful, but she wouldn't stop insisting that it was static. The cuttings of the feathers woven together, assembled in eye-bending combinations to suggest not only a picture (the watermill, the dragon, the profile) but often the absences in those pictures, too, the shadows they left, black feathers woven with dark purple ones to make surprising representations of voids. Or sometimes, there *was* just empty space, with a single dash of down to emphasise its emptiness. The eye was constantly fooled by them, happening upon shape when blankness was expected, happening upon blankness when shape was expected. They tantalised, they tricked.

'But they do not *breathe*, George.'

'They do. I'm telling you, they do.'

'You are kind. They do not.'

On repeated inspection, they revealed themselves to not always be exclusively feathers, either. She would sometimes sew a line of thread or a single mother-of-pearl button to suggest a horizon or a sun. In one, she included a flat curve of plastic which should have jarred against the softness of a feather's spray, but somehow seemed a combination both apt and eternal.

They were good. They were very good.

But, she said, 'They lack life.'

'They're gorgeous.'

'They are gorgeously empty.'

'They're like nothing I've ever seen before.'

'They are like nothing empty you've ever seen before.'

He would argue with her like this, but then she would remind him of their first day, of that first 'impertinence', as she'd called it. Her dragon in that tile had remained the same, a dragon that George refused to agree lacked any life at all. He could see malevolence in the dragon's eye, made green by what was maybe a bit of glass or garnet.

But now the dragon was threatening George's crane. The same dragon made of feather flew over the crane made of words on paper. A combination of mediums that shouldn't have worked. A combination of styles that shouldn't have worked. George wasn't even remotely afraid to acknowledge that it was even a combination of *competencies* (hers exquisitely agile, his barely managing a limp) that shouldn't have worked.

But oh. But oh. But oh.

'Holy shit,' Mehmet had said.

Holy shit indeed, George had thought.

The dragon now had purpose. The crane now had context. The dragon now had a dangerous curiosity, it had potential. The crane now had threat, a serenity about to cease. Together, they had tension. Together, they were more than two incomplete halves, they were a *third* thing, mysterious and powerful and bigger than the small black square that imprisoned them. A frame had become a film, a sentence had become a story. The dragon and the crane invited you to step in, take part, be either or both, but they were very clear that you would do so at your peril.

And she had *given* it to him.

'As a thank you,' she had said, 'if you wish it.'

'No,' George said. 'It's too much. *Clearly* too much.'

'I'll take it,' Mehmet said.

'It is finished,' Kumiko said. 'You finished it. It belongs to you as much as me.'

'I . . .' George started. 'I . . .'

'*I'll* take it,' Mehmet said again.

And then Kumiko had said, 'Tell me, do you regularly make your cuttings?'

Which really started everything.

She didn't ask him to cut anything specific, felt that that would somehow get in the way of inspiration. But George eagerly began to dedicate every spare moment to making cuttings – raiding the second-hand bookstore bins, buying proper ones if nothing was right, then sending Mehmet to the front of the shop to torture any customers who came in ('But it says red here on the form.').

He tried not to think, tried to loosen his concentration from its moorings, allow the blade to just make its marks, letting himself stay unsure of what the final assemblage would be until he put the last slice into place.

'What is it?' Mehmet asked of the first one he finished that he was even partway satisfied with.

'What do *you* think it is?' George replied, slightly baffled himself.

'Some kind of hyena?'

'I think it might be a lion.'

'Oh, yeah. One of them stylised jobbies, like they have on England sport shirts.'

'Jobbies?'

'Everything old is new again, Captain.'

'Call me Captain again and you're fired.'

Mehmet frowned at the hyena/lion. 'This isn't some mysterious allure of the East thing you've got with this woman, is it? Because I'd find that, like, amazingly offensive.'

'You're from the East, Mehmet, and I find you neither mysterious nor alluring.'

'Ah,' Kumiko said when she saw the cutting. 'A lion. Yes.'

And took it away.

He still knew very little about her as yet, what she did with her free time, who her family was, even what she did for money.

'I *live*, George,' she would say, an expression of pained perplexity glancing across her brow. 'What does anyone do? They live, they survive, they take themselves and their history and they carry on.'

Well, that's what characters in books do, he would think but not say, *but the rest of us need to buy bread and beer once in a while.*

She hinted, occasionally, that she lived off savings, but how much money could whatever kind of international aid worker she'd been have stashed away? Unless, of course, it was from before or was family money or–

'I worry you,' she said one night in bed, in George's bed, in George's house – he still hadn't been to hers ('Too small,' she'd said, frowning at herself. 'Smaller than anyone would ever believe.') – in what may have been the third week of their dating. It was a strange time. He'd look back and know they'd spent hours together but would only have clear memories of a few passing moments: her lips parting to eat a polite bite of aubergine, her laughter at the bread-hungry geese who disappointedly followed them around a park, the bemused way she took his hand when he looked uneasy at being surrounded by teenagers in a queue at the cinema (to see a film which vanished like vapours in his memory).

She was almost a half-remembered dream, yet not.

Because here she was, in his bed, mirroring his caresses of her, running a finger from his temple to his chin and saying, 'I worry you.'

'I know so little about you,' he said. 'I want to know more.'

'You know everything important.'

'You say that, but . . .'

'But what?'

'For example, your name.'

'You know my name, George,' she said, amused.

'Yes, but is Kumiko Japanese?'

'I believe so.'

'Are *you* Japanese?'

She looked at him teasingly. 'In the sense that my name is, yes, I suppose I am.'

'Is that an offensive question? I don't mean it to be–'

'George,' she said, sitting up a bit more, looking down at him on the pillow, her finger continuing down through the greying hairs on his chest.

'Things were not easy for me, before,' she said, and it was as if the night itself stopped to listen to her. 'There were hard days, George. Days that I loved, of course, days that I lived to the end of every minute, but more often they were hard. And I do not wish to live in them again.' She stopped, her finger poking playfully at his belly button, her voice anything but that same playful. 'There is more of me to know, of course there is.' She glanced up at him, and he could have sworn her eyes were somehow reflecting golden moonlight that was actually coming from behind her. 'But we have time, George. We have all the time we can steal. And so, can it wait? Can I be revealed to you slowly?'

'Kumiko–'

'I feel safe with you, George. You are safety and softness and kindness and respite.'

George, who had been uneasy with how this conversation was going already, suddenly felt twice as dismayed. 'Softness?'

'Softness is strength,' she said. 'Stronger than you know.'

'No,' he said. 'No, it isn't. People say that because it sounds nice, but it's not really true.'

'George . . .'

He sighed. He wanted to hold her now, wanted his arms around her, his too rough hands skimming gently over the skin of her back, her thighs, even her feet and hands. He wanted to completely surround her somehow, be a cave for her, be in fact the very respite she had called him, the very respite he resisted being called.

'My ex-wife,' George said, regretting introducing her into the bedroom but pressing ahead. 'She always told me I was too nice, too friendly. Too *soft*. She didn't mean it in a bad way, not at all. In fact, she's still a friend.' He paused. 'But she left me. Every woman eventually has. I've never done the breaking up with a single woman I've ever dated.' He ran his hand up the side of Kumiko's arm. 'People want niceness in their friends, but that's a different kind of love.'

'Niceness, George,' she said, 'is everything in the world that I want.'

And though George heard the words *right now* silently

94

added to the end of that sentence, he genuinely had no idea if it was because she'd intended them or if they were supplied by his own fearful heart.

He framed the dragon and crane, took his time considering how. A simple flat frame couldn't even come close to properly doing the job, the depth of the tile's physical construction preventing it from merely being pressed under glass. Besides, basic frames were for brilliantly toothed children and their Golden Retrievers, not something as challenging, as *alive*, as this.

After trying and failing at a number of approaches – unglassed, mounted on matte or gloss, set flat to be viewed from above – he finally placed it inside a shallow glass case so that there was empty air around it, a hint of diorama. The case itself had a tarnished gold edge around the corners, like the picture inside might have been in there for hundreds of years and might crumble to dust upon opening. It seemed like a relic from some alternate timeline, an artefact accidentally tumbled through from some other place.

But then, where to put it?

He hung it at home, but for some reason that didn't seem right. Above his mantelpiece it looked indefinably wrong, a foreign visitor smiling politely and wondering when on earth this dinner party was going to end. The walls of the rest of his rooms were too crowded with books to give it enough space to breathe, so he tried hanging it above his bed. One startlingly incoherent sex dream later (landslides and grasslands and armies running over his very skin), he took it right back down.

So finally, that only left the shop, where at least he

would be able to see it every day and where it looked strangely comfortable, watching over him, not at all out of place, somehow, among the best examples of his shop's work. And this was where he'd met her, of course. So maybe this tile, a crossroads of their two differing arts, just looked most natural hung in the same crossroads where their lives had intersected.

He hung it above his desk, on the back wall, distant from the front counter, slightly too far to be seen clearly, he thought.

But.

'What on earth is *that*?' the man in the suit said, picking up some freshly printed training folders because, he'd said, his secretary was sick. George looked up from his desk, from the small cutting he was making that seemed to be a still life of fruit (or possibly a spaniel) taking shape in front of him.

'Don't ask me,' Mehmet said, still resentful the tile hadn't been given to him. 'I don't think we'd call that art in Turkey.'

'Then the Turks would be very foolish indeed,' said the man in the suit, a kind of stunned dazzle in his voice. 'Is it yours?' he asked, looking at George keenly, as if on the verge of confirming something he'd always wanted to know. And he meant *Is it yours?* both ways, George realised. Had George made it? But also, George was curious to hear, did George own it?

'The crane is mine,' George said. 'The dragon is . . .' He paused for a moment, Kumiko's name precious on his tongue. 'Someone else's.'

'It's extraordinary,' the man said, simply, without undue emphasis, his eyes never moving from it.

'Thank you.'

'How much is it?'

George blinked, surprised. 'I beg your pardon?'

'How much are you offering?' Mehmet said, crossing his arms.

'It's not for sale,' George said.

'But if it was?' both Mehmet and the man said at exactly the same time.

'It's not. The end.'

'Everyone has a price,' the man said, looking slightly annoyed now, having been denied something he wanted, the injustice that outraged the modern world above all others.

'That's about the most hostile thing I've heard all day,' George said.

The man's posture shifted. 'I'm sorry. I genuinely am. It's just that it's so . . .'

George waited to hear what the man would say. Mehmet seemed to be waiting, too.

'. . . right,' the man finally said.

George was astonished to see the man's eyes now swimming behind incipient tears.

'Are you sure?' said the man.

'I'm sure,' George said, but respectfully.

'I'd pay good money,' the man said. 'More than you think.'

And then he named a figure so extravagant that Mehmet actually gasped.

'It's not for sale,' George said.

Mehmet turned on him. 'Are you *crazy*?'

'You know,' said the man, 'I do actually understand. I wouldn't part with it either.' His hand idly patted the pile of training folders on the counter, a motion that contained so much disappointment, so much recognition that he'd bumped up against one of life's worst limits, George found himself standing. To do what, he didn't know. To offer the man comfort? To apologise? To simply recognise the importance of the moment?

He would never find out, because the shop door opened and Kumiko came in, smiling up at George in greeting.

'I hope you do not mind,' she said, setting her suitcase on the counter beside the man's folders, seemingly oblivious to his presence. She took out another black tile, hiding its contents from George for the moment. 'I have taken your lion,' she said. 'And I have used it.'

She flipped the tile over with a silently delighted *ta-da*.

The lion now prowled the watermill. A conjunction even more jarring than the dragon and the crane, but one that somehow, against all possibilities, worked just as well. The trueness of the watermill, which carried history in every glistening feather filament, was now imbued with a warning. *Lions alone welcome here*, it seemed to say. *Lions made only of words.* But perhaps *this* lion, this one here, who had clearly prowled the watermill for so long that it and the watermill were one home, one history, perhaps it might make an exception for you, the viewer. It might still eat you, but then again, it might not. Like the dragon and the crane, the risk would be yours. Would you take it?

'It's . . .' George said.

'Holy . . .' Mehmet said.

'That's . . .' the man in the suit said.

And then he named an even more extravagant sum.

'*Goodness*,' Kumiko said, as if seeing the man for the first time. She glanced at George, astonished. 'Is he offering to buy it?'

The man didn't wait for George to answer and increased his extravagant sum by another extravagant amount.

Kumiko giggled, actually giggled, looking at George as if they'd somehow stepped into the middle of an unexpected comedy sketch. 'What on earth shall we do?' she said.

George felt unwilling, almost savagely so, to let the lion and the watermill out of his sight, even after this single glimpse of the way it lived there on the tile.

The man doubled his second extravagant sum.

'Sold!' Mehmet cried.

'George?' Kumiko asked again. 'The money would be useful to me. For supplies.'

George tried to speak, but it came out in a croak. He tried again. 'Anything,' he stumbled. 'Anything you say.'

Kumiko watched him for a moment. 'I will not hold you to that,' she said. Then she turned to the man. 'All right. A deal.'

As George, in a daze, wrapped the lion and the water-mill in tissue paper the man in the suit began to cry, unembarrassed. 'Thank you,' he kept saying, as Mehmet ordered up a dummy invoice the man could charge his credit card against. 'Just, thank you.'

'*How* much?' Amanda said, the next time she dropped JP off at his house.

'I know,' George said. He hoisted JP up to eye level, bouncing him in his arms. 'You thought your *grand-père* was crazy, huh? Cutting up books like that?'

'*Désolé*,' JP said.

'No, seriously, Dad, *how* much?'

'She gave me half. I said no. I *insisted* no, but she said we'd made it together, that it was nothing without my contribution – though that's patently a lie, Amanda, my contribution is tiny, a tenth, a thousandth of hers.'

'But she still gave you half.'

'Said it would turn the art into a lie if I didn't accept it.'

'When the hell am I going to meet this woman?' Amanda demanded.

George was confused for a moment, but then he realised that Kumiko and Amanda still hadn't actually met. Somehow it had always worked out that they were never there at the same time. Strange. Though, to be honest, when he was with Kumiko, George tended to forget about the existence of anyone else on the planet, forget momentarily they might be important at all. He felt a flush of shame and improvised a lie.

'Soon,' he said. 'She suggested a cocktail party.'

'A *cocktail* party? Where? 1961?'

'Cock-tail,' JP said, making shooting noises with his finger.

'She can be a bit old-fashioned,' George said. 'It's just an idea.'

'Well, I do want to meet her. This mystery woman who's just earned you a month's salary in a day.'

'I had a little part in it. I did make the lion.'

'Whatever you say, George.'

Kumiko had a second set of tiles she was reluctant to show him. There were thirty-two of them, she said, and they sat quietly in the corner of her suitcase in five separate stacks tied together with white ribbon, a single sheet of tissue paper between each to keep them from rubbing together.

'It is a larger project of mine,' she said.

'You don't have to show me,' he said.

'I know,' she said, a small smile playing on her lips. 'Which is why I perhaps will.'

She finally did late on a Saturday in the print shop. George had returned JP to Amanda after her second weekend in a row counting traffic queues in Romford or Horsham or whatever town with a great-aunt-sounding name it was, and George had come in to relieve Mehmet, who hated working alone and swore he had a Saturday afternoon call-back for 'swing in *Wicked*', which George assumed was a lie but let him off anyway.

He hadn't seen Kumiko for the previous two nights. Their get-togethers were unpredictable. She now had a phone number she never seemed to answer, and often she would just show up in George's shop, wondering if he'd like to join her for company that evening.

He always said yes.

Today, she waited until nearly the end of opening hours to make her way inside. Still with the suitcase, still with the white coat draped over one arm, no matter how much colder this winter seemed to be getting.

'My daughter would very much like to meet you,' he said to her as she opened the case.

'The feeling is mutual,' Kumiko said. 'Perhaps if we have that party you were speaking of.'

'Yes,' George said. 'Okay, yes, then definitely, let's–'

'It is a kind of story,' she said, interrupting, but so delicately it was almost as if she'd done so by accident, as if he had asked her about the pile of unseen tiles seconds ago rather than many nights before. She reached into the suitcase and, instead of showing him the new picture she'd made of his latest donated cutting (a closed fist, but one drained of potential violence, one clearly clasping its last beloved thing), she picked up a packet of tiles tied with ribbon.

'A sort of myth,' she said, setting the packet down but not yet unwrapping it. 'A story I was told as a girl, but one that has grown in the telling over the years.'

Yet still she didn't move to untie the ribbon.

'You don't have to,' George said.

'I know.'

'I'm willing to wait. I told you I was willing to wait for anything.'

She looked at him seriously now. 'You hand me too much power, George. It is not a burden, but it might become one, and I do not wish that.' She touched his arm. 'I know you do it out of your abundant kindness, but there may come a day when both you and I would wish that I treat you less carefully. And that must remain a possibility, George. If there is never a chance of hardness or pain, then softness has no meaning.'

George swallowed. 'All right, then,' he said. 'I'd like to see the tiles.'

She opened her mouth in a little square of delighted surprise. '*Do* you, George? And my immediate thought was to say no to you. But how wonderful. Of course I will show you.'

She untied the ribbon, and showed him the first one.

It was almost completely covered in feathers. They fanned out, looping in and out of one another in a spray of brilliant white. Within, a single feather, also white but of just different enough tone to stand out, was cut and woven into the shape of an infant.

'These are not for sale,' she murmured, hesitant just yet to show him the rest.

'No,' George said, in almost silent agreement.

'But what might you add?' she asked. 'What does it lack?'

'It lacks nothing,' George said, his eye following every contour of the white, every slightly different contour of the infant.

'You know that not to be true,' she said. 'And so I ask you to think on it.'

George studied the picture again, trying to detach from his conscious mind, trying to let the image float there, let other images attach themselves to it.

'I'd add an absence,' he said. 'An absence made of words. There is loss here.' He blinked, recovering himself. 'I think.'

She nodded. 'And will you cut the absence for me? Will you cut others, too, as you've been doing?'

'Of course,' he said. 'Anything.'

They turned back to the tiles. 'What's happening here?' he asked. 'You said it was a myth. What myth?'

She merely nodded again, and he thought she wasn't going to answer.

But then she spoke, as if at the beginning of a story.

'*She is born in a breath of cloud,*' she said.

And continued speaking.

The following Monday, after a weekend spent with her, again lost in specifics but with generalities of serenity and comfort and a sweet yearning, George hung in his shop the third tile they'd made, the latest of the ones separate from her private thirty-two.

She had taken the closed fist he'd made, the one bled of power and vengeance, the one that seemed resigned and perhaps welcoming of its ultimate fate, and paired it with the feathered cuttings of the cheek and neck of the woman looking away from the artist. It was a more jarring conjunction than even the lion and the watermill. It had intimations of violence, fist against face, no matter how calm the fist, but this dissipated quickly. The fist became no longer a fist, but simply a closed hand, withdrawing, empty, from its final caress of the woman's face. The caress may, in fact, have been of a memory, the closed hand reaching into the past to feel it again, but failing, as the past always fails those who grasp at it.

'It's just a picture,' George kept saying to himself, as he tried to find a spot on the wall to display it. 'It's just a picture.' Trying to somehow surprise it out of its power, reduce its impact on him, keep it from making his stomach tumble.

But he failed. And was happy that he did.

The door opened behind him. For one amazed moment, he thought it was Mehmet being unprecedentedly punctual, particularly after a weekend following whatever a 'swing from *Wicked*' audition might have entailed.

'You're early,' he said, turning, the third tile in his hand.

But it wasn't Mehmet. It was the man who had bought the second tile for such an extravagant sum. He wasn't alone. A slightly plump but fiercely professional-looking woman was with him. Short blonde hair, expensive earrings and an open-collared shirt of a cut so simple and elegant it probably cost more than George's refrigerator.

Her face, though. Her face was nearly desperate, her eyes blazing at George, slightly red at their edges, as if sometime this morning she had been crying.

'Is this him?' she asked.

'This is him,' the man said, a step behind her.

The woman looked down to the picture he was holding. 'There are more,' she said, relief flooding her voice.

'Can I help you?' George mustered himself to ask.

'That picture,' she said. 'That picture you're holding.'

'What about it?' George said, raising it slightly, ready to defend it.

And then the woman said a number that George could only ever really have described as extravagant.

After she finally, *finally* finished the last of the dreariest Essex queue counts in the history of dreary Essex queue counts, and after she'd picked up a cranky, under-slept JP from yet another Saturday with her father, who was weirdly distracted and mumbled something about getting back to his cuttings, and then having at last arrived home after going to two separate supermarkets to find the only kind of juice JP was drinking this week (mango, passion fruit and peach), there was a knock on Amanda's front door.

She ignored it, as she usually did. Who knocked on the doors of flats these days? Salesmen, for the most part, explaining the sensual pleasures of double-glazing, or rosette-wearing fascists in summer hats seeking her vote in the next election or, once, in a Cockney variant so thick that even as an Englishwoman she had trouble following it, a man asking if she'd like to buy fresh fish from the back of a van. ('Who would ever do that?' she'd asked him.) It definitely wouldn't be the building supervisor at least, not on a game day, and it was too late for the post,

106

so when the knock came a second time she ignored it all over again.

'Whatever happened to the Jehovah's Witnesses, do you think?' she asked JP, tucked behind 3D glasses in front of their decidedly non-3D telly. 'You never see them much any more. It's like they've passed into myth.' She grabbed another handful of sticky toys to be tidied away. 'Though probably not one of those myths with breasts and bacchanals and swans having it off with maidens.' She turned to her son, who had not answered, mostly because he was four years old and in front of the TV. 'What do you suppose a Jehovah's Witness myth might be like, poo-poo? I picture quite a lot of lighthouses.'

'Hush, Mama,' JP said. 'Wriggle dance!'

Which meant the Wriggle dance was coming up agonisingly soon on the Wriggle video download, danced by the childlike dinosaur Wriggles in their Wriggle costumes on Wriggle Beach under Wriggle rainbows springing forth from Wriggle applications on Wriggle computer pads. The dance involved very little more than wriggling, but JP was a fierce devotee.

The knock came a third time, along with a muffled call. She paused, a sticky action figure in one hand, a sticky fire truck in another. She debated whether to risk it, but that fish salesman had also been calling things as he knocked ('Fresh fish!' she assumed, but would it really matter?). She waited, but whoever it was didn't try a third time. She dumped the toys into the toy box and, with a sigh, decided the room was clean enough and all she really wanted was to get her beautiful boy off to bed after his weekly call with Henri and watch crappy Saturday evening telly by herself with a cup of tea and some sarcastic tweeting to her sixteen followers.

'Wriggle dance!' JP shouted, leaping to his feet and commencing to wriggle vigorously.

Amanda's mobile rang. She stepped into the kitchen to rinse the sticky off her hands before taking it out of her pocket.

The display read, to her mild surprise, *Henri*.

'You're early,' she answered. 'He's–'

'You are home,' Henri said, his accent, as ever, a surprising combination of spiky and warm. 'I can hear the television. Why do you not answer your door?'

'It was unexpected,' he shrugged over a cup of tea. 'I am back on the Eurostar tomorrow evening, and we only come because Claudine's mother got trapped in her hotel room.'

Amanda paused in her own tea-sipping. 'Trapped?'

Henri made a dismissive Gallic wave. 'For most people, this is surprising. For Claudine's mother . . .' He shrugged again, a burden he was willing to put up with.

(JP had been beside himself at Henri's appearance. '*Papa! Papa! Je suis tortillant! Tortiller avec moi!*' And indeed, Henri had been up for a bit of paternal wriggling. It had taken ages to get JP down to bed after that, but Henri had asked to do it himself, even giving him a bath and reading him a story – *Le Petit Prince*, of course – before JP finally drifted off. Amanda had even tried not to feel irritated at how pleased with himself Henri looked after completing the tasks she did daily to no audience whatsoever.)

'So where's Claudine now?' she asked.

'On her way back to France,' Henri said, and Amanda thought there was nothing more French in the world than

108

a Frenchman saying *France*. 'Her mother is using my ticket. I could not get another until tomorrow.'

'It took both of you to save her mother?'

Henri rolled his eyes as if asking for mercy from the gods. 'You will have to believe yourself very lucky not to have met her. *Your* mother, so different, so English, so *nice*. I very much love Claudine' – he was looking away so he didn't see Amanda's small flinch – 'she is like the oboe playing Bach, but her *maman* . . .'

He took another sip of his tea. 'Thank you for allowing this intrusion.' His voice was without cynicism or hidden meaning. He really was grateful. 'I really am grateful,' he said.

'You're welcome,' she said, in a small voice.

There was a short, careful silence. 'May I ask how are you?' he said.

'You may.'

He smiled back at her, in a way that made her stomach sink down to her toes. She loved him, she loved him, she loved him, she hated the French motherfucker, mostly for how *much* she loved him, but oh she loved loved loved him still, the handsome bastard. 'So, how *are* you?' he asked again.

She opened her mouth to say 'I'm fine', but what came out instead was 'I can't seem to stop crying lately'.

And to her surprise, it was true. She'd never considered herself much of a crier, but lately, oh, just lately. Crying when she talked with her father, crying at the slightest bit of TV sentiment, crying when a lift door closed before she reached it. It was infuriating, which weirdly only made her cry more.

'Are you depressed?' Henri asked, not unkindly.

'Only if that means being angry all the time.'

109

'I think the word for that is *Amanda-esque*.' He raised his eyebrows in a way that only the French ever bothered with, but it was still friendly. This detente was still fairly new. Henri visited often enough to be sure JP kept his physical presence fresh in his memory, but it had, for the first couple of years, been like the exchange of nuclear secrets between hostile agents, with her, if she was honest, by far the more hostile. Over time, though, it had become too tiring to stay so constantly mad at him. She had thawed from strained to curt, from curt to polite, from polite to this almost friendliness, one which, in a way, was almost harder to take, because if she could be this calm with him, then that probably meant the spark had completely gone, hadn't it? All that furious passion had at least been *passion*. The thought made her frown, and Henri mistook her expression.

'Forgive me,' he said, setting down his cup of tea. 'I do not wish to offer you reason to shout at me.'

'Is that all you think I did? Shout at you?'

'There was quite a lot of shouting.'

'There was quite a lot to be shouting *at*.'

He grinned. 'And we are nearly there again. But please, I did not come for an argument. I came to see my son, and I would very happily do so in peace, if we can agree?'

Amanda said nothing, just swished the last bit of cold tea across the bottom of her cup as she looked at him. He was annoyingly tanned, his salt-and-pepper hair cropped very short to downplay a receding hairline. It only made him look sexier, though, as did the slightly French cut of his t-shirt and the slightly French wisp of chest hair over its collar.

'This bothers me, the crying,' he said, leaning towards

110

her on the settee. 'It cannot be good for you. It cannot be good for Jean-Pierre if his mother is sad.'

She thought for a moment. 'I really don't think they're entirely sad tears. They're more angry.'

'These are not very different shadings.'

He was still there, leaning close enough to smell, an achingly familiar scent that was partly the honey soap she knew he was partial to, partly the cigarette he'd no doubt had on the walk here from the Tube, and partly just Henri, the individual smell that anyone had, made alluring or off-putting only because of the person who wore it.

Alluring. Or off-putting. Or alluring.

Goddamn him.

She reached up and ran a hand across his cheek. The stubble softly scraped her fingertips.

'Amanda,' Henri said.

He didn't back away as she neared him, didn't back away as she unquestionably entered his personal space, didn't back away as her lips touched his.

But then he backed away. 'That would be a bad idea.'

'Claudine is under twenty-five miles of water,' Amanda said, still close, though not quite sure what she was doing, feeling tears just seconds away, trying to make sure they didn't arrive. 'And think how well we already know each other. We could skip all the stuff neither of us like.'

He took her hand and kissed it. 'We should not.'

'But you're thinking about it.'

He smiled and gestured to his lap, where an impressive area of strained fabric made his physical interest plain. 'But we should not,' he said. 'We cannot.'

She waited another second to see if he would yield (and *yield* was the right word, she was asking him to yield to her, not just to see if he would, but because her need was clearly so much greater, so much greater at that moment that it felt as if she was falling off a cliff and desperately wanted him not to save her from falling, but to fall *with* her, and if they survived, well, then, afterwards there could be more fucking cups of fucking tea) and then she sat back on the settee, trying to smile casually, as if it was just a passing fancy, no big deal, some mature adult fun they could have had, but nothing to regret, nothing to worry about.

She had to bite her bottom lip to keep from crying. Again.

'I love you, Amanda,' Henri said, 'and I know, despite what you might shout, that you love me as well. But I love Claudine now and she is able to love me in a way that doesn't cost her as much as it costs you.'

'It was nothing,' Amanda said, annoyed at the thickness in her voice, trying to turn it into a false brightness, knowing neither of them believed her. 'Passing fancy on a Saturday evening.' She sniffled and looked away from him as she took a sip from her empty teacup. 'Just a bit of fun.'

He watched her for a moment. She knew he was fighting between trying to look noble about everything – he'd always had a pompous streak – but also truly trying to delicately, kindly, not embarrass her, if it was at all possible. It wasn't, and she just had to wait until he realised that.

'I should go,' he finally said, standing, but he didn't move away from her when he stood. Their proximity was suddenly very close, him standing, her sitting, both of them aware again of the still-present strain against his trousers.

They breathed for a moment.

'*Merde*,' Henri whispered, and pulled his shirt off over his head.

Later, when it was over, and he sat on the edge of the settee wearing nothing but a cigarette and his now inside-out underpants, he gestured towards JP's room. 'I miss him,' he said. 'Every day, I miss him.'

'I know,' was all Amanda could manage.

She didn't cry after he left, didn't feel angry or sad or anything at all, just watched brightly coloured people suffer brightly coloured hysteria all across the Saturday night telly. When it was finally time to turn all of that off and go to bed, *that's* when she cried.

Sunday passed in a grind of chores: a week's worth of dishes (she was ashamed to admit), slightly more than a week's worth of laundry (she was even more ashamed to admit, JP was on a third rotation of a certain pair of dungarees), plus a break to feed the ducks at a nearby pond, which JP refused to do wearing anything but his Superman costume, complete with fake muscles.

'Ducks, ducks, ducks!' JP said, throwing an entire slice of bread at a goose.

'Little bits at a time, sweetheart,' she said, bending down to show him. He watched her hands, almost panting with bread-anticipation.

'Me!' he said. 'Me, me, me!'

She handed him the bits and he threw them all at the goose in a single motion. 'Duck!'

She was lucky, she knew it, told herself so with annoying repetition. She'd found an affordable nursery near work that JP seemed to love and which was even mostly covered by Henri's child support. Her mother could pick him up at the end of the nursery day if Amanda's work overran and watch him until Amanda collected him on the way

113

home. George, too, was always more than happy to take him in at odd times when needed.

And look at him. Christ, just *look* at him. Sometimes she loved him so much she wanted to eat him alive. Just put him between two slices of this stale duck bread and munch on his bones like a fairy-tale witch. The juice stain around his lips, the way he was brave about almost everything on earth except balloons, the way his French was so much more punctilious than his English. She loved him so much she'd tear the earth apart if anyone ever dared harm–

'Okay,' she whispered to herself, feeling the tears coming again. 'Right then.'

She leaned forward and kissed the back of his head. He was a little bit stinky because bathtime was another chore running late today, but he was still purely him.

'Mama?' he asked, turning round, hands out for more bread.

She swallowed the tears. (What was *wrong* with her?) 'Here you go, sweet cheeks,' she said, handing him another batch. 'This one, by the way, isn't actually a duck.'

He turned back to the goose, amazed. 'It's not?'

'It's a goose.'

'Like Suzy Goose!'

'Yes, of course, I forgot we read that–'

'She's not white, though.'

'There are lots of different kinds of geese.'

'Is that different than goose?'

'One goose, two geese.'

'One moose, two meese.'

'This one's a Canada goose, I think.'

'Canada moose,' JP said. 'What's Canada?'

'A big country by America.'

'What do they do there?'

'They chop down trees and eat their lunch and go to the lavatory.'

JP was thrilled at this news.

'Is that a goose, too?' he said, pointing.

She followed his finger to a great white bird wading through the pond. It had a splash of red feathers across its head and was looking carefully at the water between its feet, as if hunting.

'I'm not sure,' Amanda said. 'A stork maybe?'

Then a thought occurred. A startling one.

But no, that had just been George's dream, hadn't it? She hadn't believed that had actually happened. He hadn't called it a stork either. He'd called it a *crane*, that was it. Did England even *have* cranes? She didn't think so, but she'd certainly never seen a bird like this before. The size of it, for one thing–

JP coughed, and the bird glanced up at the noise. A bright golden eye, crazy like the eyes of all birds, caught hers briefly and held it for one second, two, before returning to its hunt.

Amanda felt briefly like she'd been judged. But then, she felt that most days.

'Is Papa coming to feed the ducks with us?' JP asked.

'No, baby, Papa had to go back to France.'

'Claudine,' JP said, proud of his knowledge.

'Indeed,' Amanda said. 'Claudine.'

JP looked back at the goose he'd been feeding. It had nibbled up the last of the bread and was poking its long neck at them in a request that managed to seem both embarrassed and assertive. JP just stood there, hands on his hips, foam Superman muscles bulging. 'A goose,' he said. '*I* am not a goose.'

'No, you're not.'

'Sometimes I am a duck, Mama,' he explained, 'but I am not ever a goose. Not even once.'

'Why do you suppose that is?'

'If I was a goose, I would know my name. But when I am a goose, I don't know my name, so I'm not a goose. I'm a duck.'

'You're a JP.'

'I am a Jean-Pierre.'

'That, too.'

He stuck his sticky hand in hers (how? How was it sticky? All he'd been handling was *bread*. Did little boys just ooze sticky resin, like snails?). Amanda glanced again at the stork/possibly crane thing, watching it until it disappeared behind the branches of an overhanging tree, still scanning the water for food.

'Surely the fish are hibernating this time of year?' she asked, then rolled her eyes at how stupid it sounded. She was becoming increasingly worried she was turning into one of those single mothers you saw on trains, speaking in a loud, clear voice to their child, as if pleading for somebody, *anybody* to please join in and give her something else to talk about besides goddamn wriggling.

'What's hyperflating?' JP asked.

'Hibernating. Means sleeping off the winter.'

'Oh, *I* do that. I get into bed and I sleep the whole winter. And sometimes, Mama? Sometimes, I *am* winter. *Je suis l'hiver.*'

'*Oui*, little dude. *Mais oui.*'

By the time she'd got JP to bed that night, she found she was so tired she couldn't be bothered to even make lunch for the next day. She was supposed to have time off in lieu for all these idiotic Saturdays out in soul-sapping

116

middle-of-Essex nowhere, but Head of Personnel Felicity Hartford had made it clear that 'time off in lieu' was like the gold standard: worth the world, as long as no one ever asked to spend it.

She called George that evening instead, and they talked about Kumiko – who Amanda *still* hadn't met; it had got to the point where it seemed George was purposely keeping her secret – and about the astonishing amount of money he and Kumiko were suddenly being offered for the art they made together, a development Amanda instinctively mistrusted, like telling everyone you'd won the lottery before doing the final verification of your numbers.

'You remember that bird you said you saved?' she asked. 'What was it? A stork?'

'A crane,' he said. 'At least I'm pretty sure it was a crane.'

'Did that really happen? Or did you just dream it?'

He sighed, and to her surprise, there was a real annoyance in it. She pressed on quickly. 'Only I think I may have seen it today. At the park with JP. Tall white thing, hunting for fish.'

'*Really?* That park near your flat?'

'Yeah.'

'Gosh, wouldn't that be something? Gosh. It wasn't a dream, no, but it sure felt that way. *Gosh.*'

She talked to her mother next, mostly about her father. 'Well, almost none of that makes sense, dear,' her mother said about Kumiko and the art and the money and the crane. 'Are you sure?'

'He seems happy.'

'He always seems happy. Doesn't mean he is.'

'Don't tell me you still worry about him, Mum.'

'To meet George once is to worry about him forever.'

Just before she lay down in bed to pretend to read, Amanda picked up her mobile again and clicked 'Recents'. *Henri* was third down, after her father and her mother. She hadn't spoken to anyone else the entire weekend. She thought of calling Henri to see if he'd made it home safely, but that, of course, was impossible, for so many reasons. And what would she say? What would *he* say?

She put the phone back down and turned off the light. She slept. And dreamt of volcanoes.

Work on Monday morning involved an analysis of the data she'd collected at the weekends – numbers of cars, how long each had waited on average, possible alternate traffic signalling or routing or directional changes that might help. She never tried to explain this part of her job to others, not after seeing how their faces stretched back in terror that she might keep talking about it.

But, well, people were dumb, and she found the job interesting. The sorting out of traffic may not have been all that dynamic, but the solving of a problem could be. And these were problems she *could* solve, was even developing a certain flair for solving, even possibly so well she may have been shifting Felicity Hartford from anonymous loathing of her into reluctantly approving awareness.

Though Rachel – who was, after all, her immediate superior – was starting to prove a real obstacle.

'Have you finished the analysis yet?' Rachel asked, standing at the end of Amanda's desk reading a report, as if Amanda's work was too boring for eye contact.

'It's 9.42,' Amanda said. 'I've only been here forty-five minutes.'

'Thirty-*one* minutes?' Rachel said. 'Don't think your tardiness hasn't been noticed?'

'I worked all day Saturday.'

'Queue counts should only take the morning? I hardly think that's *all day*?'

It had been like this since the picnic. Nothing obvious had changed, no big gestures or declaration of eternal enmity, just the slow withdrawal of lunch invites, an increased brusqueness to work requests, a general chilling of atmosphere. Refusing to look at her was new, though. They must have entered a new phase, Amanda thought. All righty then.

'How's it going with Jake Gyllenhaal's brother?' she asked, turning back to her screen. Out of the corner of her eye, she at least saw Rachel look up.

'Who?'

'The boy from the park,' Amanda said, faux-innocently. 'The one who threw olive oil all over you.'

'Wally is fine?' Rachel said, a little frown (plus, Amanda was thrilled to see, a little frown *line*) briefly scarring her immaculate face.

'He's called *Wally*?' Amanda said, for what was the third or maybe fourth time. 'Who's called Wally these days?'

'It's a perfectly normal name?' Rachel said. 'Unlike certain other names I could mention? I mean, Kumiko for someone not even Japanese?'

Amanda blinked. 'What a weird thing to remember. And how do you know she's not Japanese?'

'Not really weird?' Rachel said. 'You talk about it, like, incessantly? Like you have no life of your own so you've got to live through your father's? It's sad? Is what it is?'

'Sometimes, Rachel, I don't know how you think–'

119

'The *report*, Amanda?' Rachel said, green eyes flashing.

Amanda gave up. 'By lunchtime,' she said, then put on a huge fake smile. 'And hey, maybe we can have a bite and go over it together. What do you say?'

Rachel made a fake disappointed sound. 'That would have been super? But I've already got plans? Just on my desk by one?'

She walked away without waiting for Amanda's response. *We could have been friends*, Amanda thought.

'And yet somehow, no,' she said to herself.

'Out of the *way*, fat ass!'

The cyclist's elbow sent Amanda's coffee flying towards a pavement heaving with City workers on their lunch breaks, including a businesswoman who'd picked the wrong day to wear cream. The cup hit the pavement at the woman's feet, splattering her with a wave that reached all the way to mid-thigh.

The woman stared at Amanda, mouth agape. Amanda, torn between the embarrassment of having so many people hearing her called 'fat ass' and the embarrassment of having practically *thrown* coffee at an innocent bystander, tried to seize the initiative.

'Fucking cyclists,' she said, feeling the sentiment truly but also hoping the woman would follow her on the shift of blame.

'You're standing in the *bike lane*,' the woman said. 'What did you expect him to do?'

'I expected him to give way to a pedestrian!'

'Maybe your ass was too fat for him to avoid.'

'Oh, fuck you,' Amanda said, giving up and walking away. 'Who wears cream in January anyway?'

'You're paying to clean this!' the woman said, stomping after her.

Amanda tried to push her way through all the suits, male and female, that had slowed to watch the altercation. 'What are you going to do?' she said. 'Have me arrested for dry-cleaning?'

A handsome Indian businessman stepped solemnly in front of Amanda. 'I really think you should offer to pay for the woman's cleaning,' he said, in a thick Scouse accent. 'It's the proper thing to do, like.'

'Yeah,' said a second handsome man. 'It was your fault, after all.'

'It was the *cyclist*'s fault,' Amanda said. '*He* knocked into me, and now he's miles away, no doubt cresting the wave of his own self-righteousness.'

The cream-wearing woman caught up and grabbed her by the shoulder. 'Look at me!' she said. 'You're going to pay for these.'

'Don't worry,' said the handsome Indian Scouser. 'She will.'

Amanda opened her mouth to fight. She was even ready, she found to her surprise, to physically threaten this woman in some way, ready maybe even to follow through on an actual slap (even an actual *punch*) if the woman didn't take her *goddamn* hand off Amanda's shoulder. Amanda was tall enough and big enough not to be messed with and by God people should just go ahead and learn–

But when she opened her mouth to start, she found herself, once again, overflowing with tears.

Everyone was looking at her, their faces angry that she'd brought injustice into their day, waiting firmly to see it righted. She tried to speak again, tried to explain

121

in no uncertain terms what the woman could do with her cream trousers, but all that came out was a choked sob.

'Seriously,' she whispered to herself, 'what is *wrong* with me?'

Moments later, though they seemed like hours, Amanda had exchanged business cards with the woman, under the disdainfully triumphant eyes of the two handsome men. She left them to whatever high-finance *ménage à trois* they'd end up with and took the rest of her lunch to a small green-space near the office, only realising as she sat down on the one remaining open half of a bench that she now no longer had a coffee to go with it.

They're angry tears, she told herself as she cried into her cress sandwich, made in a hurry this morning without mayonnaise because she was late for JP's nursery. *They're angry tears*.

Henri was right, though. Not very different shadings.

'Are you all right?' said a voice.

It was the woman sitting on the other half of the bench, a woman Amanda had barely registered as she sat down, a woman also, bafflingly, wearing cream. Seriously, it was fucking *January*, people.

But this time, at least, it was a cream outfit embracing a kind face, yet one that had (Amanda was surprised to find herself thinking) also seen the world, and had returned knowing maybe not so much about the world but more about herself than Amanda could learn in a lifetime.

'Long day,' Amanda coughed out, confused. She turned back to her sandwich.

'Ah,' said the woman. 'Myths tell us the world was created in a day, and we scoff and we call them metaphors and allegories, but on a day like today it seems as if we could break our backs the whole morning to make the universe and someone would still ask us to come to meetings in the afternoon.'

Amanda smiled back politely, feeling the first inklings of alarm that she'd sat next to a mad person. But then again, no. This odd little woman seemed, somehow, to have understood and was merely saying so. In an odd way, yes, but one that was also oddly comforting.

I keep saying 'odd', Amanda thought. The woman's accent was also oddly ('and again') unplaceable, clear but foreign in a way that suggested not a country but a kind of ancientness. Amanda shook her head. *No*, she thought, *she's probably just Middle Eastern. Or something.*

'I am sorry,' the woman said, three words, not the usual contraction, but even then it wasn't an 'I am sorry' that meant 'I'm sorry'. It was an 'I am sorry' that meant 'Excuse me'.

Amanda looked back over.

'This seems scarcely credible,' the woman said, 'but is it at all possible that you are Amanda Duncan?'

Amanda froze mid-chew.

'I am sorry,' the woman said again, and this time it meant 'I'm sorry'. 'This is quite amazing, is it not?' she said. 'We have not met, but I feel as if we have.'

Amanda sat up straighter, astonished. 'Kumiko?'

For all of a sudden, it could only be her.

A cyclist – possibly the same one from earlier for all Amanda knew, they all looked identical, with their crotch-fitting tights and their air of ethical entitlement – raced past, perilously close to the bench, causing them both to rear back. Amanda's cress sandwich tumbled to the pavement, lying there like a murder victim.

'Fucking *cyclists!*' she screamed after him. 'Think they own the world! Think they can do whatever they like!

Complain you're in their way even when you're on a FUCKING PARK BENCH!'

Amanda sat back, lunchless, drinkless, furious that the tears were coming again, furious that everything felt like it was sliding apart, that it was doing so for *no good reason*, that nothing had changed except something slight, something she couldn't put her finger on, something that took everything that was her life and placed it slightly higher up on a mountainside so she had to climb for it, and when she got there, there was only more mountain, there was only ever going to *be* more mountain for as long as she lived, and if that was the case then what was the goddamn *point*? Of *any* of it?

A handful of tissues nudged gently under her nose. Unnerved by where that chain of thoughts had run from and how quickly it had reached its alarming destination, Amanda took the tissues from the woman, from *Kumiko* it now seemed impossibly to be, and wiped away her tears.

'I know,' Kumiko said. 'I hate them, too.'

It took Amanda a moment to realise what Kumiko meant. When she did, she looked up in wonder and burst into fresh tears.

Which at least weren't angry.

'**D**uncan Printing?'
    'Is that the famous artist George Duncan?'
'. . .'
'That's him, isn't it?'
'. . .'
'Oh, come on, George? No need to be shy? I saw you on the internet?'
'It's over. I thought we–'
'No, it isn't over? I've seen the ones you've got for sale? Right here in front of me on my computer screen? It's not over at all, is it, George?'
'I mean *this* is over. And you know it is. *You* wanted it to be. And for once, I agreed–'
'But that was before you became *famous*?'
'Hardly famous, look, I–'
'And these *prices*, George? That's being a bit of a tall poppy, isn't it?'
'Those aren't our websites. Those aren't our prices. We don't even know how that all started. It's just sort of exploded–'

'"*We* don't even know"? You and this Kumiko person? That's her name, isn't it? Kumiko?'

'I'm going to hang up now, Rachel, and I don't want you–'

'A couple who works together? Isn't that nice?'

'You've really got to stop this upward inflection. It makes you sound like an imbecile.'

'. . .'

'I'm sorry. I didn't mean–'

'Screw you, George. I'm just trying to be *nice*. I'm just trying to be *friendly*. I mean, you broke my heart–'

'That's not even a little bit true. Clandestine meetings. Sworn to secrecy. You never even seemed like you were having a good time.'

'That's really not fair? The secrecy was for both of us? I mean, I'll *happily* tell Amanda all about us now, if that's what you want–'

'Is that meant to be some kind of threat?'

'. . .'

'I'm going to hang up now. I really am.'

'Wait. Wait? I'm sorry? I know how harsh I can be. I do. But . . .'

'But what?'

'I can't bear you being cruel, George. That's the last thing you ever are.'

'I'm sorry, I–'

'Because that's the thing I can't stop thinking about. That you're not cruel? Because cruelty is so *common* these days, you wouldn't believe it. Every man I go out with, it's like I'm in a competition with him. Who's the meanest? Who's the rudest? Like we're competing from the first hello to prove how tough we are. And then the actual dates are like a, like a, like a, what are those things?'

'A joust?'

'Yes! Like a joust! And the only thing you're allowed to do is show the other person how tough you are and how hard you are and how you're laughing at their weaknesses. That's what it is. You're *laughing* at them. You're laughing at how stupid they are? And you're trying your goddamn hardest to make sure they're *never* going to laugh at how stupid *you* are. And don't even get me started on the sex?'

'I would really hope not to—'

'Because the sex is all about pretending that, no matter how great it is? No matter how much work and, like, *skill* they put into it? That it's only okay? That you've had better? That it wasn't, like, *bad*, but they shouldn't feel too proud of themselves?'

'Rachel, I don't know what you want from—'

'It's awful, George. I *hate* it. And I've been with this guy, Wally?'

'*Wally?*'

'And every minute is like that! Every minute! Like we're on *Gladiators*? It's *exhausting*. I'm so tired of it. I'm so, so tired of it? And you weren't like that.'

'. . .'

'. . .'

'. . .'

'George?'

'I'm with Kumiko now.'

'I know. I know? I mean, I do know? Your daughter won't shut up about it? So I know? But I was just thinking. I was thinking how much I missed you.'

'. . .'

'. . .'

'I don't know what to say to—'

127

'You don't have to say anything? I just–'

'I'm with Kumiko–'

'Miss someone who's–'

'And I really have–'

'Someone who's actually *kind*–'

'Fallen in love with her.'

'You were so nice to me, George. Hardly anyone is.'

'Well, you weren't exactly nice yourself.'

'I know I wasn't that nice to you–'

'No, nice *to* yourself. You didn't treat yourself well.'

'You were the first person to ever suggest that could even be a possibility, George. And I've been dating this Wally, who's really, really *cute* and all but–'

'Rachel, I have to–'

'But I just keep thinking, *He's not as nice as George.*'

'It was a *fling*, Rachel, and I think we both know what a mistake it was. I'm too old for you. I'm too boring for you. You said so yourself. I'm not even that good-looking–'

'So what if all that's true? Sometimes you need more than that.'

'And this has nothing to do with me being with someone else? Nothing to do with me being in the news a little bit?'

'You're being mean again, George. And it doesn't suit you?'

'I'm genuinely going to go. I'm going to wish you well–'

'See? Niceness.'

'But I'm really going to go now.'

'I'd like to see you.'

'Rachel–'

'Just for old time's sake?'

'No, I don't think–'

'I could show you a proper good time.'

'. . .'

'You know I can, George.'

'I'm so sorry, Rachel.'

'You will be if you don't let me–'

'I'm so sorry you're this lonely.'

'George–'

'I wish happiness for you. I listen to you and I hear hurting and I hear cries of how much you want to–'

'Wait just a *second*–'

'–connect with someone, *really* connect.'

'I *do*, though? I–'

'And I'm sorry it can't be me. But it can't. It really can't.'

'George–'

'And I wish you well–'

'*George*–'

'But I have to go now–'

'I'm pregnant.'

'. . .'

'. . .'

'. . .'

'. . .'

'Except, of course, you're not.'

'George–'

'Goodbye, Rachel, and I'm sorry.'

'George, I just–'

The lady flies for a lifetime and more, landing when the growing earth calls to her, flying when it does not. Both are enjoyable, and enjoyment is, despite her tears, something she seems to have an aptitude for. She grants absolution wherever she lands, piercing hearts with her forgiveness, for of what do we ever ask forgiveness if not our offences against joy?

The world enters its adolescence, the land stitching itself together into a recognisable whole, though not without its pains and eruptions. She does not avoid the volcanoes when they spew, recognising in them the same anger as the water, of effort directed outward, into nothing.

'Not long,' she tells the volcanoes. 'Not long before your reach will dig its long muscles into the earth, binding it tightly as a world. One arm clasping another clasping another, holding the burden of life on your collective shoulders. Not long.'

And the volcanoes believe her, calming their angry flows, directing them more usefully, dragging the world together.

All volcanoes, save one.

'I do not believe you, my lady,' says the volcano, his green eyes flashing in a malevolent merriment she finds puzzling. 'The point of a volcano is anger,' he says. 'A calm volcano is merely a mountain, is it not? To calm a volcano is to kill it.'

Lava and heat and destruction flow from him in waves, the denizens of this young earth fleeing before his burning laughter. She flies away in distaste, before circling around again to confirm her distaste. Then circling round again.

'The purpose of a volcano is to die,' she says. 'Is this not what you strive for?'

'The purpose of a volcano is to die, my lady,' says the volcano, 'but as angrily as possible.'

'You do not seem angry,' she says. 'You smile. You jest. You speak from desire, from flirtation. I have seen it the world over.'

'I speak from joy, my lady. Angry joy.'

'Is such a thing possible?'

'It is that which creates us all. It is that which fires the magma of the world. It is that which drives the volcano to sing.'

'Is this what you call your destruction? A song?'

'I do, my lady. And a song can never lie.'

'Unlike you,' she says and flies away.

The volcano casts a sail of lava after her retreating form.

It does not reach her. It is not meant to. 'You will return, my lady,' he says. 'You will return.'

10 of 32

She returns. She is older, wiser. The world is older, too, though surprisingly not that much wiser.

'You still erupt,' she says, flying a wide circle around the volcano.

'And you still forgive,' says the volcano, atop his chariot of horses, 'where forgiveness is not warranted.'

'You have become an agent of war,' she says, keeping beyond his reach, for she has learned more about volcanoes in the passing time, learned as we all must to stay out of range of their exertions.

'I am a general now,' says the volcano. An army spreads out before him, swarming over the world, consuming forests and cities and deserts and plains.

'You have not died like all the others and become a mountain.'

'I have not, my lady. There was no future in it.'

He raises his whip, a long chain of glowing white heat, and lashes his great and terrible horses. They whinny in agony and trample farms and bridges and civilisations under their hooves, his innumerable, ravenous armies flowing like burning rivers in their wake.

She flies with him for a time, watching in silence as he grinds this corner of the world to ruin. She says nothing to him. He says nothing in return, save for the occasional glance in her direction. Those green eyes, tracing her path.

'I will forgive you,' she says, 'should you ask.'

'I will not ask, my lady,' says the volcano.

'And why not?'

'I do not require anyone's forgiveness, and neither do I recognise your authority to offer it.'

'The authority to offer it is given by he who asks.'

He smiles at her, his eyes bright. 'This does not contradict me, my lady.'

II of 32

Guided by a feeling she declines to recognise, she swoops down low over the volcano's advancing army. It has encountered another and, up close, it is impossible to tell which side is which. The battle is nothing more than a twisting, spattering pan of butchery, turned in on itself to boil and burn.

She sweeps back up and around, circling the volcano for a last time.

'Before you leave, my lady,' says the volcano. 'I wonder if you will tell me your name.' He smiles again, and reflected in his eyes the world is dying in fire and terror. 'So that I may call it to you when you next see me.'

'I will not see you again.'

'As you wish, my lady,' the volcano says, bowing his head at her. 'Yet I will tell you mine.' He opens his mouth and a roar of pain and mischief is hurled from it. The leaves on nearby trees curl up just to hear it, birds fall from the skies, black locusts spiral from cracks in the ground.

'But you, my lady,' says the volcano, 'may call me—'

'I shall not call you anything,' she says, ready to fly away, but not leaving, not just yet. She says, for the second time, 'I will not see you again.'

The volcano says, also for a second time, 'As you wish, my lady.'

He raises his whip, but she is gone before it lands.

'Father?' she says, flying through the clouds. She knows he will not answer. He never has, not at any point as the world has grown older. She neither knows nor in fact believes that he might be out there listening to her, for a cloud shifts and gathers and rains itself out many times over the course of a single day let alone a world's lifetimes, and even the daughter of a cloud cannot tell one from another.

They might be her father. They might just be clouds. They are not her father. They are clouds.

Yet still, 'Father?' she says.

She says nothing further, unsure of what her question might be. Her head is filled with the volcano, with arguments they have never had, defeats of him she has never achieved, the final sweet forgiveness she can offer as she grants him his last wish of a release he has not asked for.

She flies through the clouds, letting the drops of moisture cool her brow, wet her clothes in sweet relief, soothe the aching muscles of her flying.

All the while, her father watches her, whispering her name only when she has finally left the clouds and is too far away to hear it.

G eorge began to dream strange things.

Kumiko still wouldn't let him see her work, would still barely let him past the front door of the small flat where she lived – which didn't matter so much as she was almost always at George's now anyway – but he began to dream of locked doors and knowing she was beyond them, knowing also that the locks were only there at her request and his observance of that request. He could look any time he chose. But in his dreams, he stayed behind the door. In agony.

Or he dreamed of finding her in a secret white room with no locks, gathering feathers to herself in the shape of a woman, draping and trimming long white wings back into arms and fingers, disguising a beak behind her nose, putting pale brown contact lenses over her golden, golden eyes. When she saw him watching her, she wept for him, for all they were about to lose.

Or he dreamed of fire, rising up through the earth, spilling out in seams of lava, chasing him, with her running behind, but in the dream he could never be sure whether she was running from the fire, too, or if she was leading it to him, so that it could swarm down and consume him.

When he woke, he forgot every fact of the dreams, but a residue of unease remained.

And began to accumulate.

The first purchase he made with the tile money was a massive new printer for the shop.

'Not a raise for me?' Mehmet asked, arms huffily folded.

'And a raise for you,' George said, watching the delivery men move the printer into place.

'How much?'

'Pound an hour.'

'That's *it?*'

George turned to him. 'Pound-fifty?'

Mehmet looked as if he was about to protest, but then his face broke into a disbelieving smile. 'How have you made it this far in life, George? How do you not get eaten alive by the world out there?'

'I do okay,' George said, his eyes back on the printer.

It didn't gleam; its parts were plastic and its rollers looked like what they were, cogs in an enormous piece of industrial machinery. But oh, it *did* gleam. In his heart's eye, it gleamed. It was faster than George's old printer, but that was just a technical point. Its colours were more vibrant. The sheens and complex texture combinations it could do were almost laughably luxuriant. Its programming could re-adjust itself in an instant, *faster* than an instant, could *anticipate* your coming instant and do what you wanted before you even asked.

It was everything George had ever wanted for his shop.

And it had paid for itself from the art that hung above

it. Art that Kumiko mostly made but for which she insisted his part was vital, and for which she continued to give him half.

Which was turning out to be half of quite a lot. After they'd sold the second tile – of the closed hand beside the profile of the face – to the woman brought in by the first buyer, they'd sold a third and a fourth within the week to friends of those first two buyers. Despite being obviously moneyed and occasionally intimidatingly cool, neither of the new buyers had seemed to want the tiles out of any sense of fashion – how could they, the tiles were far too new – but instead behaved with the same sort of desperate longing the first buyers had shown. One, a creative accounts exec who wore an expensive black tie over an expensive black shirt under an expensive black blazer, had said almost nothing beyond a whispered 'Yes' as he gazed on the newest tile, which showed Kumiko's feathered horses plummeting down a hill towards a river of George's words, before handing over a large wad of bills to the scandalised Mehmet.

Then someone, presumably one of the buyers, had tipped off a small but influential online arts journal, which had featured a brief interview with George – but not Kumiko, who had asked him to please be whatever sort of public face the tiles might need – as a 'potential rising star', and before the end of that week they'd not only had a number of enquiries to buy the at-that-point still-unfinished fifth tile, but also offers of initial meetings and even representation from different art dealers.

George had declined, mainly because Kumiko seemed reluctant to involve others, but by then it hardly mattered. Word was spreading, without George seemingly having to do anything to make it spread.

'You've got buzz,' Mehmet said, in an annoyed way, after they'd shipped off the fifth tile to a buyer in Scotland who hadn't even seen it in person. 'God knows why.'

'If God does know,' George said, 'he's not telling me.'

Kumiko, meanwhile, kept out of the way, letting George handle all the selling while she kept on working industriously, taking whatever cuttings George offered her and somehow turning them into breathtaking compositions that seemed to have always existed, merely waiting to coalesce and reveal their ancient, fully formed shape rather than just being newly made. She worked on further tiles to sell but also added George's cuttings to her private stack of thirty-two that even he hadn't seen all of. These were kept secret and off-sale, but for the others there was already a growing queue of people who snapped up the sixth and seventh tiles within hours of them being finished, paying increasingly preposterous prices.

Preposterous enough, for example, for a substantial down payment on this top-of-the-line, affordable-only-by-proper-publishing-folks printer.

It was gorgeous. It was his. It barely seemed real.

'It seems somehow . . .' He turned to Mehmet. 'Am I missing something here? How did this happen?'

'I don't know, George,' Mehmet said. 'I'm not sure anybody does.'

'Don't you find it strange?' he said as Kumiko lathered up his hair.

'Lean back,' she said, to keep his head over the sink.

'The *speed* of it,' he said. 'The *hunger* for it. It seems . . .'

He didn't finish the sentence. He didn't really know *how* it seemed.

'I am surprised as well,' Kumiko said, rinsing off the shampoo with a measuring cup. She squeezed out the excess water, then sat him up and started combing out his wet locks, a pair of short, sharp scissors in her hand.

'I suppose I'm just dazed,' he said.

He felt a small hesitation in her hand, so small as to hardly even be there, before she gathered up a line of his hair and snipped its ends cleanly away.

'Dazed in a good way or a bad way?' she asked.

'I'm not sure it's either good or bad. It's just . . . *dazzling*. There was nothing. Just this idle hobby of mine that meant *nothing*. And then there was you.' He looked at her. She gently guided him back into a more suitable position for the haircut. 'And all of this, too,' he said. 'And . . .'

'And?' She took another snip of his hair, moving with the confidence of a professional.

'And nothing, I suppose,' he said. 'Just that this extraordinary thing has happened. *Is* happening.'

'And that unnerves you?'

'Well, *yes*.'

'Good,' she said. 'It unnerves me, too. I am not surprised at the hunger you mention. The world has always been hungry, though it often does not know what it hungers *for*. But the suddenness, yes. It *is* rather remarkable, isn't it?'

She combed his hair again, ready for more snipping. This haircut had happened simply. He'd said he was going to visit his local barbers – a pair of Brazilian brothers, surprisingly young, outlandishly handsome, utterly gormless – and she'd said, 'Let me.'

'Where did you learn to do this again?' he asked.

'On my travels,' she said. 'Plus, it isn't so far from what I do in my work, is it? They are complementary skills.'

139

'I wouldn't want to try cutting *your* hair.'

He could almost feel her smile, feel the warmth of it behind him in his little kitchen, as he sat in this chair, an old sheet wrapped around his neck, newspapers on the floor to catch the clippings. He closed his eyes. Yes, he could feel her. Feel her against him. Feel the brush of her breath against his neck as she leaned in close.

'I love you,' he whispered.

'I know,' she whispered back, but it didn't feel like a rebuke. Her knowledge felt like delight, and he knew that this was enough.

But then there was an accompanying feeling that it wasn't enough. *Do you love me?* he wanted to ask, and it shamed him. Even when she said the words to him – which she did, though not as often – he always had to stop himself from asking for confirmation.

He knew so very, very little about her. Still.

But it wasn't as if he'd told *her* everything either. Rachel had gone unmentioned, for one, though that was more for his daughter, who he suspected, almost certainly correctly, would be crushed if she knew. There were also, of course, the whole host of bad habits kept secret in the early days of any relationship – the toenail ablutions in bed, the *laissez-faire* approach to whisker maintenance, that whole dabbing himself with a square of loo roll after peeing thing – but even compared to that, Kumiko had given him almost nothing. It was unreasonable, it was untrusting, it was–

He pushed it down, fought it away.

'I once tried cutting Amanda's hair,' he said, 'when she was little.'

He heard Kumiko chuckle. 'And how did that go?'

'Not bad, I thought.'

140

'And yet still it was only once.'

'Well, little girls, eh?' He frowned, his chest slightly over-filled with love for his difficult daughter. 'Though Amanda was never a very usual little girl. Funny, always funny, and Clare and I thought that meant she was doing all right.'

'I like her,' Kumiko said. 'She makes very much sense to me.'

'I still can't believe you met like that.'

'The only unnatural thing would be if there were *no* coincidences, George. I could have walked into any print shop, for example. But I walked into yours and look at the upheaval that has resulted.'

He turned to her. 'So you feel the upheaval, too?'

She nodded, turning him back again. 'I have not as much time as I would like to work on my own story.'

'Yes,' he agreed, thinking once more of the thirty-two tiles, of what he had seen of them – the lady and the volcano, the world they were making – and of all the ones he had yet to see. She hadn't even told him how the story ended yet. 'Are you okay with that?'

'For now,' she said. 'But you know this yourself. A story needs to be told. A story *must* be told. How else can we live in this world that makes no sense?'

'How else can we live with the extraordinary?' George murmured.

'Yes,' Kumiko said, seriously. 'Exactly that. The extraordinary happens all the time. So much, we can't take it. Life and happiness and heartache and love. If we couldn't put it into a story–'

'And explain it–'

'No!' she said, suddenly sharp. 'Not explain. Stories do not explain. They seem to, but all they provide is a starting point. A story never ends at *the end*. There is always after. And even within itself, even by saying that this version is the right one, it suggests other versions, versions that exist in parallel. No, a story is not an explanation, it is a net, a net through which the truth flows. The net catches some of the truth, but not all, *never* all, only enough so that we can live with the extraordinary without it killing us.' She sagged a little, as if exhausted by this speech. 'As it surely, surely would.'

After a moment, George asked, 'Has something extraordinary happened to you?'

'To me,' she said, 'and to everyone. To you, too, George, I'm sure.'

'Yes,' he said, feeling the truth of it.

'Tell me,' she smiled, a smile so kind he felt as if he could live in it for the rest of his life.

He opened his mouth to tell her about the crane in his backyard, a story he'd been shy of up until now, especially given Amanda's sceptical reaction to it, but maybe now was the moment to tell her of the strange bird whose life he may have saved, whose origin he could never know, whose appearance had marked the beginning of this impossible segment of his life, a segment his heart was in continual danger of breaking over in fear that it would end.

But instead, he surprised himself by saying, 'When I was eight years old, I was run over by a car. But that's only one version of it.'

And as she cut his hair, he told her.

'There once was a lady,' George said, holding JP's hand as they walked together around the pond, 'who was born in a cloud.'

142

'Well, *that* can't happen,' JP said.

'It can. She was born in a cloud. Like this one.' He blew out a warm, steamy breath into the cold air.

JP's eyes lit up and he did the same, puffing out long streams of clouds, then a row of small ones. 'Are clouds made from breathing?'

'I wish they were, kiddo, but it's something to do with evaporation over the ocean.'

'But *I* breathe clouds. *I* make clouds.'

'Maybe you do.'

'*Grand-père?*'

'Yes?'

'Does farting make clouds?'

George glanced down at him. JP's face was entirely sincere.

'Mama says farting is just stinky air,' JP said, 'and that everyone does it, even the Queen, but she also says my breath is sometimes stinky so that makes it stinky air, too.'

'Impeccable logic so far.'

'So, and if, so, if my *breath* makes clouds . . .' JP paused, letting the conclusions line up in his little head. He looked up with a grin. 'If I farted, it would make a cloud, too.'

'A stinky cloud.'

'A stinky cloud where the lady was born.'

'A cloud she'd want to leave very quickly.'

'Did you bring bread?'

'Did I what?'

JP pointed. 'For the ducks.'

A few shivering geese who should really have flown somewhere for the winter by now were looking hopefully up at them.

'Damn,' George said.

'Is that a swear word?'

'No. It's something beavers make.'

'Beavers have flat tails,' JP said. 'And buck teeth.'

'*You* used to have a flat tail.'

'NO!' JP said, astonished.

'Yeah, we were all worried about it. It fell off after you were born.'

'After I was born in a cloud?'

'Absolutely. A stinky cloud.'

'*Je suis une nouille*,' JP sang.

'You're a noodle?'

'A cloud!'

'Ah,' George said. '*Nuage.*'

'That's what I said!' JP said. '*Je suis une* cloud!' He ran around in a circle for a moment, arms out, shouting it over and over, before stopping suddenly. '*Grand-père*!' he said, thunderstruck. 'You spoke French!'

'Not really. I just remember a little from high school.'

'What's high school?'

'Secondary school. It's what they call it in America.'

JP's eyes dimmed a little as a very-small-person's calculation was made. 'You were American?'

'Still am.'

'Whoa.'

'That's how most people react. Now, I need your help, remember?'

'The tall bird!' JP said and looked ferociously across the pond, standing on tiptoes to see over the heads of the geese who thought his circle-running was some kind of prelude to feeding. 'I am not a goose, *grand-père*!' JP shouted.

'If you're too loud, you might scare the tall bird away.'

144

'I am not a goose,' JP whispered, very loudly.

'I believe you.'

'I am sometimes a duck.'

'I believe that, too.'

'I don't see the bird, George.'

He looked down at his grandson. '*What* did you call me?' he asked, a bit too sharply.

JP's face fell, his mouth stretching tight across his little jaw. 'That's what Mama calls you,' he said, two tiny tears fleeing down his cheeks.

'No, no, no,' George said, kneeling down. 'I'm not mad, JP. I'm just surprised.'

'She calls you that because she loves you. Is what she says.'

'That she does, little one,' George said, taking JP in his arms and picking him up. 'But for you? For you, the best love I feel is when you call me *grand-père*, and you know why?'

'Why?' JP sniffled.

'Because you, Jean-Pierre Laurent, are the only person in this whole wide world who can call me that.'

'The only one?'

'The only one.'

'I'm the only one,' JP said quietly, trying it on for size.

'How do you like them apples?'

JP's smile blazed. 'I LOVE apples! Pink Ladies are the best! Sometimes *I'm* a Pink Lady!'

'Aren't we all?' George said, setting him down and taking his hand. They walked back along the path by the pond, but all they saw were the increasingly disappointed geese, several sleeping ducks, and the inevitable startled pigeons.

No crane, nothing unusual at all.

'What happened to the lady in the cloud?' JP asked.

145

'She met a volcano,' George said, slightly distracted, still looking out across the empty pond. 'There were complications.'

He dreamed again. That he was flying.

The world was islands floating in the air, connected by rickety bridges or rope walkways. The crane flew beside him, its legs trailing behind it. 'Which is typically crane-like,' the crane told him. Pieces of the world spun beneath them, and they flew past flat stone saucers with rivers that flowed in rings, past ball-shaped stones where JP and Henri, both dressed as the Little Prince, walked in a happy circle, waving to him as he flew by.

'People don't dream like this,' George said, setting down on a rock shaped like a football field.

'You mean a football *pitch*,' said the crane, landing next to him.

George frowned. 'No, actually, I don't.'

The crane shrugged, then looked away as George peered at it more closely.

'Your eyes are wrong,' George said.

'Eyes are eyes,' said the crane, still not quite looking at him. 'Especially in a dream.'

'Especially *not* in a dream, I would have thought.' George stepped closer to the crane. It flapped its wings and flew back a few steps.

'Manners,' it said.

'Your eyes are green,' George said. 'When they should be gold.'

The crane looked at him full-on. Its eyes were indeed green, a burning, flaming, sulphurous green. 'And what do you know of gold?' it asked, its voice different, wrong.

'Who are you?' George demanded, angry, but fear rising in his chest.

'A question that needs no asking,' the crane said. Lava erupted from its eyes and poured down in great cataracts towards George.

Who ran. Or tried to. The rocky surface hurtled beneath him at great speed, rushing him away from the tidal waves of molten lava, though in actuality he couldn't quite seem to move, to make any motion except a sort of lumpy *gesture* at running.

'Okay, *this* feels like a dream,' he said.

'No,' the volcano said, rising beneath him, putting a fiery fist around George's neck and lifting him into the air. 'You were right the first time.'

'Please,' George tried to say. 'Please, stop.'

But the volcano wouldn't listen, lifting him higher and higher, its face blocking out the stars with smoke and flame. 'I will not stop,' the volcano roared. 'I will *never* stop!'

It reared back and threw George across the sky at impossible speed, rocketing past the melting world, past scalding clouds that used to be lakes and oceans, past the cries of the doomed in their burning cities. George flew fast as a comet, until he could see his target, see the white silkiness of it, see the great muscular motion of its wings furling and unfurling across the impossible expanse.

He hit it, piercing it.

And it destroyed him.

He woke. Not with a cry or a sudden sitting up in bed, heart pounding. Nothing so dramatic. He merely opened his eyes.

They were wet with tears.

'Kumiko?' he asked of the solitary darkness of his room, knowing she was at her own home tonight, knowing this was a night where he slept alone.

He asked it again anyway. 'Kumiko?'

But there was no answer.

'I want you,' he said. 'Oh, how I want you.'

And, being George, he was ashamed of his greed.

III.

Amanda brought it to work with her. Not every day, but often. Which wasn't even remotely appropriate given the money certain people seemed increasingly willing to spend on them, but also because it was precious to her for deeper reasons, ones she couldn't properly articulate to herself, much less be able to explain if anyone asked. Which was the risk of bringing it to work. If anyone saw it, they'd *definitely* ask.

So this morning, when she left the flat, she made the firm decision not to bring it. And then, like she had a number of times before, she changed her mind.

It was the usual black tile, like the one she'd seen in her father's shop, and upon it had been placed segments of white feathers, cut and trimmed and woven to suggest a horizon and a sky, and in that sky, against a bed of shimmering down, a bird in flight. A white bird against a white sky, but definitely separate, definitely *soaring* but somehow, also, still. At rest.

Below the bird, one of her father's cuttings from the pages of a book, which she (and, to be fair, often he) had always dismissed as 'aimless natterings', but here given new power, new context. These words – and words they were, bold ones, earthy ones, sometimes literally, a *fungus* here, an *eggplant* there and just down at the bottom, tucked away so you almost couldn't see it, a plaintive little *arse* that moved her somehow, every time – these words made a mountain, as solid and present as the eternal earth, anchoring the tile in place, solidifying the stillness of the bird. There was peace here, with hints somehow that it was perhaps ragged, perhaps hard-earned, but peace nonetheless.

She hid it in the top drawer of her desk and, opening the drawer to look at it now, she felt the same as the first time she'd seen it, that she was atop a precipice and about to fall, that though it was dizzying and frightening, there was also a possible liberation in the falling.

Looking at it actually made her short of breath.

Because it also felt like–

Well, it was a stupid word, wasn't it? Worse, a stupid *notion*, one that clearly hadn't been intended, though kindness obviously had, but she could never say it out loud, never think on it too long even in the privacy of her own head.

Because it also felt like–

Well, goddammit, it felt like *love*. Like *forgiveness*, somehow, which maybe were the same thing sometimes.

At which point she always told herself that it was just a tile, for God's sake. She really, *really* wasn't the kind of person who was Moved By Art. (This was almost embarrassingly true. She had once managed the entire Louvre in an hour, a feat even Henri, through his horror, had been impressed by. 'We've seen the Mona Lisa, we've seen the winged victory of Samothrace, and now I just want a crêpe.' They'd then, for reasons she couldn't quite remember, moved on to Belgium, where everything was so much crappier than France, not least that the crêpe vendors had been replaced by carts selling waffles. It was like wanting to buy air and being sold peat.) Here, though, now, in her little cubicle, she could see why word was spreading so quickly about the tiles, why the people who saw them reacted so strongly. She could barely stop herself from touching hers, from running her fingers over the top of it, from holding it close and–

'What is *that*?'

And before she even looked up, she was cursing herself for being stupid enough to bring it anywhere on earth that Rachel might see.

The tile had been a present, unasked-for and unexpected. After getting over her initial shock on that unlikely morning on the park bench – that here was *Kumiko*, in a forlorn, barely green square lined with scraggly bushes and the requisite statue of a forgotten man on a forgotten horse – they'd begun to talk. And *how* they'd talked. Of their shared hatred for cyclists ('All that self-righteousness,' Kumiko had said, allowing a frown to make her face even prettier, 'and then they act like it is your fault when they run the red light and nearly knock you down.' '*And* they smell,' Amanda had said. 'Just because you change out of your gear at work doesn't actually mean you've had a *shower*.' 'And the fold-up ones,' Kumiko continued, to Amanda's increasing delight and astonishment, 'they put it in your way on a train and it seems as if you are supposed to treat it with the respect of an elderly relative.' 'I *know*!'); how they both, contrarily, felt weirdly protective of those charity people with the clipboards who had turned eye contact into such a risk on the High Street ('They are only trying to do a job,' Kumiko said. 'And they're all so *young*,' Amanda said, 'and all probably out-of-work actors.' 'It is certainly better than being forced to watch them *act*.'); and Amanda had even ventured her opinion on the Animals In War Memorial. Kumiko, remarkably, hadn't heard of it, so Amanda explained it to her.

'Well, that sounds like an incredible waste of money,' Kumiko said.

Amanda could have cried.

And then, too soon, lunch hour was nearly over. It was time for a ravenous but also somehow satisfied Amanda to go back to the office, and that's when Kumiko said, 'I would like to give you something.'

'Can I eat it?' Amanda asked, having suffered the loss of both her coffee and her sandwich. She'd declined Kumiko's offer to share her rice and fish, but she was severely regretting that choice now.

Kumiko smiled. 'You *could* eat it,' she said, opening the small suitcase she carried instead of a handbag, 'but the flossing afterwards might be lengthy.'

And handed Amanda the tile.

'I couldn't possibly,' Amanda said, stunned. 'I really mean it, I couldn't *possibly*.'

'Do you like it?' Kumiko said shyly. Amanda was flabbergasted to see that the question was meant sincerely. She looked back down at the tile, at the improbable beauty of it, at its unlikely uplift, at the way she didn't seem to be looking at it but already dwelling within it. She couldn't help but try to decline it as a *far* too valuable gift, but her heart, oh, how her heart wanted it, wanted it, wanted it . . .

'Do I like it?' Amanda whispered, unable to take her eyes off it now. 'Do I *like* it?'

She kept looking at it. And looking at it again. And more.

'It feels like . . .' she whispered. 'It feels like . . .'

She looked up to say either 'love' or 'forgiveness', unsure of which was about to come out of her mouth, and was astonished to see that Kumiko had gone. A small cloth bag, obviously meant for carrying the tile, lay on the bench.

And somewhere, maybe even on the wind, was the permission to keep it.

Further meetings with Kumiko had been strangely difficult to come by.

'She was just *right here*, Dad,' Amanda had said in a call to George made as she stood up from the bench (after carefully, but quickly, putting the tile in the bag; it was already getting lingering looks from other bench-sitters). 'I mean, how is that even possible?'

'I don't know, sweetheart.' His words were a close whisper, over what sounded like a particularly unhappy customer in his shop. 'But did you like her?'

'*Like* her? I want to *marry* her!'

George made a sound of relief so boyish, Amanda felt momentarily overwhelmed by a need to somehow hug her father over the phone. 'What's going on there? Mehmet misspell someone's order on purpose again?'

'Just someone who had put down money for the next tile,' he said, a bit of strain in his voice. He paused as the door of the shop was slammed so hard Amanda could hear it over the phone. 'We were supposed to have a new one ready today, but at the last minute Kumiko decided she couldn't sell it. It didn't go down too well, as you might imagine.'

'Does she often do that?' Amanda asked carefully, holding the bag in front of her, trying to keep it from getting nudged as she weaved through the crowded pavement on her way back to work. 'Decide not to sell?'

'Not really,' George said. 'Well, never, actually–'

'Did she think something was wrong with it?'

There was a surprised silence from George. 'I don't know,' he said. 'I didn't actually see it. She just called, said she didn't think it was for sale, and that was that. I tend to just trust her on these things. She didn't say anything to you about it, did she?'

'No, no,' Amanda murmured. She kept looking at the bag as George talked on, giving monosyllabic but positive responses to his questions about Kumiko, all the while fighting her unexpected reluctance to tell him about the tile she'd been given.

'It's all passingly strange,' she finally said, and ended the call.

Next time, she thought. *I'll tell him next time.*

But she was wrong.

In the weeks that had followed, not only had Amanda been unable to arrange a further meeting with Kumiko, her father became harder to get hold of, too, even to look after JP. He was either on a brief holiday with Kumiko to the Highlands (of all places) or busy making his cuttings or buying new equipment for the shop. He did finally set a date for the party where he'd properly introduce her to everyone, including some of the art buyers – who'd apparently been applying increasing pressure about meeting her – and it was gratifyingly soon, but Amanda found herself hungry for more, though she was never quite clear on more of *what*.

'He says he's nearly made enough to pay off the last bit of his mortgage,' she told her mother one evening, who sounded personally offended at the news.

'How is that even possible? Are they *that* good?'

'Yeah,' she said, looking at her tile again. 'Yeah, they really are.'

'Is it wrong for me to be upset that George is finally out-earning me now that we're divorced?'

'It's been nine years, Ma.'

Clare sighed. 'Feels so much shorter.'

'How's Hank?'

'Oh, you. I'm not jealous, and I don't suddenly want him back now that he's rich. George is nice, but he's nice all the way through. I need someone who'll push back or I'll just turn into a bully, and who wants that? I'm just surprised is all. Surprised but pleased. Yes, pleased.'

'You sure?'

'Darling, wouldn't *you* want to be the person who'd made someone do that well? Wouldn't that be a nice feeling?'

'Hank's loaded.'

'He was loaded when I met him. I get no credit.'

'But you're not jealous.'

'Stop with the teasing. You say this Kumiko is lovely, and I believe you. I'm happy for him. For *them*. She's lucky to have him.'

'And he's lucky to have her,' Amanda said firmly.

And wondered for a moment exactly what she meant.

* * *

When she was at home, she hung the tile over the television, not for any other reason than that there was a hook there already for an old French movie poster that had been there so long she almost literally no longer saw it. She took it down and hung the tile in its place.

'What *is* it?' JP asked the first time, wide-eyed.

She went to answer, but everything suddenly seemed too complicated to explain in terms of animal characters, so she just said, 'Art.'

'Okay,' JP accepted solemnly, and didn't even launch into the avalanche of questions she had braced herself for. He merely looked at it for a long, quiet moment, and then he said, 'Can I watch Wriggles in the Jazz Age?'

Amanda stared at him for a confused moment. '*Stone* Age.'

'That's what I said.'

'Yeah, you know how to work the thingy.'

As JP grabbed the array of remotes required to bring up the downloaded Wriggles on the telly, Amanda watched the tile, watched the bird and the mountain, thinking that maybe they were Kumiko and her father and then again, maybe not. She also thought that, though it was hardly bigger than a dinner plate, it was also somehow bigger than the room, bigger than her whole life, and the more she looked, the more it threatened to spill over from its world into hers.

And as time passed, she never actually got around to mentioning the tile to either of her parents. From the things he said, it didn't seem as if Kumiko had told George about it either. Nor did JP ever bring it up to him, and while she certainly wasn't going to ask her wee little son to lie, somehow, without her even trying, it was never an issue. It became a secret they'd all wordlessly agreed to keep.

So she just kept looking at it.

In those same weeks, even before she caught the glimpse of the tile, Rachel had grown strangely friendlier.

'You want to join us for lunch?' she'd asked one day, Mei in tow.

Mei was astonished. 'Really?'

'Really?' Amanda echoed.

'Girls in the office?' Rachel said. 'Need to support each other? Not let stupid stuff get in the way?'

'*Really*?' Mei said again.

'Yes, really,' Rachel snapped. 'We're all grown-ups here?'

'Thanks,' Amanda said, 'but I've got plans.'

'Suit yourself,' Rachel said, and off they went.

But that hadn't been the end of it.

'Thought we might go to the cinema tomorrow?' Rachel said, appearing on a Friday morning. 'Make fun of Anne Hathaway's accent? Then knock back a few cocktails?'

Amanda had watched her, suspiciously. 'Is that an invitation?'

Rachel's face made an angry, scoffing shape but quickly recovered. 'Look,' she said, 'how many times do I need to say I'm sorry?'

Amanda opened her mouth, closed it, opened it again. 'Once?'

'So? The cinema?'

'I've got JP–'

'No worries.' And off she went again.

It was weird, and in a way worse than when they were

just friends who hated each other. Rachel was as unreasonably demanding as ever about getting work in, but the invitations kept coming, until finally she'd relented and gone for lunch at the latest gourmet burger chain.

'Do you think this is actually Emmental?' Amanda asked, lifting up the bun.

'I can't *believe* they put cheese that fancy on a burger,' Mei said.

'*Fancy?*' Rachel sneered. 'Who says "fancy"?'

Mei looked slightly confused. '*I* just did?'

'How's it going with Wally?' Amanda asked, taking a bite of the burger.

'Wally is like a huge prick?' Rachel said, cutting her own veggie burger in two.

'*Is* a huge prick,' Amanda said, 'or *has?*'

Rachel slammed down her knife and fork, startling everyone, even nearby tables. 'You know what?' she nearly shouted. 'I'm a good person!'

A quiet fell over their section of the restaurant. Mei looked at Amanda, then back at Rachel. 'Well,' Mei said, 'I mean, you're *okay*–'

'Who says you're not a good person?' Amanda asked, actually interested, though not so interested that she failed to take another bite of burger.

'I know I'm difficult? All right? But I think you have to be? To be a woman in business? And to make it in life and not be a, be a, be a–'

'Chump?' Mei suggested, sipping from her pistachio milkshake.

'Yes, not be a chump! I thought that was the whole point?'

'What are you talking about?' Amanda asked.

Rachel sighed heavily, and there suddenly seemed to be

actual tears in her eyes. 'Don't you just get tired of having to hate everybody?'

'I *don't* hate everybody,' Amanda said.

'Yes, you do!' Rachel said. 'You complain about everybody and everything! Like, all the time?'

'Well . . .' Amanda sat back. 'Not *everybody*.'

'Who do you like? Tell me.'

Rachel's insistence was so nakedly hungry, Amanda answered almost as if to defend herself. 'I love my son so much I sometimes miss him even when he's sitting right there.'

'Oh, me, too,' Mei sympathised. 'My daughter–'

'Child,' Rachel said, curtly. 'Doesn't count.'

'I love my dad.'

'George,' Rachel nodded.

'I loved Henri.'

'Did you?' Mei asked, eyes wide.

Amanda looked down at her burger, suddenly a little less hungry, remembering that night he'd stopped by, the night he hadn't mentioned again on any of his subsequent calls to JP. 'Yeah.' She looked back up at them. 'Yes, more than I can say.'

'So you're lucky then,' Rachel said. 'At least you've *had* somebody. I'm just so tired of hating everyone and myself and the two of you–'

'Hey!' Mei said.

'Oh, please,' Rachel pffted. 'I don't even know why I'm here. Do you? I don't even know why I'm trying to–'

She stopped, her face scrunching up in some really, really unattractive crying. She stood suddenly, so quickly the chair behind her fell over. She took one look at it and fled the restaurant. Yes, Amanda thought, *fled* was the right word.

161

'Wow,' Mei said, turning back to Amanda. 'Do you think you should go after her?'

'Not me,' she said, shaking her head. 'You.'

Mei acknowledged this was probably true, grabbed her bag and left without saying goodbye. Or paying for anyone's share of the bill.

Amanda stayed, pondering the conversation and finishing her burger. And what the hell, a few bites of Mei's, too.

Back at work, Rachel pretended the outburst had never happened, which wasn't a surprise, but she still kept up the almost-friendliness campaign, which *was*. And should also have been a warning, should have given Amanda greater pause before even thinking about risking the tile at work, because here, inevitably, was the moment that probably almost had to happen: Rachel standing there, her eyes laser-like on the now-hastily-being-shut drawer.

'That was–' Rachel started to say.

'None of your goddamn business, is what it was,' Amanda said sharply.

'I've never seen one in person?'

Amanda stared her down. 'I don't know what you're talking about.'

'Amanda–'

'Can I *help* you with something, Rachel?'

And then, once more, there was a strange moment. Rachel's eyes seemed to flicker and she hesitated. Then she looked down, crestfallen, at the papers in her hand and started walking away. *Who are you,* Amanda thought, *and what have you done with Rachel?*

But as she watched Rachel's unfeasibly shapely bottom shuffle off in defeat, Amanda found herself feeling an emotion so unassociated with her that it took her a minute to identify it properly. It was pity. Worse, it was *recognition*. She looked at Rachel and suddenly saw a fellow-traveller across that baffling, hostile landscape she knew all too well, the one whose entire set of rules seemed to exist for you to never properly learn and therefore be forever excluded, no matter how much you pretended it didn't matter.

For Rachel, it might have even been worse, because she *had* known the rules for a long time, had thrived on them, and had maybe now – if her equally unprecedented lunch outburst was anything to go by – found them empty. What happened to a person then? If she was trying this badly to be friends with Amanda, of all people, and doing it this incredibly incompetently, then what did that mean? Amanda realised she knew. As much as she still didn't actually *like* Rachel – because that seemed several bridges and an ocean too far – she glimpsed a harrowing sliver of understanding about her.

Rachel was lonely. And where Amanda had known that feeling her whole life, Rachel seemed to have just woken up to the possibility she'd been lonely all along.

'Rach?' she found herself saying.

Rachel turned back, her green eyes watery, but ready to be defiant. 'What?'

Amanda's hand hovered over her desk drawer before deciding that no, she couldn't do that. No matter how much pity she had for Rachel, it wasn't enough to share *this*, not yet, probably not ever, not something this private, this *hers*.

So she found herself inexplicably doing the next best thing, regretting it even as the sentence fell clumsily from her lips. 'My father's having a party to introduce people to Kumiko. There'll probably be artwork there.' She swallowed, as if to stop herself, but somehow the words kept being spoken. 'Do you want to come along?'

Rachel's smile of acceptance was any number of things. It was grateful, it was unnervingly bright, but mostly, Amanda's heart quailed to see, it was triumphant.

'You have changed,' the lady says.

'I have,' says the volcano. 'And I have not.'

She flies in her usual cautious circle around the open skies above his factories. 'You are a man of peace.'

'I am not currently a man of war, my lady. It is not the same.'

'Yet you create, you build, you add to the world.'

'It is what volcanoes do. Until we are tamed into mountains.'

'You tease me.'

'And you taunt me, my lady.'

She lands, placing her feet on the peaked roof of a factory. The billowing black smoke it produces does not sully her clothing or her skin. It flows around her, leaving her untouched.

'Taunt you?' she asks. 'How is this true?'

'My thoughts are filled with you,' he says. 'You enter my dreams, yet you stay out of arm's reach.'

'You enter my dreams,' she says, crisply, 'and you do not.'

The volcano smiles, and she sees, again, the malevolent merriment behind his blazing eyes. 'My lady dreams of me?' he says.

She takes off in flight again.

14 of 32

'Wait, my lady!' he calls after her. 'A gift!'

She soars around behind him, over the vast countrysides of factories and mines that have replaced the nations he once warred upon. 'What gift would I accept from you?' she asks. 'You are a volcano. You destroy.'

'And create.'

'And destroy again.'

'And create again, my lady. You know this to be true.'

'What is your gift?'

'Alight once more, so that I may give it to you.'

'You are dangerous to me.'

'You are just as dangerous to me, my lady. If I harm you, you will turn me into a mountain. It is a risk to us both. Either we both live, or we are both destroyed. And I wish to live.'

She considers this. After a moment, she lands.

'What is your gift?' she asks.

'An unexpected truth, my lady.'

Across the length of a continent, he holds out his hand for her to step onto.

A fraction of a second more quickly than she would have liked, she does so.

The volcano erupts, causing the world to crack in two. Factories, towns, cities, nations fall into chasms in the earth. The skies fill with ash and fire. Rivers of lava make the seas boil. All is darkness and flame and destruction.

'But you, my lady,' he says, as she stands on the palm of his hand, 'are unharmed. I cannot, do you see?'

He brings up a wave of lava to fall on her, but it parts as it does, leaving her untouched. He waves his hand to spin a torrent of fire around her, but again, it does not touch her skin. He brings a burning fist down to smash her in his palm, but it stops before harming a feather on her head.

'I wish to destroy you, my lady,' he says, 'so that I may create you again. But I cannot, despite what we both have believed.' He holds her up high, over the ruined world, up to his green, green eyes. 'Do you see what this means?'

'I do,' she says. 'And my answer is yes, I will marry you.'

On the palm of the volcano's hand, grass begins to grow under her feet.

They set about recreating the world. They call it their child, a joke that neither is particularly comfortable with, especially when the speaking of it makes it true. He raises lava to build new plains. She brings in seasons to wear them down, plant them, fill them with green.

Their regular couplings are violent yet unsatisfying. His hands wish to burn her, blast her to steam, and hers wish to turn him to stone, sending sheets of rock crashing to earth. But they cannot harm one another. He must constantly, viciously boil, she must constantly, violently forgive, but the fruits of their efforts are as naught.

Yet it works. For a time.

17 of 32

Neither ceases to be what they were before.

She suspects he is behind the wars that blight the face of their child, and when he returns from absences his horses sweat fire and blood, as if they had run to the end of time and back.

He suspects, in turn, that her absences are spent bestowing her forgiveness on others, and when she returns from periods away there is a contentment to her, a glassy-eyed satisfaction she is slow to stir from.

He has thought himself too big, too all-powerful for jealousy. She has thought herself too free, too quietly sure of her place in the world for jealousy to even occur to her.

They are both wrong.

18 of 32

She begins to follow him on his trips across their child, keeping distant and out of sight, but watching him raise armies that swarm across the land, watching him build factories that belch black smoke into the sky, watching him create a kind of link amongst all the creatures living there so that, by their own choice, they allow themselves to be more easily controlled.

He, meanwhile, hides in hot springs and geysers, travels

via ash falls and earthquakes, dances across tectonic plate stresses and the slidings of continents to follow her, watching her deal with the people of their child, watch them try to take from her, watch her forgive them with her touch, releasing them from their burdens in an exchange more intimate than any of their own closenesses could ever be.

Their child senses their disquiet, as any child would. It frets and turns and soils itself under their increasingly neglectful eye. Occasionally, it shames them into submitting to its needs, and they repay it in caresses, in seasons of peace and fair weather, in nights of endless moonlight and days of crisp sun.

But it is never long before their eyes return to one another, and when that happens the world knows to cower and take itself early to bed.

'Are we ready?' George asked.

'Would it matter if we were not?' Kumiko replied, reaching up to straighten his tie, which needed no straightening and made the gesture almost ironic, a mockery of an infinite number of black-and-white TV housewives straightening an infinite number of black-and-white neckties on an infinite number of patiently loving black-and-white advertising executive husbands.

But it was also affectionate. *Yes*, George insisted to himself.

'They're going to be surprised,' he said.

'A good party needs a few surprises. Is that not what people say?'

'I've never heard that.'

'Then it is possible you have gone to the wrong parties.'

He moved to kiss her but there was a knock on the front door. 'Already,' he sighed.

'They have to arrive sometime. Your friends.'

'But not yours.'

A faint strain furrowed her forehead. 'I do wish you would not–'

170

The knock came again. He released her and moved to the front hallway, the tension from Kumiko staying with him, like a rung bell. He stopped in front of the door for a moment, took a deep breath.

He opened it.

'Sweetheart!' he said, greeting his daughter. He leaned down to pick up his grandson, and as JP launched into a breathless analysis of a paradigm-shifting cast change in the Land of Wriggle, George found his eyes not quite believing who he saw behind Amanda, here as an apparent guest, gift bottle of champagne in her hand.

'You remember Rachel?' Amanda said, innocent as baby poo.

And the party was under way.

'Who on earth *are* all these people?' Clare said, arriving with Hank and finding Amanda in the rapidly building *mêlée* of George's sitting room. The furniture had been pushed back, but even so, it was only 7.40 and they were crammed into the space like a disco.

'Not a clue,' Amanda answered, embracing her mother and kissing Hank on both cheeks.

'How you doin'?' he said, his voice deep and friendly as a talking forest. 'Where's the munchkin?'

'Helping with the coats. Which means pretending they're seals and he's a penguin.'

'I'll go and find him,' Clare said, taking off her jacket and relieving Hank of his.

Amanda was left alone with her stepfather, which was absolutely fine, he was lovely – kind to her mother, warm to JP, sane – but she felt keenly aware, as she did all too often with Hank, that she was talking to the only black

171

person in the room. There was also the additional problem that she'd now spend the rest of the evening worrying about whether to apologise for it on behalf of England.

'So,' he said. 'Where can a Texan get a drink?'

'Mehmet's here,' Amanda blurted out.

Hank stared at her. 'Is he now?'

'I think he's in the kitchen.'

'Remind me of how I might know a Mehmet.'

'He works for George. He's Turkish.'

Hank understood and placed a hand on either of her shoulders. 'I'll make sure to find him to celebrate the rainbow nation. Can I bring you a refill?'

She sighed, but relaxed. 'Glass of white wine? Maybe two.'

'Not on my account.'

'No,' she said, tapping her wedding ring on her glass, a wedding ring she was almost only now realising she still wore. 'There's an odd vibe here. I mean, look at everyone.' She leaned forward in a whisper. 'Does George know them, do you think? Or are they just, you know, art people?'

'Why would you invite strangers to your *house*?'

Amanda knew Hank's question was actually, *Why would you invite strangers to* this *house?* She loved that he was a little bit of a snob – it was always so socially unexpected in an American – but she knew what he meant. The house was too small, too rundown and, the real issue, far too many miles out of Zone 1 for the way some of the folk here were dressed, a few of whom were currently looking in wonderment at George's utterly non-flatscreen telly.

Hank headed to the kitchen, and Amanda saw a thunderstruck Clare returning downstairs, JP in tow. 'She's moved in,' Clare said.

For a second, Amanda couldn't compute the meaning of this. 'Who?'

Clare lowered her voice to a whisper. '*Kumiko.*'

'*Has* she?'

'You didn't know?'

'No. How do *you* know?'

Clare frowned, guiltily. 'I looked through his wardrobe.'

'*Mum–*'

'It was half-full of lady's things. So either she's moved in or George has something very interesting to tell us.' Clare looked around the small, crowded room, and they heard the voices of more guests arriving. 'Where is she, anyway? What does she even look like?'

'She's got brown hair . . .' Amanda started but then wasn't quite sure where to go next.

'Thank you, darling,' her mother said. 'That narrows it down to almost everyone.'

The party spread quickly, moving into the kitchen and even the garden, despite the coldness of the night.

'Welcome,' George said, pouring wine into rented glasses. 'Welcome.'

A woman he'd never met before pinned him with her stare, an almost pleading look in her eyes that he'd come to recognise. 'I don't suppose you could direct me to the host?'

George blinked. 'The host?'

'This George Duncan person,' she said, drinking the wine, making a face at it. 'I came all the way out here to talk to him about his extraordinary art, and instead I'm standing in a freezing garden in–' she made another face '–the *suburbs*.'

'Yes, well,' George said, 'when I see him, I'll be sure to send him your way.'

'I mean,' the woman continued, gesturing with her cigarette at George's precarious breeze-block garage, 'is this some kind of prank? Or do you suppose this whole place is an extension of his art?' She turned to him, suddenly inspired. 'Like Rachel Whiteread! Yes, except instead of the empty spaces of a house, we have the house *itself*.'

'No, I think he just lives here.'

The woman snorted. She turned to the man next to her, who George had also never met, and said, 'Do *you* think he lives here?'

'Don't be ridiculous,' said the man. 'When do you think they're going to bring out the new tiles?'

George felt a hand at his elbow. He turned. Kumiko.

'The house is *full*,' she said.

'Is it?' He looked at his watch, and accidentally spilt a good portion of the bottle of wine onto the back patio. Men and women whose names he didn't know jumped back in complaint. 'It's barely eight o'clock.'

'Who are they all?' Kumiko whispered.

George wished he knew. It wasn't supposed to be anything like this, just friends and family, plus a few people from this new world they'd suddenly found them-selves in, art buyers who kept saying how connected they felt to George and Kumiko through the tiles, all coming together at the comfortable intersection of his home. A simple party. Small.

Not this.

'Well, the guy who bought the first tile asked if he could bring a friend along, and I guess it just snow-balled–'

Kumiko looked around at the crowds, but even her alarm was mild. 'We will not have enough tiny sausages.'

'They don't really look like tiny-sausage people—'

'George?' Rachel said, appearing at his shoulder like poison gas. He tensed, so much he was sure Kumiko could see it. He'd come out here because it was the furthest place he could get away from Rachel without actually leaving the neighbourhood. The light from the kitchen window caught her eyes, and they blazed green for a second. *Like devil eyes in a photograph*, George thought.

'And you can only be Kumiko?' Rachel said.

'Yes,' Kumiko said. 'That is who I can only be.'

George realised it was the first time he'd ever heard her speak to someone else in a way other than completely friendly. It made his stomach hurt, not least because he felt as if it could only be his fault.

He refilled his own glass of wine and drank it, quickly.

'It's not like they're even that good,' Mehmet said, enunciating in the careful way of the marginally too intoxicated. 'You know what I mean?'

'I've only seen pictures of them,' Hank said, skilfully mixing a gimlet for Clare, 'but they look pretty amazing to me.'

'Yeah, okay, I'm lying, they're brilliant. Can you make me one of those?'

'I could, but I'm guessing you haven't exactly been pacing yourself this evening.' Hank waited near the refrigerator door until the man in front of it noticed him and hurried apologetically out of the way. It was one of the things he liked about this country, the solicitude. People apologised if you stepped on *their* foot. Though it probably helps if you look like me, he thought. He pulled out a bottle of white and judged its label with a raised eyebrow. 'Oh, well,' he said and started looking for a corkscrew anyway.

'I mean, I shouldn't even *be* here,' Mehmet said. 'I'm missing a party for this.'

Hank gestured with the corkscrew at the bodies pressed into the surprisingly narrow kitchen. 'This is also what many people would call a party.'

'George said he wanted me to come in particular tonight, since I was there when he met her first.' Mehmet gave him a shifty look. 'I think there's going to be some big announcement.'

'Oh?' Hank said, feeling slightly interested as he poured himself the mediocre Pinot Grigio. He didn't *much* care. George was a nice enough guy, but so far in his acquaintance George's actual friends – as opposed to the alarming number of art buyers and hangers-on currently besieging Bromley – seemed limited to women and this slightly drunk gay person. George wasn't exactly a man's man, and though Hank wasn't so much of a Texan that he wore a cowboy hat, he *was* a Texan. On the other hand, Clare still liked George, and if there was gossip to be had, Hank was more than happy to be the one to deliver it to her. It would make her smile and, fool that he was, Hank's heart would thump quite off rhythm when that happened.

'They've moved in together,' Hank said, re-corking the wine and shooing the same man out of the way of the fridge again. 'Something like that.'

'Can't you feel it, though?' Mehmet said. 'It feels like something's coming.'

'I'm guessing for you it's a hangover.'

'Please. I'm not even straight-girl drunk.'

'I genuinely haven't the slightest idea what that means.'

'Something's on the horizon. Something about where this–' Mehmet mimicked Hank's corkscrew gesture to include the party and all the events leading up to it '–is headed. Something big. Something wonderful and, I don't know, *terrible*.' He leaned back on the counter. 'I'm just saying.'

'You're just saying.' Hank picked up the drinks and made to head back into the sitting room.

'Hey, wait,' Mehmet said.

'Yes?'

'Did Amanda tell you to talk to me because I'm Turkish?'

Hank looked thoughtful. 'She more implied it.'

'*There* you are,' Amanda said, entering George's bedroom. Kumiko was using her fingers to eat what looked like a rice dish out of a large bowl. Amanda held up JP. 'Mind if I put him down for a little snooze?'

Kumiko nodded at the avalanche of coats on the bed. 'He will be warm, at least.'

'8.43,' JP said, reading the red digital clock on the side of the bed.

'Can you say it in French?' Amanda asked him.

'Papa says time isn't French. Papa says time is only ever English.'

'Either way, sparky, it's *way* past your bedtime.' She tucked him under a long trenchcoat, and he pulled several more down on top of himself until only his nose and the top of his head were poking out. 'Don't suffocate.'

'I won't.'

She turned to Kumiko. 'He'll be out in a minute, you watch.'

'He is a lovely boy,' Kumiko said.

'Yes. Thank you.'

Kumiko gestured to the bowl. 'I am taking a quiet moment. Hiding from the party so that I can face it again afresh.'

'They're all dying to meet you. All those strangers with money.'

'It is not, perhaps, a mutual feeling.'

They smiled together and Kumiko said nothing more, just ate another fingerful. This was actually the first time Amanda had laid eyes on her since the gift of the tile, and she felt herself almost bursting with everything she wanted to say, everything she'd been holding for all this time. It was like when she used to return home from school, filled with so much new knowledge to share with her mother and father that it felt like she was going to pop open and bleed it out onto the dinner table along with her guts and blood and brains. She wondered, not for the first time, if that was something that happened to only children, if brothers and sisters knocked that kind of enthusiasm right out of you. She stroked JP's already sleeping head and wondered if he'd come home in a year's time, at death's door with the need to tell her about dinosaurs or triangles.

But where to even *begin* with Kumiko? Had she really moved in, for example? And who the hell *were* all those people downstairs and were they going to be a permanent part of everyone's life? And where did the images in the tile Kumiko gave her come from and why did they make her feel so helplessly, painfully, agonisingly hopeful? Why did she cry when she thought about it? Why had she *stopped* crying about everything else?

And where had Kumiko been? Where had she been? Where had she been? Where had she been? And how could Amanda miss someone this much who she'd only seen once before?

When she opened her mouth, though, all that came out, even before a simple thank-you for the tile, was 'What's that you're eating?'

'A kind of sweet rice pudding,' Kumiko said, but held up a finger to check the knowing nod Amanda was giving her. 'Not the kind you think. This is something from my childhood.'

'A recipe from your mother?'

She shook her head. 'My mother. Not much of a cook. Would you like some?'

'Oh, no, thank you,' Amanda said, though she couldn't quite take her eyes off the bowl. 'Have you moved in with my father?'

There was a pause in the rice-pudding eating. 'Only a little. Is that all right?'

'Of *course* it's all right,' Amanda said. 'I mean, it's quite quick, but . . .'

'But what?'

'But nothing. Just, you've really bowled him over. Our George.'

'I hope that is exactly what I have *not* done,' Kumiko said, taking another stab of rice. 'George is like a rock in the ocean to me.'

'And you're the waves?'

In answer, Kumiko merely smiled again. Then she frowned. 'Your friend.'

'My friend.'

179

'The one you brought this evening.'

Amanda made a worried face. 'Well, she's not exactly my *friend*–'

'Really?'

'I know her from work. She seems to be having some sort of breakdown, so I felt sorry for her and invited her. I hope that's okay.'

'A breakdown.'

'Yes. Like she's been wound so tight the coils are starting to snap. It's weird. I'm sorry, I should have asked.'

'Do not be sorry, if it was a kindness. Are you sure you do not wish to have some? You keep looking at the bowl.'

'It's what fat women do. Stare at food.'

Kumiko looked surprised and, oddly, angry. 'You are *not* fat,' she said. 'You, who speaks the truth even when it harms you, how can you not see this?'

'I was making a joke,' Amanda said quickly. 'I really don't think I'm–'

'This, I will never understand,' Kumiko carried on over her. 'The inability of people to see themselves clearly. To see what they are *actually* like, not what they fear they are like or what they wish to be like, but what they actually *are*. Why is what you are never enough for you?'

'For who? Me? Or everyone?'

'If you could only see the truth of yourself–'

'Then we wouldn't be human.'

Kumiko stopped, as if slapped, and then looked strangely delighted. 'Is that it? Is that what it is?'

'To be human is to yearn, I think,' Amanda said. 'To want. To *need*. What you already have, most of the time. It kind of poisons everything.'

'But it is a sweet-tasting poison?'

180

'Sometimes.'

'There, you see?' Kumiko said. 'Your frankness. It is what I like about you the best.'

'Well, you're pretty much the only one.'

Kumiko held out the bowl again. 'Please. I know you wish to. It is a sweeter-tasting poison than most.'

Amanda waited for a moment, then stepped around the end of the bed and hesitantly peered into the bowl. 'And I just eat it with my fingers?'

'Like this.' Kumiko took a little snitch of it and held it up to Amanda's mouth. 'Eat.'

Amanda stared at it for a moment, felt the weirdness of eating out of Kumiko's hand, but maybe it didn't feel so weird after all, not any weirder than everything else about Kumiko, if she was honest. Besides, she found herself really, really wanting to. She enveloped Kumiko's fingertips in the lightest of kisses and ate the bite of pudding . . .

. . . and felt suddenly swept away, suddenly on air, *of* air, the wind rushing past her, the earth far below, ancient yet young, covered in bursts of cold steam, the sweetness on her tongue light as a wish, as an eyelash, as the wash of spray from a nearby wave . . .

. . . and Kumiko was flying by her side, was offering something . . .

(Or *wanting* to be offered . . .)

'Amanda?' Clare's voice cut through the bedroom and Kumiko's fingers were leaving Amanda's mouth (as was the longing, the strange, milky longing, not of lust, not for the flesh, not even for love, but for what? For what?) and Kumiko was asking, 'Do you like it?'

Amanda, in a daze, swallowed. 'It's not what I expected.'

'It never is.'

'Everything all right here?' Clare said, eyes bright, questioning.

'Perfectly,' Kumiko said. 'Why do you ask?'

'I–'

'I must get back to the party,' Kumiko said. 'Even if most of them are strangers to me.'

She nodded farewell to them both, set down the bowl, and then moved past Clare and down the stairs to the noise of the gathering. Amanda felt cool but also flushed, as if after a brisk hike up a mountaintop. She breathed through her mouth, the lingering taste on her tongue confusing, drawing her thoughts away.

'So that was her?' Clare said. 'What on earth was all that about?'

But Amanda could only pretend to check on JP again as an unfathomable blush started rising from her neckline.

'You're avoiding me,' Rachel said, cornering him outside as he carried a tray of dirty glasses.

'Of course I'm avoiding you,' George said. 'What else would I be doing?'

They were slightly away from the rest of the party-goers, some of whom had started, thankfully, to leave, now that a couple of hours had passed and no new artwork had been displayed or auctioned or whatever it was these mysterious people thought was going to happen. The announcement was still coming, but no one leaving would be interested in it or even know it was on its way. Though right now he'd have traded a dozen of them in exchange for not having to talk to Rachel.

'I'm not going to cause trouble, George? If that's what you think?'

'That actually is what I think,' George said, trying to sound calm. 'That's exactly what I think.'

'Well, I'm not?'

He regarded her again for a moment, trying to really see her there. That freakish trick of the light from the kitchen window was making her eyes glow green again. 'Rachel–'

'Look, I *know*,' she said. 'I know you're with Kumiko and Amanda says you've moved her in and there's this really camp Turkish guy who keeps going on about some big announcement on the way–'

'*Rachel–*'

'I'm just saying I know, okay? I'm not trying anything? I can see how close you are to her? How she must give you everything I couldn't? Everything I can't seem to give to anyone?' She made a face, looking above George's head at the cold moonlight, and he could see, with a shock, that she was trying not to cry. 'I'm just so confused lately, George? I couldn't give myself to you when we were together, like you gave yourself to me. I can't do that with anyone? And that's why you left me, I'm sure–'

'You left *me*–'

'And now here's this exotic new woman and she's just everything I'm not. Everything I want to be, obviously? Beautiful–'

'You *are* beautiful, Rachel, don't pretend–'

'And smart and talented–'

'You're those things, too–'

'And *nice*.'

'. . .'

'And clearly she can just open herself up to you.' Rachel was looking at him hard now, unblinking. 'Clearly can give back to you all the things you give her.'

George found that his mouth had gone dry. He mumbled something.

'What's that?' Rachel asked.

'I said, she *doesn't* give me everything of herself.'

'She doesn't? But I thought you two looked so happy?'

'We *are* happy–'

'I thought you'd finally found someone to match all that was wonderful about you, George.'

'I have–'

'But she holds something back?'

'Rachel, I am not having this conversation with you– '

She stepped closer to him. He remembered too late that he should step back.

'But how is that better than me?' she asked.

She stepped closer again, close enough now for him to smell her, her perfume triggering all kinds of memories of kissing that neck, that too-young neck that made no sense at all for a man like him to be kissing. He could also smell the wine on her breath. That weird green glint in her eye hadn't faded, but she was still Rachel, beautiful and brutal.

'I'm trying to change,' she whispered. 'I don't know what's happening to me. I want to *give*. I've never *given*, George? I've only taken? But now that I *want* to give, there's no one I can–'

She lunged forward to kiss him.

He leaned back, though perhaps not as far or as quickly as he could have (he instantly, guiltily thought), and it became less a kiss than a glancing blow. There was only the one attempt, but when Rachel stepped away, he could see Kumiko over her shoulder, leaning out the back door, looking for him in the dim back garden.

184

'George?' she called.

But in the low light, he couldn't tell whether she'd seen anything at all.

'I wonder if we could have everyone's attention?' George said, standing near the doorway of the kitchen so that everyone could hear him, Kumiko by his side.

'About time,' Amanda heard from a man who introduced himself only as Iv. ('As in short for Ivan?' she'd asked, to which he'd answered 'No.') He'd spent his entire conversation with her talking about 'interplays of medial and indeed medium dynamics' in George and Kumiko's art while ignoring every bit of Amanda's scoffing incomprehension.

'Kumiko and I just want to thank everyone for coming,' George said, putting his arm around Kumiko's shoulder.

'*That's* Kumiko?' a woman in a suit whispered nearby. 'I thought she was a *maid*.'

'We welcome our friends and family,' George said, raising his glass towards where Amanda was standing with Clare and Hank, Mehmet a foot or two behind. 'And all our new friends, too.' He paused, coughed. 'We have a little announcement to make.'

There was an almost audible creak of tension in the room, Amanda thought, as all the well-dressed strangers simultaneously straightened their postures a quarter of an inch.

'It'll be the tile series,' Amanda heard, in another whisper.

'It won't be,' someone immediately contradicted. 'That's only a rumour.'

'*What* series?' a third person whispered.

The first two tutted at the third's display of ignorance.

'I know this will come as a shock to some of you,' George said, specifically looking at Amanda.

'He's *not*,' Clare said, behind her.

'Not what?' Hank asked.

And just as Amanda realised what her mother meant, George said the actual words.

'Kumiko has graciously agreed to be my wife.'

'Why didn't you tell me?' Amanda said, standing almost aggressively close to him.

'Good night,' George said to the slightly disgruntled faces filing out. He could hear some muttering, particularly among all those who had approached him after the announcement, asking with stricken faces when the sale would start. They'd been almost universally disbelieving when he'd said he had no intention of selling anything tonight.

Though, in hindsight, he could probably have made a mint.

'*George*,' Amanda insisted. 'You nearly gave Mum a heart attack.'

He looked at her, and had to blink several times before he could properly see her. Which was strange, as he didn't think he'd drunk *that* much.

'Why would she be upset?' he asked. 'We've been divorced for–'

'Why didn't you *tell* me?' said Amanda again, and the angry hurt on her face was almost too much for him to bear. She looked exactly as she did as a twelve-year-old, when he and Clare had used what little extra cash they'd had to replace a badly worn-out cooker without even

186

knowing how much Amanda had been counting on finally getting contact lenses to replace her glasses, a wish neither of them knew existed up until the moment Amanda burst into furious yet extraordinarily sorrowful tears behind her spectacles. They'd found contact-lens money the next month, but the cloud of worry they shared over their difficult, unexpected daughter was never quite manageable again after that. He still worried the same about her *now*.

So why *hadn't* he told her?

'I just . . .' he said. 'It was all very sudden.'

'She's moved in, though, and you didn't mention that either.'

'She hasn't *really* moved in. She's still got her flat–'

'And I've only met her once. *Once*.'

'And you said you liked her. Good night, now! I think he made a rude gesture at me, did you see that?'

'I *do* like her. She's . . .'

Amanda stopped and her eyes seemed to focus on some internal image with an expression he could only describe as unnerved reverie. And then he wondered why he was feeling so hot all of a sudden? His skin was shedding sweat like a natural spring.

'I'm sorry, sweetheart,' he said. 'I really am. I just . . . I have so *little* of her, do you see? So much of her is just completely unknowable. And I get greedy for any tiny bit of her I can have.' He looked down at the wine glass he still seemed to be holding. 'I didn't tell you because I wanted it to be something only *I* knew. A part of her that was only mine. I'm sorry if that sounds awful, but she's *so*–'

'I understand, Dad,' Amanda said, but gently. She looked past him over to where Kumiko was handing Clare,

Hank and a woozy-looking Mehmet their coats. 'I think I actually do a bit.'

He touched her gently on the arm. 'I like it when you call me Dad.'

She turned back to him, and he caught a glimpse of such heartbreak in her eyes that he wanted to take her in his arms and never let her leave this house again, but then she gave a brittle smile and it was gone. 'I've got to get JP,' she said.

'Bring him by tomorrow, will you?'

'I will, Dad,' she said and started to ascend the stairs.

'Amanda,' he said, stopping her.

'Yeah?'

'Did your friend leave?'

A *that's-a-good-question* expression crossed Amanda's face. 'She must have got a lift or something.' She shrugged. 'Weird. But kind of typical.'

She carried on up the stairs, and George moved to his last remaining guests, all of whom, mercifully, he knew and, in their own different ways, loved.

'Well, you're a dark horse,' Clare said. 'Actually, you're completely *not* a dark horse, ever, which is why I've found this all vaguely upsetting.'

'Aren't you happy for me?'

'Ecstatic, darling. I haven't the slightest idea how you managed to get her to look at you, but now that you have–'

'Congratulations,' Hank said, shaking George's hand in that too-hard way George suspected was reserved for his wife's ex-husband. 'Maybe fewer guests next time?'

'I know. We're a little baffled as to who exactly–'

'Art junkies,' Mehmet interrupted. 'Like those starling murmurations. They rise up out of nowhere in their millions, dazzle you for like seven minutes, then gone again into oblivion.'

There was a silence at this. Then George said, 'Mehmet, that was–'

'I *told* you there was something on the way,' Mehmet said to Hank, wavering slightly from the vertical. 'Something wonderful.'

'You said it would also be terrible,' said Hank.

'Well,' Mehmet says, looking back at George, 'I'm sure that's on the way, too.'

'Gosh,' George said, collapsing onto the settee after the final stragglers had left.

Kumiko sat down next to him. 'We made it.'

But – unless George was imagining it, which was entirely possible – there was an awkwardness between them somehow, a new one, as if now that they'd made their announcement to his family and a roomful of bastards, they were strangers once again. He desperately hoped it wasn't anything to do with Rachel.

'Is there anyone on your side we need to tell?' he asked.

She smiled wearily at him. 'I have said to you many times. There is only me. Except that now, there is only me and you.'

He breathed out through his nose. He was still unfeasibly warm. His sweat had soaked through three layers to drench his blazer. 'Is there really me and you?' he asked.

'What do you mean?'

He was surprised to find himself near tears. 'You keep so much of yourself from me. *Still.*'

'Please do not get too greedy, George,' she said, and

he was shocked by her use of *greedy*, the same word he used with Amanda. 'Can we not have what we have now?' she continued. 'Even as husband and wife? Can you not love me with all my closed doors?'

'Kumiko, it isn't a question of *loving* you–'

'There are things that are hard for me to answer. I am sorry.' She looked unhappy, and he felt as if there was nothing in the world he wouldn't do to stop her looking like that, murder, destruction, betrayal, if only she would pour sunshine on him again.

'Don't be sorry,' he said. '*I'm* the one who should be sorry. I actually don't feel all that great. I wonder if I have a little fever–'

She cut him off, almost gently. 'I have finished a new tile.'

He was taken aback. 'Well, but. But that's *wonder*–'

'It is here.' She went to one of his bookcases and fetched it out from where it was hidden behind a row of books. 'I had it ready for the party, but there seemed no moment.'

She handed it to him.

'It's from the story,' George whispered, the tears gathering again with full force as he looked down on her clipped and gathered feathers, his clipped and gathered words. 'Kumiko, it's . . .'

But he could only look.

The lady and the volcano circled one another warily, both now made of a combination of feathers and words, as their world cowered beneath them. And the tenderness as they watched one another, the anger, the heartache about to erupt, were almost too much for George. He was going to have to lie down in a moment and deal with this strange fever, but for now he just looked and looked, staring at the elegant, bird-like curves of the lady, at the blazing green stones Kumiko had given the volcano for eyes.

'The story,' he asked. 'Is this the end?'

'Not yet,' Kumiko whispered, her voice like a breath of cloud. 'But soon.'

Amanda dreamed she was an entire army eating the earth. Her hands were twisting streams of soldier ants and soldier men, destroying but also dissolving, then re-forming as fingers to grab, fists to pound, her body stretching from horizon to horizon, flattening everything in her path, approaching a city, yes, approaching it and raising a mighty tidal wave of a hand to sweep it all away–

But hesitating now, holding herself back from the final destruction–

And learning in an instant the fatality of this hesitation, because already she is dissipating, already she is falling to pieces, atom by painful atom–

She woke, not with a start, but with a simple opening of her eyes (never knowing this was an exact mirror of how her father woke from nightmares). She reached across the bed to place a hand on the bare skin of Henri's back, an action that always re-anchored her after a troubling dream, bringing her back to earth, settling her again for sleep.

But Henri wasn't there, of course. Not for years.

She breathed out slowly across night-dried lips and tried not to let wakefulness take hold. She shifted in the bed and sensed the wetness of night sweats on her sheets. She'd been fighting off a low fever for at least a week, culminating in a lovely new cold sore that now, as she yawned, cracked painfully at the corner of her mouth, like the punishment of an irritable god.

Even in her grogginess, it felt like a punishment she deserved. The days since the party had been fractious and stormy, not least in her own head. She found herself thinking of Kumiko almost constantly, wondering what she was doing that moment, wondering if she was with George, wondering especially when she herself might see her again. It was ludicrous. On one level, it felt like nothing so much as a crush, a surprising one as Amanda had never been attracted to other women – she kept mentally pressing those buttons to see if she had any feelings that way, but so far nada, which was both confusing and slightly disappointing – but the longing didn't seem physical. Or no, that wasn't right, it did seem physical but not *that* kind of physical. It was almost like the foods she had craved when she was pregnant with JP, her body telling her with unstoppable force that she had to eat peanuts and pineapple or die. Yes, that seemed to be it, Kumiko was a vital element that Amanda needed to keep on living.

Which made no sense. Nor did the anger she felt when further meetings with Kumiko proved difficult to arrange. Nor did her growing jealousy of George for the time he got to spend with her. She knew all of it was irrational, but what good did rationale ever do in the face of need?

'We've had to start saying no to people about the tiles,' he'd said on the phone. 'It was getting too much, so we just told everyone to leave us alone for a bit. Frankly, I'm happy for a breather. Everything's been so fast.'

'Yes,' Amanda replied, surprising both of them with the heat in her voice. 'That's what the rest of us have been thinking. How fast it's all been.'

She'd winced to herself about how petty she sounded. But didn't quite apologise.

'No need to sound quite so put out about it,' George said. 'I hope you don't mean the marriage?'

'Yes, George, the marriage is what I mean.'

'But Kumiko is–'

'Kumiko is marvellous. Kumiko is wonderful. She's like no one I've ever met before.'

'She *is* that–'

'But it's barely a couple of months,' she heard herself saying, harshly, pointlessly. 'How well do you really know her?'

He paused at that, and she thought she could hear his discomfort, even in the silence. 'Well enough. I think.'

'You *think*?'

At which he'd grown suddenly stern. 'What I really think is that this isn't your business, Amanda. For too long you've thought you had the right to just come into my life and tell old George what to do. Well, you *can't*. I'm forty-eight. I'm your *father*. I've met a woman I love and I'm going to marry her and I don't need your permission or your approval, all right?'

Almost by reflex, Amanda waited for him to say he was sorry, like he did every other time he'd snapped at her, possibly across her entire life.

Except, this time, he didn't.

'We barely knew Henri before you married him and you didn't hear *us* complaining.'

'Well, Mum complained a little—'

'And we didn't know about the divorce until he'd already moved back to *France*, so don't talk to me about too fast.'

'That was different. I was young. Young people do that stuff when they're finding themselves.'

And then he said the meanest thing he would ever say to her, all the more painful for being one hundred per cent true.

'The slash-and-burn way you go about it, Amanda, you'll be looking for yourself the rest of your life.'

For that, he *had* immediately apologised, blaming some kind of vague, lingering man flu for his temper, but it was too late. It felt as if he had shot her with an arrow. Worse, an accurate one. They hadn't spoken since. It wasn't quite that dramatic, she'd speak to him again soon, she was sure, and she certainly wasn't going to get in the way of JP seeing his rightfully adored *grand-père*.

No, what hurt was that she realised what she'd said to Kumiko at the party was right. Amanda yearned, even for the things she already had. And it was poison, not even sweet-tasting.

The insane dreams weren't helping. Regular, with content so weird it almost felt like her personality was being disassembled. She always woke from them exhausted. It might only have been the fever, but lordy. She lay awake now, her bladder deciding to not so gently insist that, if she *was* awake, there were matters that could use tending, another similarity to her father she'd go to her grave without knowing. The clock read an obscene trio of numbers, 3.47. Work was in a few hours, and she needed

195

to get some sleep. She sighed and got up, hoping to make it quick.

But thinking of work made her think of Rachel, and as she moved down the hallway she woke up some more whether she wanted to or not. Rachel had grown even stranger since the night of the party, buoyed up, it seemed, by an apparent happiness that bordered on the deranged.

'He's too hairless,' Amanda had been saying to Mei just this morning, chatting about a reality TV star who'd cross-pollinated to another reality show set in a jungle. 'It's like looking at a really hunky ten-year-old, and who wants that?'

Both Mei and Amanda had physically recoiled at the explosion of Rachel's laughter nearby. They'd been unaware she was even listening. 'Maybe Michael Jackson?' she'd said, leaning in with a slightly terrifying smile.

'Um, that's not funny?' Mei said, anxiously. 'He's dead now? And I like him?'

'Sweet Jesus,' Rachel said, looking at Mei in astonishment. 'Talking in questions really *is* annoying.' She'd turned to Amanda. 'By the way, Amanda, good work on Essex. I've been telling Felicity you're out for my job.'

She'd laughed out loud again, and Amanda watched her go with her mouth open, for once feeling exactly as amazed as Mei.

Maybe Rachel really *was* having a nervous breakdown. It wasn't that the cheerfulness was unwelcome but – Amanda didn't know the word, *sparkly* would do – Rachel had an uncomfortably sparkly feel to her, like she was a grenade well past the point where she should have exploded. All you could do was keep a safe distance and hope for the best.

Amanda stumbled into her bathroom and sat down on

her freezing toilet, gasping at the temperature. She put a hand on the radiator to try and get some heat flowing through her. The bathroom was, bizarrely, in the corner of the building. Instead of putting the sitting room here to give it a nice double-sided view, the architects had elected to use it for the one place in the flat where you regularly got naked and expelled things.

She didn't turn on the light, though the hopes of keeping a minimal level of consciousness were fading with both the train of her thoughts and the cold on her bottom. The gorgeous moonlight coming through the windows would have added several per cent to her flat's resale value if it could have been seen romantically over the back of a settee. It was almost bright enough to read in here.

She finished peeing, dried herself, flushed and stood, pulling the elastic of her sleeping-alone knickers – which were getting far too much wear recently – up to her waist.

Then she stopped.

What the hell? she thought, and turned and vomited down the still-spiralling water.

Well, she was wide awake *now*.

'Seriously,' she whispered, genuinely startled. 'What the hell?'

She knelt there for a chilly second, waiting to see if there was more to come. She hadn't drunk anything this evening or eaten anything dodgy. She still felt slightly feverish, true, but there'd not been any nausea over the week and–

She stopped.

Then she forced herself to complete the thought.

And she'd used a condom with Henri.

(Hadn't she?)

197

Yes.

(Yes?)

She sat back. Yes, of *course* she had, there's no way they'd risk a thing like that, it was automatic. Wasn't it?

When was her last period? It had always been an irregular guest, but surely she'd–

'Okay, now you're just freaking yourself out,' she whispered into the moonlit darkness. She couldn't quite remember her cycle this late at night and they *had* used a condom. Of course they had. This was just a tummy thing. *That was all.*

She waited to see if she needed to vomit again, but didn't and got up. The violent opening of her mouth had made her cold sore ache, so after she swished some mouthwash to get rid of the taste, she reached for the anti-viral cream.

That's when the sound came, so unexpected and so quickly over it was like being doused with ice water.

She froze.

There was only silence now, and she wondered if she'd imagined it. And then got annoyed with herself because who *ever* imagined a sound? It was one of those idiotic things people said in movies when they were about to be killed by a bear-trap-carrying torturer.

No, she had heard something, something loud, outside the building.

But what?

An animal's call? She looked out the window framing the beautiful moon, a window that unfortunately overlooked a less beautiful car park and too-busy street beyond. She was on the fourth floor, and even with the silence of a city at 3.47 in the morning, it seemed quite a distance over which to hear a fox, which it hadn't really sounded like anyway. Foxes were like silent film stars about to be ruined by the advent of sound, beautiful but with the most affronting croak.

She put her face close enough to the glass to catch the steam of her breath. There was nothing out there, just the usual grazing cars in the car park, lit by a single yellowish streetlight. Nothing stirred in the road beyond either, not even the hourly nightbus that took her three months to learn to sleep through. She leaned over the bath to look out the other window, which really only showed another corner of the same car park and the roof of a building that had held a series of fleeting, dodgy-sounding businesses.

Nothing. All she could hear was her own breathing and the ticking of the radiator.

What could it have been? It had felt oddly sorrowful, like a cry of mourning or heartbreak. Or perhaps a cry for a lover who would never answer–

'Oh, please,' she said to herself, shivering. 'It was a fox. Not an operetta.'

Nothing continued to happen, so she gave up and left the bathroom, pausing only when she felt her stomach rumble again, queasily poking at her like a separate person down there–

No! Not like a separate person. Not anything remotely like that whatsoever. Just queasiness. That's it, that's all, queasiness. Aside from the whole having-sex-with-his-ex-wife-while-his-girlfriend-was-tending-to-her-mother thing, which, granted, wasn't exactly a plus for him, Henri was a responsible and considerate man. He wouldn't have dreamt of risking something like that. Besides, *she'd seen him put it on.*

Had she?

'Oh, shit,' she whispered.

She tried to picture it happening, tried to see him doing it that night on her sofa, and yes, there he was in her mind's eye, his hand rolling it down over himself as she unhooked her bra. But the whole episode had been so quick, so *unhinged*, that had she really seen it or had he just been stroking himself in the way that men seemed such prisoners to when they had their erections out in the open? And where would he have got a condom anyway? She didn't have any in the flat and why would he be carrying one if he'd been with Claudine for the past couple of years–

'Stop it,' she said to herself firmly. 'Just *stop*.'

Annoyingly, she couldn't even call him to clear things up because they'd been quarrelling as well. Over JP, naturally. Henri wanted him to come to Montpellier for two whole weeks so he could be 'properly introduced to France'.

'No way,' Amanda had said.

'You cannot just say *no way*, Amanda,' he said. 'That cannot be how this conversation begins.'

'He's *four*. He gets homesick if we're gone for a long afternoon. When he's older–'

'When he's older, I will already be a stranger. I am a stranger *now*–'

'No, you're not. I can't get him to *shut up* about you– '

'You see, you are trying to shut him up about me!'

'*Henri*,' she'd growled in frustration. 'He is too young for a two-week trip–'

'One week, then.'

'He's too young for a one–'

200

'This is about me. You must admit this at least, Amanda. You are angry with me over what happened–'

Then she said, somewhat ironically given the current circumstance, 'Oh, *God*, why are men so endlessly stupid about sex?'

They'd then spent a few minutes swearing at each other in French before hanging up with the issue of JP's visit completely decided on her part and 'still to be discussed' on his.

She stopped by JP's room now and looked in on her son. Still far too small for his new big-kid bed, he was sprawled as much as he could across a Wriggle duvet and even then he barely occupied more than a tiny corner of it. She went in and re-covered him.

'*Ce sont mes sandales,*' he mumbled, without opening his eyes. '*Ne pas les prendre.*'

'I won't, booboo,' she said, kissing him on his sweaty little forehead, avoiding her cold sore. 'I promise.'

He nestled back into his Wriggle pillow and was soon deep asleep once more. He was so beautiful there in the moonlight, Amanda found herself near tears again.

'For God's sake,' she whispered.

At least being pregnant would explain all this weird emotional stuff lately. The jealousy of her father over Kumiko. The inexplicable yet tremendously upsetting feeling that somehow Kumiko was being taken away from her. It might even explain the intoxicating memory of Kumiko feeding her the rice pudding, the feel of Kumiko's fingertips in her mouth, a connection utterly unexpected, utterly – as far as Amanda was concerned – taboo and surprising, but a connection that pulled at her very guts, so much so she occasionally put her own fingertips in her mouth to replicate it.

It was childish, maddening, but George marrying Kumiko felt like she had somehow missed the best chance of her life. Everything after would be diminishment. She still guarded the devastatingly beautiful tile Kumiko had given her (because *devastating* was right, wasn't it? She looked at it and was devastated) with a fierceness that bordered on desperation. She kept it in a sock drawer now, hidden away and never taken to work again, and she didn't speak of its existence to anyone, not even George.

If she was honest with herself, which was difficult because the truth was so markedly uncomfortable, she admitted she was probably guarding all these things – the tile, the fingertips, her jealousy – against the thin, flickering hope that one day Kumiko might share all her unknowable secrets with Amanda. And perhaps that meant one day Amanda might be able to share *hers,* to finally show someone the flaw underneath the carapace of her personality, to maybe, possibly, even discover it wasn't a flaw after all . . .

Which was all impossible now because of *course* George would be the person Kumiko confided in now that they were marrying. No matter how dear her and Kumiko's friendship might grow, Amanda would never be the one with whom Kumiko discussed all those impossible things. And that made her sad enough to well up, *again.* None of it made any logical sense, and oh God, if pregnancy was the explanation–

'Mama?' JP asked from his bed. 'Are you crying?'

'No, no, sweetheart,' she said, wiping her eyes quickly. 'It's only the moonlight. It's so beautiful, don't you see?'

'I am sometimes the moon. When I sleep, I am.'

'I know,' she said, brushing away a lock of his hair.

'That's why you're always so hungry in the morning.'

He smiled and closed his eyes. She stayed for a moment to make sure he was settled – and to make sure she neither needed to cry nor vomit any more this evening – and headed back to her own bedroom, feeling her way down the darkened hallway, her thoughts crowding up despite her best efforts.

Because what if she *was*? Oh, hell, what if she was?

She put her hand on her stomach, not knowing how she felt about it in the slightest little particular. It'd be eternally awkward to explain to people why JP looked so very much like his brother or sister, and it would be a very, *very* long secret to keep from Claudine–

Who was she kidding? It'd be a disaster. A wreck.

Which was okay, because she *wasn't pregnant*. The end. A single night of regretful sex that ended in pregnancy was another thing that only happened in movies.

Except it would have its good points, too, of course. She loved JP more crazily than she'd thought herself able, and a second boy or a girl . . .

She sighed. It was practically a case study of the term 'mixed blessing'.

'But you're not,' she whispered to herself, slipping back into bed, finding a cool spot in the sheets. 'You're not, you're not, you're not.'

Which was when the sound came again.

It was much clearer this time, so deep and sonorous and unearthly she practically leapt from the bed to look out the window.

She saw nothing, just stilled cars again. No movement, not even in the shadows, though there were plenty of corners where anything could have been lurking.

But her heart was still pounding because whatever it was hadn't sounded like it had come from four storeys below. It had sounded like it was right outside her window. There was nothing there, of course, and not even a proper ledge on which something could have been standing, but the sound, the call, the *keen*–

Where had that word come from? It seemed right, though. It had been a keening sound. Old-fashioned, more than old-fashioned, *ancient*, but not ancient like Egypt, ancient like an old forest which you suspected was only sleeping. Something had keened right outside her window, and she didn't know why or for whom, but it hit her heart so purely she gave up trying not to cry altogether, even as she lay back on the pillow, and it felt proper this time, like the right thing to do, the right sadness to be holding.

Because what was sadder than the world and its needs?

She dreamed again of a volcano, but this time she alternately *was* the volcano and being ravished by it – a word she thought of, even in her dream, *ravished*, yes – his hands trailing up her naked torso, his thumbs marking the upward curve of her burgeoning belly, reaching her breasts, which were now somehow under her *own* hands as she leaned her head back against the hills and cities of her neck, and feeling the importance, somehow, that the volcano should open his eyes, open them so they could be seen, but no matter her entreaties, he refused, keeping them closed even as he entered her, and before she could object, before she could demand again, he was doing what all volcanoes must inevitably do, erupting,

erupting, erupting, the stupid pun of it making her laugh, deeply, raucously, even in the dream, even while it kept happening–

She didn't wake this time.

Mainly because she didn't want to.

And so comes the final day.

She has followed him to another war. The earth splits apart in seams and crevasses, spouting fire and lava and steam, chasing the volcano's minions who race through the narrow streets of some city or other, killing its men, raping its women, dashing its babies to the pavement.

She flies through the carnage, the looting, the pillaging, skating her fingers through pools of blood. She weeps for the world that is their child but was never their child, she weeps for her love and wonders if it is lost. She does not wonder if it was true. It was true, for both, that much is obvious.

But is it enough?

The volcano is everywhere and nowhere in the war, all things to it at all points and therefore, in an important way, absent by ever-presence. She finds instead this army's small general, one who thinks he leads his troops, when of course he no more leads them than horns lead a stampeding bull. His chin is covered in blood where he has been feeding on an enemy.

At the sight of her, the small general drops his enemy and bows to her respectfully. 'My lady,' he says.

'You know me?'

'Everyone knows you, my lady.'

'You fight for my husband.'

'Aye, my lady.' He gestures to his disembowelled enemy, now grasping at his viscera and trying to shove them back into his body. 'But so did he. We all fight for your husband, my lady.'

'Are you not tired?' she asks, stepping around him in a slow circle.

He looks up, surprised. 'Aye, my lady,' he says, his voice full of weariness and disappointment.

'You do not seek war,' she says, behind him now.

'No, my lady.'

'You seek forgiveness.'

He answers nothing for a moment, but when she comes round again to his face, he pulls himself up to full height and looks proud. 'As you say, my lady.'

'Shall I forgive you?' she asks, slightly puzzled, a hesitancy forming around her.

The small general unbuttons his uniform and exposes the skin over his heart. 'As my lady wishes.'

She goes to him. His eyes give nothing away. She is unsure still, and hesitates.

'This cannot be done in anger,' she says. 'It can only be done out of love.'

'Would it help my lady if I wept?'

'Very much.'

The small general weeps.

'Thank you,' she says, and plunges two fingers into his exposed breast, piercing his heart, stopping it.

21 of 32

He does not die. He does not even thank her.

'I shall bite out your eyes now,' she says, the uncertainty lingering.

'Please, my lady, as quickly as you can, to end my suffering,' he says, and his words sound true.

But they suggest a different kind of suffering than the mere pain of death.

Confused, she moves to bite out his eyes, but at the last moment, she sees.

Deep within them, deep down past who this general is, deep beyond his youth and birth, behind the history of the-world-their-child who brought the general to this place, in this city/abattoir, on this battlefield, deep behind that—

There is a flash of green.

22 of 32

'We are the same, my lady,' says the volcano, looking out of the general's eyes.

'We are different,' she says.

'We are the same and we are different.'

She opens her mouth to contradict him, but finds she cannot.

'You have betrayed me with this small general,' she says instead.

'And you have betrayed me with him as well.' He steps from behind the general's eyes, blasting away the flesh to spatter the concrete walls. Nothing splashes on her. 'And you see, my lady, I still cannot hurt you.'

'Nor I you.'

'We must end this,' he says. 'We cannot be. We do not fit. Our end is only one of destruction. That is how it must be, that is how it always must have been.'

'I cannot.'

'You can, my lady.'

23 of 32

He kneels in front of her, his green eyes burning with sulphur and potassium, hotter than the centre of the earth, the centre of the sun.

And his eyes weep. They weep lava enough to fill an ocean. The city around them is reduced to ashes and boiling rock.

'I have betrayed you, my lady,' he says. 'From the day we met until the seconds that pass as I speak this sentence, I betray you. It is what a volcano does, my lady, and I cannot change as certainly as I cannot harm you.'

The sky blackens. The world shudders beneath them.

'And so, my lady,' he says, 'the day has arrived. Our last day. Ordained from when we first set eyes on one another.'

He pulls the flesh away from his left breast, landslides and lava spilling to earth. He exposes his beating heart to her, pumping with rage, bleeding with fire.

'You must forgive me, my lady,' he says.

209

'I . . .'

But she cannot speak further.

'You must, my lady, or I will find a way to destroy you. You know this to be true. We are not meant for each other.'

'We are only meant for each other.'

'That is also true. We are the same and we are different and every moment that passes where I cannot burn you and melt you and destroy you utterly with my love for you is a torment unsurpassing. And because it is a torment unsurpassing, I will continue to take it out on our child, this world.' He leans forward, his exposed heart beating faster now. 'Unless you forgive me, once and for all, my lady.'

'I cannot.'

'You know what I speak is true, my lady.'

'I do.'

'You must act. Pierce my heart. Bite out my eyes.'

'I cannot.'

His eyes burn. 'Then you do not love me.'

24 of 32

She gasps. She raises her hand to plunge it into his heart.

'Do it, my lady,' he says, closing his eyes. 'Forgive me. I beg of you.'

Her hand is raised, ready to fall, ready to end this torment, which she will admit, if only to herself, is as bad for her as it has ever been for him. She loves him and it is impossible. She hates him and that is impossible, too. She cannot be with him. She cannot be without him. And both are burningly, simultaneously true in a way that grinds the cliché into dust.

But what she cannot do, what she cannot do that has no

opposite which is also true, what she cannot ever, ever do—

Is forgive him.

For loving her. For burning her. For desiring her. For making her do all these things in return by his very existence.

She cannot ever forgive him.

She will not end his torment. She will not end hers.

She lowers her hand and lets him live.

'You should go.'
'...'
'...'
'You mean it?'
'I mean it.'
'It's three– No, it's nearly *four* o'clock in the morning– '
'I want you to go.'
'...'
'...'
'You're breathing very heavy, George. Are you feeling all right?'
'Please, I'm asking you to–'
'What would be the point? What could possibly be the point in me leaving right now instead of in two hours?'
'Rachel–'
'You said she wasn't coming over tonight, that she was working at her flat. Which, amazingly, you still claim to have never properly seen.'
'I *haven't.*'

'What a weird combination of strength and complete weakness you are, George.'

'You're talking differently. Have you noticed?'

'People change. People become.'

'People . . . *what*?'

'Do you know why I'm here? Do you know why you let me come here tonight?'

'So I could possess you.'

'So that you could– Well, yes, okay, you beat me to it. That was weird. But, so, no, actually, it was so that I could *let* you possess me. Big difference. And in doing so, don't you see, I also possessed *you*. And that's what you're afraid of, isn't it? That you don't possess her.'

'That isn't any of your–'

'And if you don't possess her, how can she possess you? Does she even want to? That's what you're thinking, isn't it? You're thinking, on the one hand, she's obviously the very best thing that will ever happen to you in your sad little life, but on the other hand, *damn* her and her elusive-ness and her secrecy. *Damn* her. And you were angry and you called me, remember, I didn't call *you*–'

'Rachel, I would really like you to leave now–'

'But there's a deeper question. If she won't let you possess *her*, how will she ever want to possess *you*? And we all want to be possessed, don't we, George?'

'Take your hand off that, please. I asked you to leave.'

'The thing is–'

'Get off me–'

'Make me. The thing is, I know exactly what you're feeling. I know exactly what all this feels like.'

'Rachel, I said–'

'One last time, George, because we both know there won't be another. I'm on the pill, there won't be any accidents, don't you worry. That's it, that's the response I was hoping for, one last time and I'll go.'

'. . .'

'. . .'

'. . .'

'But before I do–'

'*Rachel*–'

'I have to say this to you. All these years, I've been treating possession as a game, don't you see? Something only to be withheld. But do you know how lonely that is, George?'

'I–'

'You don't. You actually don't. You think you know loneliness, but you don't. Because you allow yourself to be possessed. And everyone loves that about you. Granted, sometimes after they possess you they have their fill and move on, but that's not what I'm saying. I'm saying that when they *first* meet you, you offer yourself, George. That's what you do. You open your arms and you say, this is me, take me, have me.'

'Rachel, are you crying?'

'Aren't you?'

'This light. The moonlight. Your eyes reflect so strangely–'

'And by being possessed, you *possess*, because that's how love works. So what are you going to do with Kumiko? A little faster now, George, we're almost done.'

'Rachel–'

'You *are* crying. Good. You should. That's what I didn't understand about you, George. I thought I possessed you like all those other idiots I slept with. Possession while giving nothing in return. But you. *You*, George. I possessed you, and you possessed me. And that's why I can't forgive you.'

'Rachel–'

'That's why I can't part from you either.'

'Please–'

'That's why I'm here tonight. Why. This. Is. Happening. More. I said, *more*.'

'Kumiko.'

'Yes, I know. Say her name. I'll say it, too. Kumiko.'

'Kumiko.'

'Kumiko.'

'*Kumiko.*'

'. . .'

'. . .'

'. . .'

'. . .'

'That's okay, George. You just weep. You've betrayed your best love, and weeping is only proper. I'll go now. I will.'

'Your eyes.'

'What was that?'

'Your *eyes*.'

'It's only my tears, George. And long will I cry them.'

'. . .'

'. . .'

'Did you *hear* that?'

'No.'

'It sounded like, from outside the window–'

'I didn't hear anything, George. And neither did you.'

IV.

He was making his final cutting.

He looked up from his desk. *Final*. What an odd choice of word. Not really final, of course, merely the final cutting for the last tile in Kumiko's set, the one that would make the story complete. She wanted to finish it before they married, but surely there'd be more to make after.

So, not the final cutting. Not the last ever. No.

He wiped a bead of sweat from his forehead and went back to work. Even aside from how this nagging fever made everything seem extra bright, a trill of anxiety buzzed all around him these days: the sudden rush of being engaged to Kumiko, the still-elusiveness of her as she threw herself into finishing her tiles, the quarrels he'd had with Amanda, whom he couldn't seem to speak to lately without snapping.

But most of all, he had slept with Rachel. He almost literally couldn't believe it had happened and wasn't just something he'd dreamed. It had, in fact, seemed dreamlike when he called her, dreamlike when she'd come over to his momentarily Kumiko-less house, dreamlike when they'd spent the night in his bed. The sex had been joyless and compulsive, like how drug addicts must feel at the end of their using, but Rachel had been right. He could possess her (and she, him) in a brief but total way that had never happened with Kumiko, that felt like it never *could* happen. Kumiko was unknowable, how many times did he need proof of it? She was like a figure from history or a goddess, and he'd been frightened and angry and–

'Stupid,' he whispered to himself, slashing the page he was working on and throwing it away.

He'd slept with Rachel. He'd slept with Rachel. He'd slept with *Rachel*. Kumiko didn't know about it, there was no way for her *to* know, and he felt the oddest certainty that Rachel would say nothing either. But what did that matter? The damage was done.

'You don't look very good, George,' Mehmet said from the front counter, where he was supposed to be working on a set of conference badges but was instead fiddling with the design for a flyer for some small theatrical drama in which he'd somehow nabbed a supporting role. As far as George could tell, it seemed to consist mostly of audience confrontation and full-frontal male nudity. It was being staged above a chip shop.

'I'm fine,' George lied, 'and that doesn't look like work.'

Mehmet ignored this. 'You know, we're all still waiting for the date.'

'What date?'

Mehmet gasped. 'Your *wedding* date. We'll close the shop, I assume.'

'Yeah, I guess we will.'

'Aren't you excited?'

'I'm working, Mehmet, so should you.'

Mehmet turned back to his computer. 'I don't even know why I bother.'

George looked up. 'Why *do* you bother?'

'Huh?'

'There are other jobs you could get. Even if they're not acting jobs, they'd at least be closer to it than a print shop. A theatre box office, maybe. Or a tour guide–'

'A *tour guide*,' Mehmet practically spat.

'You know what I mean.'

'But what would you do without me, George?'

'Probably much the same as now. Except with fewer interruptions.'

Mehmet swivelled back and forth on his stool, regarding George for a moment. 'You really don't see it, do you?'

'Beg pardon?'

'The way people are around you. The way they act.'

'What on earth are you talking–'

'They're loyal to you, George. You inspire that. You're best friends with your daughter. You're best friends with your ex-wife–'

'Hardly *best*–'

'And Kumiko, who is beautiful and talented and mysterious enough to probably have any man in the whole wide world, chose you. Don't you ever ask yourself why?'

George felt his skin flush, which might not have even been the fever. 'It's not because I'm loyal.'

'It's because you *inspire* loyalty. No one wants to let you down. Which, frankly, makes them all vaguely irritated with you most of the time – I know it does me – but they stick around because they want to be sure you're all right.' Mehmet shrugged. 'You're likeable. And if you like *them*, well, that means they're really worth liking, doesn't it?'

221

This was easily the nicest thing Mehmet had ever said to him, and in the midst of everything that was wrong at the moment George felt a sudden dizzying upsurge of love and kindness.

'You're fired, Mehmet.'

'What?'

'I'm not angry. I'm not even dissatisfied with your work. Well, not much. But if you stay here, you're going to end up taking over this shop, and that would be the saddest thing that ever happened. You deserve better.'

'*George*—'

'I've got a ton of money in the bank from these goddamn tiles. I'll give you a big redundancy. But you need to take the leap, Mehmet. You really do.'

Mehmet looked ready to argue, but then he stopped. 'How big a redundancy?'

George laughed. It felt like a rare thing. 'It's been a pleasure, Mehmet.'

'What, I have to leave *now*?'

'No, of course not. You've got badges to finish.'

George went back to his cutting, his momentary lightness dissipating quickly. He glanced up at the first tile he and Kumiko had made together, still hanging on the wall above him. The dragon and the crane, danger and serenity, staring him down. That miracle of first creation. How had he done it then?

And how the hell was he supposed to do it now?

The day after the party, Kumiko had quietly set out every tile of the private story she was telling, one by one, along the bookshelves of his sitting room, putting them in front of his books so the story told itself around the room. The mandala of his soul holding the tiles of hers. He counted them. There were thirty-one.

'There is one left to finish,' she'd said.

'The end of the story,' he'd said. 'Will it be a happy ending?

She smiled at him, and his heart soared. 'Depends on what you mean by happy.'

George looked across the tiles. 'It's just that it all seems sort of precarious, doesn't it? Like everyone's happiness could be snatched away at any moment.'

She'd looked at him. 'Do you think your happiness is going to be taken from you, George?'

'Who doesn't?'

She considered this as she regarded the penultimate tile. 'One more to go,' she said, 'and then this story is finished.'

One more to go, he thought, looking down at his cutting again now, wondering what the little separate bits were supposed to add up to, wondering which direction he was meant to be heading with them. This assemblage would be for that final tile, but Kumiko had refused, as ever, to tell him what she wanted. Well, *refused* was probably a bit strong, she'd more *eluded* him when he asked her about it, but as the days went on he was growing more and more anxious. It felt increasingly like a test he was failing.

'You're an artist, George,' she'd said. 'This is what you must accept. And if you are an artist, then you will know the shape when it appears under your hand.'

'But what are *you* cutting? So at least I'll know–'

'It is better if you don't.'

And then George had found himself saying, 'What else is new?'

They hadn't exactly fought after that, but a chilly

politeness had descended. It really seemed as if it *should* have been the moment they had a big blow-up, that they needed to have at least one fight that would either sunder them irreparably or – and George really did think this was more likely and not just because he hungered for it – bring them even closer together. But instead, she had (politely) insisted on going back to her own flat, saying it felt important for her to finish her work there before she took the final step of moving in completely.

He'd thought this meant just a day, but another, then another, then a few more had passed, until a full week was gone, with Kumiko still working, still demurring from making the final move to his house. It had also been a week of being battered by this fever, battered by failure after failure with his own work, and then one ugly, ugly evening, after he'd been unable to get hold of her all day long, there had dawned the single deadly thought that she didn't really love him.

And that turned out to be too frightening to bear alone.

It only took a moment, a single, inexplicable moment, but he found himself taking out his phone and dialling a number which turned out to be Rachel's.

'George,' she'd answered, as if she already knew what he wanted.

She'd come right over, despite the hour, and she'd seemed, not to put too fine a point on it, slightly unhinged.

But that hadn't stopped him.

'Is this for the big project?' Mehmet said, appearing over his shoulder, making him jump.

'Jesus, Mehmet, I nearly cut off my thumb,' George said. Then he turned to look at him. 'What big project?'

'I've just heard rumours.'

'What rumours? We're just taking a little break, that's all.'

'It's all over the right sort of digital places, George, where you wouldn't even know how to look. Word doesn't stop spreading just because you want it to.'

'What are you talking about?'

Mehmet sighed, as if talking to a slow pupil. 'The tiles were doing well already. Then you suddenly stopped making them–'

'We didn't stop, we're just–'

'Please. How do people react when they can't have something? It turns them into babies. Gimme, gimme, gimme. If you wanted to lower demand, you should have put out a million tiles, not zero.'

George turned back to the cutting. 'I have no control over any of that. There's no big project. Not for them anyway.'

Mehmet shrugged. 'Doesn't matter. Just by talking about it, they might *make* it true. That's kind of what art is, isn't it?'

George sighed and rubbed his temples. He really did feel rough. Maybe it was time to think about giving up for the day. He'd been cutting from a mould-spattered copy of *The Golden Bowl* he'd found in a £1 bin outside a charity shop. It was a book, he suspected, which could possibly have been deeply metaphorical for his situation, if he or anyone he'd ever known had actually read it. As it was, all he knew of the plot was what he'd gleaned from the back cover. A gift of a bowl meant to represent love had a crack running through it. Or something. He'd torn off the cover, thrown it away, and started cutting, trying to figure out what Kumiko needed for the last tile.

But page after page after page and nothing had appeared. Without quite realising he was doing it, his first attempts were silhouettes of women, their faces, their bodies, clothed and unclothed, even the curve and nipple of a breast once, which seemed so viciously reductive he'd crumpled it immediately and gone to lunch, embarrassed and sorrowful. What was *wrong* with him?

He'd tried animals after that. It was a crane that had first brought them together, after all, and if the word 'final' continued hovering in the air, then perhaps an animal might round things off nicely. But all his birds became penguins, all his penguins became otters. His tigers were sheep, his dragons moths, his horses barely more than geometric shapes with unconvincing legs.

'Ah, *screw it*,' he said now, throwing away what felt like the hundredth iteration. One more. One more try and then he'd give up. Maybe completely.

He tore out one final (that word again) page of dense, Jamesian prose and tried to read it to see if inspiration could be found.

She saw him in truth less easily beguiled, saw him wander in the closed dusky rooms from place to place or else for long periods recline on deep sofas and stare before him through the smoke of ceaseless cigarettes.

Yep, that seemed to fit pretty well with the little George thought he knew of Henry James. He was sure it must be brilliant, but it didn't half read like an artistic representation of writing, rather than writing itself. A painting of a page. A cutting without cuts.

And then, because he was still George, he felt a flash of guilt at thinking so much like his daughter and being unkind to a long-dead writer who was revered by thousands, or at least hundreds, and whose golden bowl no doubt stood for something richly meaningful that could almost certainly illuminate the *closed dusky rooms* of his own–

He closed his eyes for a moment. Henry James was probably the last writer you should read if you were feverish. He took in a long breath, opened his eyes, and turned the page over. He slashed a line across it with his blade.

Why had he called Rachel? What could he possibly have been thinking?

He cut another line, making two sides of an open, rough triangle.

It was as if he'd wilfully decided to sacrifice *everything* just to spite Kumiko, a spite she would, he hoped, remain forever unaware of, so it did nothing but slice at his own heart, as spite only ever did.

He cut two more swift lines, removing a shape from the page and setting it to one side.

He hadn't even been *angry* with her, not really. He'd just felt . . . *lost*. Alone. Unaccompanied even when she was right there with him.

He cut more lines from the same page, above where he'd removed the triangle. A cut here, a smaller shape from the page there.

And it was his fault alone. He had never really confronted Kumiko, had demanded nothing further from her than what she gave and therefore she had every right to think, to believe, to *trust* that George was happy with what he was given.

Cut. Tear. Cut more. Tear more.

And so he had – stupidly, *insanely* – gone to Rachel, who *had* given, and he had given in return, only to discover–

A final cut.

–that to be given everything was too much. That *something* was plenty. Or at least enough. That his world, the world of the sixty-five per cent man, was filled up to its brim by partial, and drowned by whole.

He wanted Kumiko. There was nothing else worth wanting, nothing else worth *needing*.

And oh please please please let her forgive him without knowing why. That's all he wanted from her now, forgiveness.

Please forgive me–

'That's pretty cool,' Mehmet said, still standing behind him, forgotten.

'I swear to God, Mehmet,' George barked, startled again. 'I'm suddenly very happy to waive any notice period.'

'No, but seriously,' Mehmet said. 'Nice.'

George looked down at what he'd made, arranged there on his work mat, the different shapes coalescing into a larger form. His eyes took a second to see it, but there it was, impossible now to miss.

He'd cut a volcano. An erupting volcano.

One covered in words, made from a book. A volcano that breathed fire and brimstone and ash and death. One that signalled the destruction of the world.

But also, as ever, the birth of another.

And there it was. This was it. He'd found it.

The final cutting.

The story could end.

He drove to her flat directly from the shop, the cutting pressed safely in a clear plastic folder. He was in no way

228

nervous about what she'd say, because he knew the cutting was right. It was different from the volcanoes he'd made before – stolid, peaceful, lumpen things that he'd never seen her use – and very different from the ones she made herself. It was more than just the difference between feather and paper, this was a volcano that had burst unconscious from his fingers, a volcano of George, and Henry James's bowl could go leakily hold some flowers, thank you very much, because a volcano right now was all the metaphor he needed, and not just because his fever was radiating off him like lava.

Evening was falling as he pulled up outside the building that held her flat, a flat he had only ever really stood at the doorstep of while picking her up. Which had never seemed all that weird till now, just another facet of Kumiko's mystery, that she didn't want him to see her workspace, didn't want to feel him there even in memory, she said, or the work wouldn't flow. He had believed it easily, even though she didn't seem to have any problem coming to the shop, into *his* workspace.

He hadn't called ahead, not that she answered her phone more than a third of the time anyway, but that was all right, maybe it was time for George to be a little surprising. In a good way. He parked and reached for the volcano, looking at it again. It felt so right, felt somehow so *open*, burning in his hand, a confession and an apology and so much a plea for how much he needed her that he felt she couldn't help but see it and understand it and add it to the final tile, completing their story, bringing them together, forever. He turned with a rush of hope to open his car door.

And the world came to an end.

*   *   *

Rachel was coming out of the block of flats.

Rachel.

Who lived nowhere near here.

He watched her step from the front door out onto the pavement, illuminated by the lights of the foyer and the few streetlights ticking on. He watched her look through her handbag for her keys, her face unsmiling and oddly confused.

Then she glanced up, as if she'd heard something, and saw him.

The light caught her eyes again, flashing them green as she gave him the briefest of glances. Then she immediately pretended she hadn't seen him, though there was no way that could possibly be true. She looked back into her handbag and continued the hunt for her keys while starting to move away.

But before she disappeared into the night he caught a last look of her face, and it was still strangely baffled, even disappointed.

George looked up the front of the block of flats to Kumiko's window. His stomach was tumbling, falling through his body down some kind of alimentary bottomless pit. How had this happened? How had Rachel known where Kumiko lived, when she was so particular about giving out her address to even George? Had they met before? Had they known each other all along? And what had they said to each other?

It was over. It could only be over. And it was over by *his* hand, his selfishness, and his greed, yes, *greed*, not for the money that the artwork so surprisingly brought, but for Kumiko herself. He was greedy for her. He wanted more than she was giving, and though that greed was against all his best tendencies, all the things that made everyone like him, he still felt it. He hungered for her, and she wouldn't feed him.

And now here was Rachel. In Kumiko's block of flats, probably in her very *flat*. Where George himself had never properly been.

Somehow, as unreasonable and baseless and outrageous as it was, George started to grow angry. He gripped the steering wheel in two fists, a frown twisting his mouth, the fever feeling like it was blazing now, catching him in a furious shine. It seemed so unfair, everyone else conducting his life for him, yet again, like he was so placid it couldn't possibly matter. Well, it *did* matter. It did, at last, bloody well matter.

He had to see her. This had to have some resolution. One way or another, something had to end.

He grabbed the cutting and got out of his car, slamming the door so hard the whole vehicle rocked. He strode to the entrance, ignoring the call button as he held open the door for an exiting young mother and her two children. She looked at him suspiciously, until her eyes caught the cutting under his arm and she said, 'Kumiko?'

He only answered a gruff 'Yes', before brushing past her.

He pressed the up button on the lift thirty-three times before the doors opened. He bounced angrily on his feet as the lift rose, and even now, he could feel the injustice of his anger. *He* was the one who betrayed Kumiko. She had done nothing.

In fact, that was her crime, wasn't it? That she had done nothing.

But oh, the injustice of that, too, because of course she hadn't done *nothing*. She had given him the whole world. Just not enough of herself in it.

The anger churned in him, ready to boil over, ready to erupt.

The lift doors opened and he stormed down the hallway, going straight to her door and pounding on it.

'Kumiko!' he shouted. '*Kumiko!*'

The door swung open under his fist.

He fell quiet as it slowly glided all the way open, gently tapping the opposite wall. It was silent in the flat. The lights were on, but there was no sound, no activity from inside.

'Kumiko?' he said.

In three steps, he was further inside her flat than he'd ever been, which was an absurd notion, one he couldn't believe he'd put up with for so long. No wonder women didn't take him seriously. No wonder his own daughter laughed at him and talked to him like–

He stopped, raising a slow fist to his forehead, as if to massage away a headache. Where was all this coming from? This rage, this lashing out. Who *was* he, at this moment?

What had happened to George?

'Kumiko?' he asked again, as if maybe she would have the answer.

He moved past a ruthlessly clean kitchen, almost to the point of never having been used, and then into a similarly clean sitting room, so devoid of personality it could have been a hotel.

Was this where she lived? He turned a slow circle. There was no trace of her anywhere. No art of hers on the walls – for these prints of southwestern American pueblos were surely intended only for people who considered artwork as furniture – but also not even a plant or a discarded bit of clothing.

It was almost as if no one lived here at all.

There were two doors off the sitting room, one cracked open slightly to reveal a sliver of immaculate toilet, and the other, shut tight, could only have been her bedroom, which must in turn serve as her workroom, for there was nowhere else possible in this small space. Between the two doors was a small mirror, and George caught a glimpse of his sweat-covered face in it, barely recognising his scowl or the ferocity of his gaze. Even his eyes seemed different, and he leaned forward to look. They seemed almost–

There was a sigh behind the closed door.

He moved towards it, listening, but there was nothing more. He was on the verge of saying her name again, but surely she would have heard him by now? He turned and looked back up the short hallway. Why had the front door already been opened?

Fear suddenly rushed him. Had something happened? Had Rachel grown so deranged that–?

He grasped the doorknob and burst into her bedroom, feeling a crippling headrush as he moved so quickly, and before him–

There she stands.

She is at an easel, on which rests the final tile. He sees the feathers gathered there, already cut and assembled loosely on the black square. The cutting is not yet finished, even in his briefest glance he can see that there are spaces to be filled, spaces that will complete this shape, make it cohere.

He barely takes in the room around him, can only vaguely sense an empty white space, containing nothing at all but

233

her and the easel and the tile, though that can hardly be possible, can it?

But what he sees of her can hardly be possible either.

She is wearing a thin, silky robe of a light rose colour, with inky edges and wide sleeves. The robe is open, and she has let it gather at her elbows, a swoop of cloth low across her bare back. She is naked underneath, and as she turns towards George her fingers are pressed between her breasts.

Where she is plucking a feather from her skin.

For she is not Kumiko at all, she is a great white bird, pulling out a feather to add to the others she has already plucked for the tile on the easel. The feather comes loose, as if she can hardly stop herself from finishing the action, now that she's started it.

He sees her feathery skin twitch with pain at the feather breaking away, sees as she holds it in the air between her long, slender fingers − between the edges of her long, slender beak − between her long, slender fingers.

The feather has a single drop of red blood quivering at its tip, full of potential, full of life and of death.

George looks into Kumiko's brown eyes − her golden eyes − her brown eyes. He sees the surprise and horror there, sees her reeling through every consequence of his presence.

But more than anything else, he sees a sorrow so deep and ancient that it nearly rocks him off his feet.

He knows, in an instant, he should not have seen this.

He knows, in an instant, that all would have been well, that the future would have taken care of itself, if he had never come here.

He knows, in an instant, that it is now only a matter of waiting for the end.

He woke on the small, anonymous sofa in Kumiko's small, anonymous sitting room. She stood in front of him, her robe closed around herself again, though from how she was leaning over him he could see the skin on her upper chest and down to her breast.

Smooth, of course. And featherless.

'George?' she said. 'Are you all right?'

He looked up into her face, and there was the same understanding, the same mystery that made his heart ask to be sent somewhere where it could just look at her forever in peace. 'What happened?'

'You have a fever.' She pressed her hand to his forehead. 'A bad one. You stormed into my bedroom, looking very terrible, George. I am worried. I was about to call a doctor. Drink this.'

He took a glass of water from her, but didn't drink it. 'What did I see?'

She looked confused. 'I don't know what you saw.' She pulled the robe tighter around herself. 'It seemed to disturb you a great deal.'

'What was Rachel doing here?'

'*Who?*'

'I saw her coming out the front just now. I saw . . .' He trailed off, suddenly unsure.

She frowned at him. 'It is a big building, George. Lots of people come and go. I did see an old friend this afternoon, but I can assure you beyond all shadow of a doubt that it was not that woman.'

That woman was said so pointedly that guilt throttled him, to the point where even 'old friend' seemed an unreasonable enquiry to chase at the moment, so he finally just said, 'I'm sorry.'

'For what?' she asked.

He swallowed, felt how dry his throat was, drank the water down in one. Maybe she was right, maybe his fever really was that bad. He couldn't have seen what he thought he did in the bedroom, obviously, so maybe he hadn't seen Rachel either . . .

He didn't know whether this felt like good news or not.

'You are so difficult to know,' he heard himself whispering.

'I know,' she said. 'And for that, *I* am sorry.' Her face softened. 'Why did you come here today, George?'

'I wanted to show you this,' he said, and reached for the cutting, which Kumiko had placed on the table. She took it, looking at it through the plastic. He started to speak again, but her glance stayed firmly, actively on the cutting, on the words and pages and angles and curves and voids that formed the erupting volcano.

'This is perfect, George,' she said. 'This is everything it should be.'

'I just went with what I felt. I didn't even know what it was until I finished.'

She leaned forward and put a soft hand on his cheek. 'Yes. Yes, I understand. I understand everything.' She stood, keeping the cutting. 'You rest here. Lie back, close your eyes. I won't be long.'

'What are you going to do?'

'This is the final piece of the story. I shall use it to make the last tile.'

George cleared his throat, feeling as if his whole life depended on the answer to his next question. 'And then?'

But she smiled again, and his heart leapt in a kind of terrified, vertigo-dazzled joy.

'And then, George,' she said, 'I will gather my final belongings and move into your house as your wife, and you, my husband. And we shall live happily ever after.'

She left him then, as he lay back like she'd suggested, his heart pounding, his brow still feverish but perhaps cooling, and he turned her words over and over in his thoughts, wondering how she had made 'happily ever after' sound so much like 'goodbye'.

Amanda held the pregnancy test over the toilet bowl, ready to be widdled on.

She'd had it since she first vomited, but it had remained steadfastly in its box, so tonight at least marked a sort of progress.

Because what if she was?

But what if she *wasn't*?

But what if she *was*?

In her calmest moments – or at least calm*er* – she kept reminding herself she still wasn't all that late. Her cycles had careened so wildly as a teenager her mum and dad had agreed to the pill for a while at age fourteen just to get things regulated, and when she was off it these days – having, since Henri, not much reason to be on it – it was almost as bad, especially since the birth of JP.

So she was still in her plausible window. Yes, she was. Indeed. And she hadn't thrown up unexpectedly any more, despite, all right, a vague, persistent nausea and a vague, persistent fever, which were probably just flu season and the germ factory that was any small child. Yes. All those things. And that's what the pregnancy test would tell her. Of course it would.

But.

It was past midnight, the flat dark and cold again, a waning moon shining through the windows in the toilet. She'd had another bonkers dream, woken up needing to pee again, and here she stood, not knowing whether she was going to use it this time or not.

'Or not' seemed a distinct possibility. The test was a heartlessly digital one, meant to eliminate ambiguity, but the black figures floating on the grey background inadvertently gave it a dated feel, like a pregnancy test from the late eighties. Why hadn't she gone with some warm, caring test with purple crosses or pink pluses, rather than something that might have once looked like the future to her mother?

She still had to pee, was holding it in while she debated, growing yet again increasingly awake in the cold.

She closed her eyes for a moment and shifted her awareness around her body, letting her mind slip, trying to see what her stomach was actually doing rather than just what she was worried about. And yes, okay, maybe it was a bit nauseous, though she didn't feel like throwing up at the moment and, as ever, it could have all just been the fever.

She kept her eyes closed and tried to find clues in the rest of her body. Discovering she was pregnant with JP had been a number of things, among which was the most incredible feeling of unlooked-for confirmation. The hormonal shifts, the flushes on her skin, the feeling of being full and flooded, she had *known* she was pregnant without ever knowing. Before she'd even noticed the upfront symptoms, she had known it on some elemental level, as if her body was a hundred per cent clear on things and not particularly bothered if her brain was late to the party.

And so she pushed her thoughts deep into her abdomen, into her thighs and legs, into her arms and hands, into her breasts and throat. Pregnancy didn't just happen in your womb; your whole body re-arranged itself, like country-house staff preparing for a visit from royalty. She sent out feelers and tried to listen to what they were finding.

She opened her eyes.

She arranged herself over the toilet and weed onto the stick, cleaning it and herself and setting it on the sink to wait the required three minutes.

She kept her mind as clear as she could, thinking almost nothing, just humming what eventually revealed itself to be a song by the Wriggles, a cover – or so Clare had mentioned when she'd heard JP sing it once – of an ancient pop hit about Africa. JP loved it because it had taught him the longest word he knew to date: 'Serengeti'.

Her consciousness was interrupted by a sound, muffled and indistinct, and she immediately thought of that strange *keening*. She was at the window before she even thought to move, looking into the darkened car park. But the sound continued in an insistent way that wasn't like before and wasn't, after all, even coming from outside.

It was her phone.

She glanced down at the pregnancy test, still resting on the sink, slowly revealing its results, as she dashed out the door of the bathroom. She swore in a vicious whisper as she caught her big toe on the doorjamb, and hopped into her bedroom, where her mobile was repeatedly strumming the mournful folk song she used as a ringtone.

It stopped when she was halfway across the room. She fell across her bed to read the display.

Rachel.

Rachel?

Rachel had called her at – she looked at the clock – 1.14 a.m.?

Huh?

Before she could even consider whether it could have been anything other than an accident, the phone rang again, startling her so much she nearly dropped it.

'Rachel, what the f–?'

She listened for less than twenty seconds, and even though her mind was storming with questions, she asked none before hanging up. Within another thirty seconds, she had shoved herself into jeans and a heavy jumper. Before another minute had passed, she'd crammed sockless feet into shoes on her way into JP's bedroom to pick him up as a bundle, blankets and all.

Before the clock read 1.17 a.m., she was dashing out her front door, car keys in her hand, JP in her arms, running as fast as her feet would carry her.

The lady's hand does not fall.

The volcano opens his eyes, the green at first surprised, then slowly burning, boiling, blazing to rage.

'So be it, my lady,' he says, and he rises to his feet, his head reaching to the sky. His voice shakes the foundations of creation as it whispers in her ear. 'I love you, my lady, and now my hatred for you shall be as large as that love. As large as the universe entire. Your punishment shall be that I shall never stop chasing you, never stop tormenting you, never stop asking for that which you cannot bestow.'

'And I love you,' she says, 'and your punishment will be that I will forever do so.'

He leans down to her. 'You will never be at rest. You will never be at peace.'

'Nor will you.'

'The difference, my lady,' he says, with an ugly smile, 'is that I was never at rest to begin with.'

She takes a step back from him. And another, and

another, moving faster and faster, until she turns her back on him and takes flight, racing away into the heavens.

'You may flee, my lady!' he shouts after her. 'I will forever follow!'

But then he frowns.

She is not fleeing. Her path has swooped upwards into the heavens, high up, beyond this world, beyond time.

And now she is flying back.

At him.

With increasing speed.

She races towards him as a comet, as a rocket, as a bullet fired from before the beginnings of all things. He stands taller, preparing himself for battle. Still she comes, faster now, white-hot from her speed.

And she *is* a bullet, separating from herself, watching herself fly towards him, fly towards his still-exposed heart. She slows in mid-air, watching the bullet part of herself race ahead, cutting the air, flying faster and faster.

Until it strikes.

Lodging in the heart of the volcano, knocking him off his feet. He falls with a crash that creates planets, that destroys stars, that scars the heavens with its tearing.

He falls.

But he does not die.

In fact, he begins to laugh. 'What have you done, my lady, that is supposed to have killed me?' He sits up, feeling his beating heart.

Feeling the bullet lodged within.

'I have shot you,' she says.

'It is a bullet without harm, my lady.'

'It is a bullet with a name. A bullet whose name will eventually be the death of you. A bullet whose name is Permission.'

He frowns, growing angry. 'My lady talks in riddles.'

'As long as this bullet resides in your heart,' she says, 'so will a part of me. And as long as a part of me resides in your heart . . .' She flies down close to his face so there will be no mistaking her words. 'You have permission to harm me.'

There is a silence, as the world below takes in a shocked breath.

'What, my lady?' the volcano says, his voice low and heavy.

'Try.'

'Try what?'

'Try to harm me.'

He is unsettled, confused. But she is taunting him and begins to fly annoyingly close to his face. 'My lady!' he says, cross, and half-heartedly throws a blanket of lava her way.

She cries out in pain. She turns to him, the burn growing on her arm, the skin rippling and peeling in an ugly wound.

'My lady!' he says, shocked.

But she flies out of his reach.

30 of 32

'Where is your hatred now, my husband?' she asks. 'Where is your torment? You can harm me.' She cocks her head. 'So what will you do?'

She turns her back and flies away, not too fast, not in fear, just away. Away from him.

He trembles as what she has done sinks into him. The terrible, terrible thing she has achieved, far worse than any forgiveness could ever be.

He grows angry. And angrier still.

She is disappearing into the distance, a speck of light against a night of black.

'I shall pursue you, my lady,' he says. 'I shall never cease pursuing you. I shall follow you until the end of time and—'

But she is not listening.

And he is not pursuing.

His heart aches. Aches with love. Aches with hatred. Aches with the bullet of her lodged inside.

His rage grows.

'My lady,' he says, angrily. 'My lady.'

He storms over the landscape, destroying everything in his path, but there is no satisfaction in it, nothing to be gained from the small peoples running from him, the cities sinking beneath his blows, the vast forests burning under his breath. He turns back to the horizon. She is still a disappearing spot upon it, one star among the firmament.

'My lady,' he says again.

He reaches down into the forest and rips up the tallest tree from its roots. He crushes it in his fist until it is straight and light. He reaches into the metals of the cities, into the factories he knows so well, and fashions an arrowhead from melted weapons of death. He fletches the arrow with feathers, extincting an entire species of the most beautiful bird he can find. He pulls out a bowstring from the tenderest sinews of the world, ignoring the cries of his child. He makes the bow from his own lava, allowing it to cool only into elasticity.

In the instant and eternity it has taken him to make his weapon, she has not disappeared from the horizon. She is still there, forever, like the bullet in his heart.

'This is not over, my lady,' he says, lining up his sight.

He lets fly the arrow.

It strikes her.

'Oh, my love!' she cries out, in pain and terrible, inevitable surprise. 'What have you done?'

And she falls, falls, falls to earth.

The fire began like this (1).

In the top half of the final tile, a volcano made of words erupted its fury, blasting verbs and adjectives and gerunds out into the world to consume everything they touched. In the bottom half, somewhat counterintuitively, a woman made of feathers fell from the sky. She had a single cut word – covered in down to obscure its exact letters – pierced through her heart. She fell with sorrow and resignation, but her position was such that she might also have completed her fall, thrown to earth by the angry arms of the volcano.

Kumiko set the tile on the bookshelves with the others. She had lit the room with candles in every corner, the tiles flickering in the warmth of the flames, like miniature suns in a temple for an ancient goddess.

'It seems a strange ending,' George said. 'The volcano destroying itself in anger, the woman beyond his grasp.'

'A happy release for both, maybe,' Kumiko said. 'But also perhaps a sad one, too, yes. And after all, not even an ending. All stories begin before they start and never, ever finish.'

'What happens to them next?'

In answer, she only took him by the arm and led him out of the sitting room, up the stairs, and into what was now their bed. Her intention didn't seem exclusively carnal, but she did press herself to him after they undressed, holding him to her, stroking his hair. He looked up into her eyes, lit by moonlight.

They reflected back to him, golden.

'Do I know who you are?' he asked.

To which she only said, 'Kiss me.'

And so he did.

Down in the sitting room, the candles still burned in their wax cylinders, flickering and dancing. One candle, though, had a flaw. Its flame licked and burned unevenly, and soon the wall of the candle melted away, molten wax spilling over the side, pooling across George's old coffee table. Even this was only a small danger, but the collapse unbalanced the candle just enough for it to tip, lowering its flame closer to the tabletop.

Later, after a physical intimacy so close and gentle and perfect it made George dare to think for a fleeting moment that happiness might be possible after all, he sat up in bed. Kumiko sleepily asked where he was going. 'To blow out those candles,' he replied.

But it was already too late.

The fire began like this (2).

After Kumiko placed the last tile and George blew out the candles she'd lit, they'd retired to bed. They made love slowly, almost sadly, but with a tenderness so light George felt as if they'd finally made it through some unnameably strange and mysterious ordeal, safely reaching the other side. He looked up into her eyes, lit by moonlight.

They reflected back to him, golden.

'Do I know who you are?' he asked.

To which she only said, 'Kiss me.'

And so he did.

Later, they slept, and still sleeping, George rose.

He padded down the stairs with the stumbling certainty of the sleepwalker. In his darkened sitting room, he moved towards the first tile of the story (*'She is born in a breath of cloud . . .'*) and took it down from the bookshelf. He tossed it carelessly on the coffee table. He did the same with the second tile, dropping it on the first. He repeated this action, unseeing, through every tile, one after the other, until he reached the last, set out this very evening. He placed it on top of the others, the pile now in great disarray, the feathers and his paper cuttings tearing and ripping under the slipshod weight.

Still in the dark, he reached for the box of matches with which they had lit the candles. He struck one, and though his pupils recoiled at the sudden blaze of light, he didn't wince or blink or look away.

He held the flame to the edge of one of the tiles near the bottom of the pile. It was at first reluctant to catch, the tiles being made of a particularly heavy matte bonding, but catch it eventually did, a dark blue flame oozing over it, grabbing inexorable hold of the first batch of page cuttings, then brightening, expanding, a hungry tongue sprouting two more, which each sprouted two more in turn.

George dropped the match and turned back towards the stairs, slowly climbing them as the fire grew and spread and flexed its muscles.

He would remember none of this and not believe it if he had, having zero history of somnambulism. Nevertheless, he climbed back under the covers, placed his head on the pillow, Kumiko snuggling in behind him, and he closed his eyes again, as if they had never been properly open.

The fire began like this (3).

In the darkened sitting room, while George and Kumiko slept upstairs, the tiles looked at one another across the bookshelves. They told a story of a lady and a volcano who were both more and less than what they were called. Their story was told in feathers and paper, but it was the feathers alone that now seemed to waft and shift as if in a breeze–

A feather detached itself from one of the tiles, flitting in the air, jumping and dashing in a fretful spiral–

Where it was joined by a second, a bit of feather from a different tile, swirling around the first–

And then a third and a fourth, then a flurry, then a *wave* of feathers, pouring from the shelves, twisting in spirals and helixes, coalescing then bursting apart, grabbing at each other like fists at the end of living ropes. They started to concentrate themselves in the centre of the room, and there seemed to be a kind of charge running through them, with flashes here and there, as if small electrical storms raged inside the cloud of feathers–

A spasm surged through the cloud, every bit of feather rushing towards a middle point–

Where, for the briefest of seconds, the feathers came together to make a great white bird, its wings outstretched, its neck unfurling high into the air, its head curled back in what might be ecstasy, might be terror, might be fury or sorrow–

And then it blasted apart, uncountable feathers and sparks flung across the room as it exploded–

The sparks caught cloth and books and wood and curtains as they landed in a hundred different spots, igniting them–

The fire began like this (4).

The volcano opened its green eyes and looked out across the vastness of the sitting room, a universe unto itself.

The horizon of this universe told a story.

The volcano stepped from the final tile to read it, his eyes showing first astonishment, then grief, as he read the tale along the skyline. He wept tears of fire to see the lady again, to see how things had gone.

But as he read, he also began to grow angry.

'This is not how it happened,' he said. 'There is more than what is told here.'

The volcano's anger began to make him grow, as anger inevitably did to a volcano. The valleys and glaciers along his flanks trembled and broke apart, re-forming as he grew larger and larger, taller and taller, his anger firing the furnace that burned within him.

'You have misrepresented me!' he shouted. 'You have denied the truth!'

He grew so large he filled the world of the sitting room, nations fleeing from him, cities crumbling under his earth-quakes, forests and landscapes disappearing through crevasses big enough to swallow an ocean.

'This will not stand!' he shouted, raising clenched and furious fists. 'This will not stand!'

He erupted, sending ash and fire in an unstoppable cataclysm that burned the universe entire.

The fire began like this (5).

The house was silent, asleep. Nothing stirred, even in George and Kumiko's bedroom, where they slept against one another, the blankets twisted around them like foot-hills after an earthquake.

Down below, in a still moment, the front door of George's house slowly opened, followed by silent footsteps inside. The door closed, just as quietly.

Rachel made her way into the sitting room, holding the key that George had forgotten he'd once given her in the palm of her hand. She stood, squinting in the dark-ness, trying to read the tiles.

She hadn't been feeling particularly well lately. Whole swathes of time seemed to vanish from her day without her being able to account for them, and when she *was* fully aware of what was going on, the rushes of feeling that buffeted her were both exhausting and perplexing. She had always known who she was, it had been her greatest weapon, and then, one day, after ending it with George, she had woken up and *not* known. That had proved increasingly difficult to handle, increasingly diffi-cult to live with, and there seemed no relief from it, as if she'd suddenly been given a burden to carry, one that slowed her down while the rest of life rushed away from her, leaving her behind.

Perhaps, she wondered, as she brushed her fingers against the barely visible tiles, she was going crazy.

What on earth, for example, had possessed her to go and see Kumiko? She couldn't even remember how she knew where Kumiko lived, though it can only have been something Kumiko must have mentioned at that party. But when she arrived, she and Kumiko hadn't even argued. Rachel had calmly – really quite astoundingly calmly – told Kumiko that she'd slept with George, that he'd called her over and insisted on it, and that she had done so immediately and willingly without a thought to Kumiko's feelings.

Kumiko had taken it all without visible anger, except perhaps for a slight impatience, as if she'd been expecting the news all along and it was tardy in arriving.

And then Kumiko had opened her mouth to speak, and the next thing Rachel remembered, she was downstairs, looking for her keys in her handbag. Which was *really* annoying, because she would have loved to have heard what Kumiko had to say about it, even if she couldn't remember for the life of her why she'd gone over to Kumiko's in the first place.

Then she had glanced up and seen George sitting in his car.

And oh, the shame that followed. The unbearable *shame*. It had been so painful, she'd had to sit in her car for nearly twenty minutes before the crying ebbed enough to let her drive.

Which also made no sense. She'd never much bothered with shame before. And why so *much*, especially if George was the one who–

No. No, it was crazy.

It was, in fact, further proof that she was *going* crazy.

As evidence, here she was in George's sitting room, an action that made perfect sense and also none whatsoever, and frankly she'd had just about enough of that feeling lately. She'd also had enough of the endless *dreams* she'd

253

been having – *ridiculous* dreams, of being made love to by whole countries, of flying through impossible landscapes, of being shot by *arrows*, for Christ's sake – and what it really boiled down to, she supposed, was that she was exhausted by it all. She had nothing more to give, and even she knew she'd had very little to give in the first place.

So here she was, in George's house, and an anger was rising in her. Anger at all that had happened. Anger at all that had stopped feeling familiar and liveable. Anger, too, because she couldn't even properly account for how she'd arrived here tonight. Or why.

Her eyes flashed green. On an impulse, she picked up the matches she'd seen lying on a side table.

She lit one.

The fire began like that. Or that. Or that. Or that. Or that.

And it burned.

Amanda glanced in her rearview mirror. JP was still asleep in his car seat, having not even really woken as she picked him up out of bed, jammies, blanket and all.

It was only JP that made any of this seem real. The tangibility of him was undreamable, his smell of milk and sweat and biscuits, that heartbreaking cowlick up the back of his head, and – she frowned in a little flash of shame – that stain of cranberry juice on his upper lip that she really should have washed off before bed.

She set her eyes back on the road and took a corner as swiftly as she dared. No, if he was here, then she was here. But nothing *else* about this made any sense at all. Rachel (*Rachel!*) calling at this hour of the morning, screaming her head off in terror and alarm and – this was the part so difficult to process, the part that would take so very much unpacking at some unspecified date in the future – doing it *at George's house.*

It didn't compute. Not in any way. Why would Rachel be parked outside George's house?

Why would Rachel be the one who saw the fire?

Even Rachel hadn't seemed to know. She'd said it outright. 'I don't know what I'm doing here,' she'd shouted, 'but you have to come!'

There'd been something in her urgency that had struck Amanda as utterly true, beyond all manipulation, beyond whatever crazy bullshit Rachel was entirely capable of pulling. Rachel's terror had reached right through the phone and sunk into Amanda's guts like a frozen stone.

So here she was, driving as fast as she could get away with.

'Come on,' she said, cutting across a surprisingly late night taxi. The driver gave her two fingers, which she absentmindedly returned.

Her father didn't live all that far from her, three miles at most – though in this city that usually meant thirty minutes anyway – but she sailed through the nearly non-existent traffic, cresting the small hill that took her down to her father's house.

Where she saw the pillar of smoke.

'Oh, shit,' she whispered.

It stretched impossibly high in the air, straight up, too, on a clear, windless, freezing night, like an arm reaching up to heaven.

'No,' she whispered as she took the last few turnings. 'No, no, no, no, no, no, no.'

She pulled around the last corner, expecting to see–

Not this.

There was nothing in the street. No fire engines, no neighbours out in nightgowns and slippers watching the blaze.

No sign of her father or Kumiko.

Just Rachel, frantic, beside her own car, as George's house blazed in front of her.

Amanda screeched to a stop in the middle of the road.

'*Maman*?' she heard from the back seat.

She turned to him. 'You must listen to Mama, JP. Are you listening?'

His eyes were locked solidly out the window, hypnotised by the fire.

'JP!'

He looked back at her, frightened.

'Sweetie, you do not get out of that seat. Do you hear Mama? Whatever you do, you do not get out of that seat!'

'*Un feu*,' he said, eyes wide.

'Yes, and Mama has to get out of the car for a minute, but I'll be right back. I'll be *right back*, do you hear me?'

He nodded and gripped his blanket around him. Hating herself for leaving him there, hating *Rachel* with irrational zeal – and perhaps a little bit rational, too – for being the person who brought her to this place, Amanda leapt out of the car.

'*WHERE'S THE FUCKING FIRE BRIGADE?*' she screamed.

'I called them,' Rachel said, looking stunned. 'They're on their way.'

'I don't hear any sirens! Why am I here first?'

'I'm sorry, I panicked, I called you and then it took me a minute to–'

But Amanda had stopped listening. Flames were leaping out of the sitting-room window, and it looked as if they might even have reached the stairs. There was so much smoke, though. So unbelievably much.

'GEORGE!' she screamed at the top of her lungs. 'KUMIKO!'

'They're still in there,' Rachel said behind her.

Amanda turned on her. 'How do you know? And what the fuck are you doing here?'

'I don't know!' Rachel shouted back. 'I don't even remember how I got here. I was just here, and there was a fire and . . .' She trailed off, her face so scared, that Amanda turned back to the house without pushing her further.

At last she heard faint sirens, but in the distance, too far, arriving too late.

Something was wrong here. Something *more* wrong than just the fire, which grew even as she watched it. Lights were starting to come on in nearby houses, but she had a weird feeling they'd only been woken by her shouting and *then* noticed the fire.

She looked back at Rachel, whose expression was almost that of a madwoman. She went to speak to her, to demand what she knew, but then a loud exploding sound came from the house. They couldn't see exactly where it came from, but it boomed across the night nevertheless.

The house blazed even more, almost disappearing behind smoke and fire. If Rachel was right – and Amanda knew somehow she *had* to be – then her father was in there.

George. And Kumiko.

And the fire brigade, their sirens still far in the distance, were going to be too late to save them.

She grabbed the front of Rachel's blouse with a fist so tight Rachel cried out. '*You listen to me*,' Amanda hissed, their noses actually touching. 'JP is in my car and you are going to watch him *right now*, and I swear on my life, Rachel, that if anything, *anything* happens to him, I will put a knife through your heart.'

'I believe you,' Rachel said.

Amanda let her go, ran to her car and stuck her head in. 'Everything's going to be all right, sweetie. This lady's going to watch you for a minute. I'm going to get *grand-père*.'

'Mama–'

'Everything's going to be all right,' she said again.

She leant over the seat, squeezed him ferociously for a brief second, then turned and ran into her father's burning house.

By the time they realised how very bad it was, first smelling the smoke, then seeing it push under the door with alarming force, they were already trapped.

They'd tried to run for it anyway – George still naked, Kumiko in the barest of nightslips – but they only managed two or three stairs before the smoke beat them back.

'I cannot,' Kumiko had said behind him, coughing out the words with an alarming wetness.

It wasn't just that the smoke was unbreathable, it felt like a living thing, a cloud of snakes trying to reach down your throat to not just choke you, but poison you, burn you with darkness. George understood in the worst possible instant what news stories meant when they said people died of smoke inhalation. One or two breaths of this and your lungs no longer worked, one or two more and you lost consciousness forever.

Through flashes of it, he could see flames already coating the bottom of the stairs, so there might not have been a route for them even if they could have made it down.

They retreated to the bedroom, shutting the door behind them for all the good that it did. George felt dangerously light-headed, from the smoke and from how quickly cataclysm had overtaken them.

'We will have to go out the window,' Kumiko said, almost calm, but he could see the beads of sweat pouring down her forehead. The temperature in the bedroom had risen with alarming speed.

'Yes,' George agreed, following her to it. She opened it and looked out. They were directly over the kitchen and could see smoke pouring out from the ground-floor windows below.

'It is far,' she said, 'and onto concrete.'

'I'll go first,' George said. 'I'll try and break your fall.'

'Chivalrous,' she said, 'but there is no time.'

She put a foot on the windowsill to lift herself up.

An explosion rocked the house, it sounded like from somewhere in the kitchen. Kumiko lost her grip and fell back into George's arms. They tumbled to the floor.

'Gas main,' he said.

'George!' Kumiko called out in alarm, looking behind him. The bedroom floor was starting to *sag*, as if it was melting into the room below, something that turned out to be almost unfeasibly frightening, because George only realised how much he counted on floors to stay flat when they suddenly stopped doing so.

'We must move!' Kumiko said over the roar. 'Now!'

But before they could even rise there was a sound like an angry yawn and the far end of the bedroom completely gave way. One of the bookcases George kept there (mostly non-fiction) vanished immediately into the fire below. The bed started to slide, too, down the still-tilting floor.

Kumiko grabbed the windowsill, now the only thing

261

to hold on to as the floor continued to slide away from them. The bed juddered to a halt for a moment, caught on something, and flames streaked up the mattress. George caught a quick, hellish glimpse of the sitting room below, consumed by fire, before smoke started pouring into the bedroom like a tidal wave.

'Try to pull yourself up!' he shouted. He was lying below her as the floor continued its tilt. It could only be a matter of seconds before everything went. He pushed her up towards the window, and she made it easily, one foot on the sill, her arms on the window's sides, ready to jump. She turned back to him, fear across her face.

'I'm right behind you!' he coughed, trying to rise.

But with another judder the bed fell through, taking most of the floor with it. George fell, too, catching his upper arms on the sudden ledge remaining below the window. His legs swung down into the burning lower level of his house, and he screamed in pain as flames seized his bare feet.

'*George*!' Kumiko yelled.

'*Go*!' he shouted back to her. 'Jump! *Please*!'

His mouth filled with smoke at every syllable, even the taste of it knocking his senses off-kilter. He tried to curl his legs away from the burning below him, could feel the soles of his feet blistering, the smoke, the pain, the fear, all of it filling his eyes with tears.

He looked back up to Kumiko.

Who wasn't there.

Thank God, he thought, grateful she'd jumped, grateful she'd at least got away. *Thank God*.

He felt himself succumbing to the smoke – so fast, so *fast* – his thoughts slurring and slowing, the world shimmering away.

He was distantly aware of his grip slipping.
Distantly aware of falling into the raging fire below.

Distantly aware of being caught.

In his dream, he flies.

The smoke curls around him under the swoop of two great wings. He thinks at first that the wings are his own, but they are not. He is being carried, held, he is not sure how, but the grip is firm around him.

Firm but tender.

The wings swoop again, slow but with a strength so sure he has no fear, even though a fire big enough to consume the world is burning below him. They pass through a wall of smoke, and the air is suddenly cooler, fresher, easier to breathe.

He is flying through open air now, arcing up and out like the path of an arrow.

He weighs nothing. His burdens fall away like the world below him. He glances up but he cannot see exactly what it is that carries him.

But even in his dream, he knows.

A long neck, graced with a crown of scarlet and a pair of golden eyes, turns back to look at him, just once, the eyes filled with tears of their own.

Tears of sadness, he thinks. Tears of depthless sorrow. And he grows suddenly frightened.

The arc continues its downward momentum. The ground approaches again. He touches the grass first with his feet, its coolness a sudden balm on skin that he now remembers is burnt and roiling with pain.

As he is laid gently down, he gives out a long slow moan.

He calls, he cries.

He keens.

Until long white feathers wipe away his tears, brush across his forehead and temples, and enfold him in soft, soft whiteness.

He longs for his dream to end.

He longs for it never to end.

It ends.

'George?'

He blinked open his eyes, starting to shiver almost immediately. He was naked against the frost-covered grass of his back garden.

'*George*,' the voice said again.

He looked up. Kumiko. He was lying in her arms, as she knelt behind him in the grass. Though still only in her nightslip, she seemed oblivious to the cold.

'How did we . . . ?' he asked, immediately coughing and having to spit out an alarming black tar.

When he looked back at her again, her eyes were golden.

And brimming with tears.

George felt a catch in his throat that wasn't smoke. 'I know you,' he said, and it wasn't a question.

She nodded slowly. 'You do.'

He touched her cheek, smudged as it was with soot. 'Why are you sad then?' He ran his thumb down to her chin. 'Why are you always so sad?'

There was a crashing sound, and they both looked back

to the house. The flames fully engulfed the roof now, eating his home with a terrifying ferocity.

'The tiles,' he coughed out, quietly. 'We'll have to write new ones.'

But Kumiko said nothing, and he moved his hand to brush away the tears that flowed down her cheeks–

(–like the feathers that had brushed his own–)

–and said, 'Kumiko?'

'You must forgive me, George,' she said, sadly.

'For what? *I'm* the one who needs forgiveness. *I'm* the one who–'

'*Everyone* needs forgiveness, my love. And for more years than I can count, I have had no one to offer it to me.' Her golden eyes blazed, though maybe it was just a reflection of the flames from the house. 'Until I found *you*, George,' she continued. 'You are the one who can. You are the one who must.'

'I don't understand,' George said, still in her arms, still lying across her lap.

'Please, George. Please. And then I shall go.'

He sat up, alarmed. 'Go? No, you can't go. I've just *found* you.'

'George–'

'I won't forgive you. Not if it makes you leave.'

She placed a hand on his chest, as if to calm him. She kept her glance on it, so he looked down, too. Her fingers spread out–

–and seemed to change. A splay of feathers shot from underneath them, white as the moon, white as starlight, white as a wish.

Then they were gone.

'I cannot stay,' she said. 'It is impossible.'

'I don't believe you.'

'It grows harder by the moment, George,' she said, another flash of feathers appearing under her hand. And then gone again.

George sat up further, though he had to steady himself. He was still extremely light-headed, no doubt what was causing him to see all these dreamlike things. The fire burning with impossible colours, greens and purples and blues. The night sky above them far too clear on this winter's night. The stars sharp enough to cut your hand if you touched them. And he was cold, freezing cold–

But also burning up, the fire seeming to rise from his injured feet and blaze through him, coursing a fresh rage into his blood, an anger large enough to–

'No,' Kumiko said, though not as if she was talking to him. 'You have done enough. You know that you have.'

George blinked at her. 'What?' But the burning was fading, the overwhelming feeling of eruption subsiding, disappearing into memory. He frowned. 'My eyes were green just then, weren't they?'

She leaned to him and kissed him, her own eyes still golden, even though he was between the fire and its reflection. 'I have found peace with you,' she said. 'A peace I was desperate for, a peace I hoped might have even lasted.' She looked back up at the fire. 'But clearly it cannot.'

'Please, Kumiko. Please don't–'

'I must go.' She took his hand in hers. 'I must be released. I must be forgiven. I can no longer ignore how I ache for it.'

'But I'm the *last* person who should be forgiving you, Kumiko. I slept with Rachel. I don't even know *why*–'

'It is not important.'

'It's the most important thing of all.'

He pulled away from her. Time seemed to have

dammed itself for a moment. How could this fire be blazing so heavily with no fire brigade swarming over the property? How could he no longer be freezing here on this grass? How could Kumiko be saying these things to him?

'I know you now,' George said. 'That's all I wanted. That's all I *ever* wanted—'

'You do not know me—'

'You are the lady.' He was firm when he said it, and calm. 'You are the crane. You are the crane I took the arrow from.'

She smiled at him, sadly. 'We are all the lady, George. And I am your crane and you are mine.' She sighed. 'And we are all the volcano. Stories shift, remember? They change depending on who is doing the telling.'

'Kumiko—'

'I misspoke before.' She gently wiped some ash from his cheek. 'You *do* know me, George, and I need you to forgive me for that knowledge. It has brought you into the wrong story, and it will consume you. So you must forgive me for it.' Then she repeated her words, full of sorrow, but also full of longing. 'Everyone needs forgiveness, my love. Everyone.'

George watched as she reached up to her chest and, with the nail of her index finger, drew a line down her skin. It opened like a fissure in the earth, widening until he could see her heart beating its life underneath it. She took George's hand in her own and guided it there.

'Kumiko, no,' George said, a great feeling of grief starting to press against his chest and throat.

'Take it,' she said. 'Take my heart. Free me.'

'Please don't ask me,' George said, his voice cracking, his own heart swiftly breaking. 'I can't. I love you.'

'It is the most loving thing one person can do for another, George. It is what makes life possible. It is what makes it *liveable*.'

Her heart beat there, glistening with blood, steam rising from it into the cold air.

'You'll leave,' George said.

'I have to leave either way. But I can leave either imprisoned or free. Please. Please do this for me.'

'Kumiko–'

But he found he had no further words. He also found that somehow he understood. She loved him, but even that couldn't keep her tied to this earth. She asked him to forgive her for his knowledge of her, and somehow that made sense, too. As long as it was *this* story of herself she could tell, not the one he demanded to know, all would have been well.

But he *had* demanded. He had been stupidly, stupidly greedy for knowledge of her. And he had found out.

He knew her.

But wasn't that what love really was, though? Knowledge?

Yes. And then again, no.

And now she was right, there was no choice. There was only how she would leave to be decided.

He held his hand above her chest, hesitating.

'Do not!' a voice boomed across the garden.

Rachel stood at the side gate, her eyes a green so bright George could see them even in shadow, almost as if she was burning from within. JP stood by her side, sucking his little thumb, wild-haired and startled, Wriggle blanket over one shoulder.

'Rachel?' George said. '*JP?*'

'*Grand-père?*' JP said around his thumb. 'Mama went– '

'You will not do this!' Rachel yelled, dragging JP forward so abruptly he called out in surprise. 'You will not!'

George tried to stand, but the burns made it impossible. Kumiko rose behind him, though, getting to her feet, the wound on her chest now gone (and he hadn't *really* seen it, had he? That had just been the smoke inhalation . . .). She stood strangely before Rachel, extending her arms, as if expecting a fight.

JP let go of Rachel's hand and he ran over to George. 'Mama went into the house!' he said, eyes wide.

'She *what*?' George said, looking back at the blaze, an inferno with no escape. He turned to Kumiko and shouted, 'Amanda's in there! Amanda's in the house!'

But the world had stopped.

The volcano approaches the lady across the field of battle, the world behind him burning. The lady still carries her wound, he sees, blood dripping from her outstretched wing. It gladdens him that she still suffers, but his heart breaks for it, too.

'You will not do this,' he says to her. 'It is not for you to decide. It is for me.'

'You know this is not true,' the lady says. 'You know that I have given the choice to him.' She frowns. 'No matter how you may have tried to persuade him otherwise.'

The volcano smirks. 'This body,' he says, referring to the form he wears. 'It fights back in surprising ways. I have been in it since before its birth, but it is . . .' He flashes a look, almost of admiration. 'Surprisingly strong.'

'Is it not time to free her?' the lady asks.

'Is it not time to free him?' the volcano replies.

The lady looks down at George, frozen there in a moment of time, his voice caught in a terrible plea, one she knows will need an answer.

'He loves me,' the lady says, knowing it to be true.

'That he does, I admit,' the volcano says, his eyes burning. 'Despite being given ample opportunity to destroy the love you returned. They are great destroyers, these creatures.'

'So speaks a volcano.'

'We build as well as destroy.'

'You could not come between us. Though you tried.'

'But it is inevitable, my lady. Once he knew you, he entered our story, and the harm I may do him here is so much easier to accomplish.'

'You think so, do you? You think it is that easy?'

'I have started already.' He gestures to the blaze behind him. 'This form and I have set fire to your world. To his. It is only the beginning of what we shall do to you, my lady.'

'Are you sure the fire is yours? Can you say that this is your destruction with the utmost certainty?'

The volcano frowns. 'I will not listen to your riddles, my lady.' He looks at George. 'This is not the way our story ends. You know this.'

'Stories do not end.'

'Ah, you are right, but you are also wrong. They end and they begin every moment. It is all about when you stop the telling.'

He has reached her now. They are closer than they have been for eternities, and they have also always been this close. With a shrug, the volcano steps out of Rachel's body, his green eyes gleaming, and she falls to the grass and out of the battlefield. The volcano reaches a hand to his chest and opens it, exposing his granite heart, beating in a field of molten lead.

The bullet still lodged within.

'I wish to end this, my lady,' he says, solemn now. 'The

victory is yours. I see now that it always was.' He kneels before her.

'There is no victory,' she says. 'I have made no triumph.'

'I only ask of you what you asked of him, my lady. Free me. Forgive me, at long last.'

'Then who will be left to forgive me? I do not think he will be able to let me go, in the end.'

'It is the eternal paradox, my lady. The only ones who can free us are the very ones who are too kind to do so.'

He leans his head back, closing his eyes, presenting his heart to her, beating in its crater.

'And now. Please.'

She could wait, she knows. She could stretch out their story forever, but she also knows she would never move from this moment, not until their story was finally told. The volcano is correct. There is only this end. There has only ever been this end.

And so the lady grieves, weeping larger than the heavens, filling oceans with her tears.

The volcano waits, silently.

It is, finally, an easy motion. She reaches into his chest and first removes the bullet of herself. As it leaves him, he groans in exquisite pain. She clenches her fist around it, and when she opens her hand again it is gone. He weeps for its loss. She brushes the tears from his eyes and waits for him to gather himself, returning the courtesy of patience he has just shown her.

'My lady,' he whispers.

Then she reaches into him again and, with a sigh of ancient grief, pierces his heart with her fingers. In her hand, it crumbles instantly to ash, blowing away in the wind.

'Thank you,' the volcano says, relief shedding from him in waves of fire and dying lava. 'Thank you, my lady.'

'Who will take my heart now?' she asks as he rises and solidifies, reaching for the horizon as he becomes, simply, a mountain.

Perhaps he makes to answer, but he is already stone.

Rachel collapsed to the ground at George's feet. He clutched JP tightly to him still and looked back up at Kumiko, who stood as if frozen. He shouted her name again. And once more.

Finally, she seemed to hear him. 'George?'

'Amanda's in the house! She went in to save us!'

Kumiko looked back to the raging fire. 'Yes,' she said. 'Yes, I understand.'

For a strange passing instant, she seemed to *blur*. George could think of no other word for it. He would look back on this moment, press at it, see if he could sense something more there that he could name, because it really did feel like it was *here* that the important thing happened. He didn't know, would *never* know, what it was, but this momentary blur of her, when she was somehow there and not there, seemed indelibly the moment where the story ended. It was a moment that should have lasted for an eternity, at least.

But it passed almost immediately. The blurring ceased as quickly as it had begun, though there was something different about her when she knelt down to him now, something less defined, like all boundaries had fallen from her.

'What just happened?' he asked. 'Something–'

'She is safe, George,' Kumiko said. 'Amanda is safe.'

'What? How can you know that? How can you–?'

But she was already raising her hand to the skin of her chest again, and once more she drew a line with her fingernail. The skin opened, the fissure parting to reveal–

'Kumiko, *no*,' George whispered. 'What have you done?'

She put her hands on his cheeks, the tears from her golden eyes streaming. 'You saved me once, George. And by loving me, you have done so again.'

She brought his lips to hers, and they kissed. It tasted to George of champagne and flight and flowers and the world being born and of the very first moment he laid eyes on her and she'd told him her name and it all burned bright as the raging sun, so bright he had to close his eyes.

When he opened them, she was gone.

'Why are you crying, *grand-père*?' JP asked, a moment and a lifetime later. Then he whispered fiercely, 'And why are you *naked*?'

'She's gone,' George couldn't stop himself from saying.

'Who?'

George wiped his eyes. 'The lady who was just here. She had to go.' He cleared his throat. 'And your *grand-père* is very, very sad about that.'

JP blinked. 'What lady?'

'Okay, this is weird,' Rachel said, sitting up on the grass, looking like she was trying to figure out where the hell she was. She saw the fire and looked astonished, then saw George and JP and looked even more astonished.

277

'Are you all right?' George asked.

Rachel seemed to take this question very seriously, even putting a hand to her chest as if to check her heart was still beating. 'You know what?' she said. 'I think I really am.' She got to her feet, swaying a little, but upright. 'I think I really am all right.' She laughed. And laughed again.

'*MAMAN!*' JP suddenly shouted, leaping from George and dashing towards a figure staggering, impossibly, out the back door of the burning kitchen.

(*Out the* locked *back door of the burning kitchen*, George had a second to think.)

Amanda.

Her face and clothes were black with smoke, the whites of her desperate eyes comically bright under the thick layer of soot. She was coughing into her fist but coming away seemingly unharmed from the wall of flame behind her. 'JP!' she cried and came running to meet him halfway across the lawn, picking him up in a fearsome hug. She staggered over to George. 'Dad!'

'I can't stand up,' he said. 'My feet–'

'Oh, *Dad*,' she said, pulling him into her sooty embrace as well.

George felt his last defences collapse as he was held by his daughter. 'She's gone,' he said. 'She's gone.'

'I know,' Amanda said, holding him tight. 'I know.'

'She's gone.'

And he felt the truth of it like a bullet in his heart.

Amanda held her father tight against her as he wept, JP making spitting sounds to clear the soot from his mouth where he'd kissed her, and Rachel standing there watching it all.

'Thank you,' Amanda whispered to her over George's sobbing head. Rachel gave her a questioning look. Amanda gestured to JP.

'Oh,' Rachel said, turning back to the fire and watching it burn. 'No problem.' And then as if to herself, 'No problem at all.'

There was a crash and a sudden *whooshing* sound as the fire brigade finally, *finally* started to aim hoses at the fire from the street side, a fine mist of steam drifting into the back garden. The flames at the top of the house immediately disappeared under the water, replaced by thicker smoke.

'We can't get around any more,' Amanda said, nodding to where the side of the house was now collapsing in burning slow motion onto the driveway. 'We'll have to wait back here until they put it out.'

'*Un feu*,' JP said again.

The *feu* had, by this point, been burning long enough to keep them all uncomfortably warm, so Amanda gently undraped the Wriggle blanket from around her son. 'Why don't we give this to *grand-père* for now?'

'He's *naked*,' JP said, happily.

She put the blanket around George's shoulders, covering him.

'It's all over,' he said.

'I know, Dad,' Amanda said, rubbing his back. 'I know.'

'She's gone.'

'I know.'

He looked up at her, quizzically. 'How do *you* know?'

But before she could answer, Rachel interrupted. 'Amanda?'

'Yeah?'

'Could you tell work I won't be in on Monday?'

'Are you *kidding* me–?'

'Just, please, Amanda. As a friend.'

Amanda coughed again, watching her. 'Yeah, okay, I guess.'

'In fact,' Rachel said, turning back to the fire, 'maybe you could tell them I'm not coming back at all.' She hugged her arms to herself, and it took Amanda a minute to wonder how it was that Rachel looked so different.

Then she realised it was because she looked *free*.

V.

No one needed her in a meeting for at least an hour, the corridor outside was momentarily clear, and she could probably get away with 'accidentally' locking her door for a few minutes, so what the hell? She hung the tile on the back wall of her new office, if only to see how it looked.

It looked . . . well, it looked *great*. How could it not? The mountain of words on the horizon, the bird of feathers in the night sky above, forever beyond each other's reach though – painfully, beautifully – forever in each other's sight. A picture of sadness, but also of peace and history. They could look upon love and be comforted.

At least, that's how Amanda liked to read it.

In the end, though, there was no possible way of keeping the tile here. It was far too valuable, for one thing. The market for the few surviving, already-sold tiles had skyrocketed since Kumiko's death, and even though Amanda's added to that scant total by one, the only other person she wanted to know of its existence was George, who she'd finally shown it to at Kumiko's wake. She'd been nervous, frightened even, that he'd react badly to her having kept it from him, but he'd said he understood completely, understood, too, her desire to keep it secret still.

It was something completely personal to the two of them, after all, a physical intersection where their lives crossed with Kumiko's. And who else, who *better* to share it with than George?

None better, she thought, looking at the tile for as long as she dared. *None better at all.*

She sighed and took it down, placing it carefully in the bag that Kumiko had given her and locking the whole thing in a drawer. She opened her office door again, sat down at her desk and looked out the window at her brand-new view.

It was only of a dirty canal, but it was a start.

Since the night of the fire all those weeks ago, Rachel had not only gone ahead and quit her job, but had vanished completely. Mei reported that Rachel's flat was abandoned, save for a couple of fistfuls of Rachel's clothes and a suitcase, with only the briefest calls to make her goodbyes to her putative best friend.

'What did she say?' Amanda had asked a very teary Mei over lunch.

'I just don't believe it.'

'I know, but what did she *say*?'

Mei shrugged, sadly. 'She said she had finally found clarity, and that she couldn't believe how much of her life she'd wasted. She said she wanted to see what was beyond the horizon, and that more than anything, she wished the same for me.'

'Well. That was nice.'

Mei's face screwed up in anguish. 'I know! Do you think she's had a traumatic head injury?'

Mei hadn't seemed very much surprised – or indeed to very much notice – that Felicity Hartford had gone straight to Amanda for promotion into Rachel's position, something Amanda felt almost certain Rachel had orchestrated. Well, if that was the case, then maybe accepting it in a certain spirit was required.

'I'm only doing this because you're a woman, you realise,' Felicity had said. 'We can't have fourteen male directors, apparently, despite the other candidates' manifest superiority to what I'll laughingly call your *abilities*–'

'I want my own office,' Amanda said.

Felicity looked as if Amanda had just stripped to her underpants. 'I beg your pardon?'

'Tom Shanahan has his own office. Eric Kirby has his own office. Billy Singh has his own–'

'And there are a larger number of directors who do *not*, Amanda. There will be no special treatment just because you–'

'You don't hate women.'

At this, Felicity Hartwell had blinked. 'My dear, what an *extraordinarily* odd thing to say.'

'You hate *everyone*. Which is fine with me, I'm not too much of a fan of everyone either, but you take it out on women because it's more fun, isn't it? We fight differently. More interestingly.'

'I'll thank you to change this line of–'

'So I'll make a deal with you. You give me my own office and I won't take you to a *very* uncomfortable tribunal where I'll present my recording of everything you've said so far.' She removed her phone from her pocket and showed Felicity that it was still recording every word.

'And, in return, let me just ask you this.'

Felicity's face hardened. 'You don't know who the fuck you're dealing with, Missy–'

'What do you think of the Animals In War Memorial on Park Lane?'

'I could eat a nothing like you for *breakfast*–'

'What do think of it?' Amanda snapped, feeling the nerves in her stomach twang from the tension of this gambit.

But still appearing fairly calm. Which was nice.

Felicity sat back, exasperated. She made a disgusted *fine* sound. 'I think it's a ludicrous embarrassment,' she said, 'put up there by rich morons with–'

'–more money than sense,' Amanda finished. 'It's an abomination to equate a Golden Retriever with a soldier. Not that I have anything against Golden Retrievers, mind, but they've even got a fucking *pigeon* up there. And the whole Memorial is bigger than the one for all of *Australia*, so clearly we care more as a country about pigeons than we do Australians.'

'Well,' Felicity said, still astonished, 'can you blame us?' And then, seeing Amanda's face, she gave a surprised smile. 'Oh,' she said. 'I see.'

Every woman around the office had been remarking lately how much easier – if not exactly *easy* – Felicity was to work with these days. And all it took was lunch once a week with Amanda. It had been an effort to evict a complaining Tom Shanahan from his office, but Felicity had done it and had even left an ANZAC card as a good-luck note on Amanda's desk this morning. Scarily, Amanda was beginning to think they were becoming rather good friends.

*   *   *

'I'd suggest a plant,' her new assistant Jason said, stepping into the doorway. He was very, very cute in a tiresomely fascist sort of way that stirred not one single ember in Amanda's fires. A feeling which seemed mutual; he wasn't more than five years younger than her, but had clearly cast her into the sexual outer darkness anyway.

Who cared? The outer darkness had *way* more interesting people in it.

'Plants are for the emotionally pliable,' she said, looking down, as if returning to work she hadn't actually started.

'Noted,' he said. 'Papers for you.'

He put them on the far corner of her desk. And waited. She slowly looked back up in the tried-and-tested manner of a boss indicating an employee's presence was unwelcome.

'Mei Lo asked if she could schedule a meeting,' he said.

'. . . and?'

'I said I didn't believe you had any openings on your schedule, that I didn't believe there'd be any openings all week, and that I didn't believe you cared for meetings anyway.' Jason grinned, his green eyes glinting. 'She said she couldn't believe it.'

Amanda had already been looking forward to finding ways to fire him within the month, but for now she just sat back in her chair and said, 'Do you love anyone, Jason?'

He looked surprised for a moment before the smirk returned. 'Careful there, Miss Duncan. You could have a sexual harassment suit on your hands.'

'*Love*, Jason. Not sex. Which depressingly explains so very much about you. And I know you were being sarcastic, but it's Mrs Laurent. I never officially changed it back.'

He looked impatient now. 'Will that be all, *Mrs Laurent*?'

'You didn't answer my question.'

'Because it's none of your damn business.'

She tapped her lower lip with a pen, an implement Felicity Hartford was trying to ban from the office, ostensibly because all work should have been entirely electronic by now, but really to see how irritated everyone would get. It had been Amanda's idea. 'You see, Jason,' she said, 'it's okay to think people are idiots. Because on the whole, they really, really are. But not everyone. And that's where the mistake is easy to make.'

'Amanda–'

'*Mrs Laurent*. You end up hating so many people that without even noticing, you start to hate *everyone*. Including yourself. But that's the trick, you see? The trick that makes everything survivable. You've got to love somebody.'

'Oh, please–'

'It doesn't have to be everybody, because that would make you an idiot, too. But it has to be someone.'

'I really have to–'

'I, for instance, love my son, my father, my mother, my stepfather, and my ex-husband. Which hurts a little, but there you go. I also loved my father's fiancée, but she died, and that hurts, too. But that's the risk of loving anyone.' She leaned forward. 'I also love my friends, who at this moment consist entirely of the scariest human resources woman in the history of scary human resources women, and Mei Lo. Now, she's not much, I'll give you that, but she's mine. And if you *ever* talk that way about her again, I'll pound your no-doubt-entirely-waxed little ass into the carpet so hard you'll walk funny for the rest of your life.'

'You can't talk to me like–'

'Just did.' She smiled. 'Get out. Go find someone to love.'

He left with an angry sneer. Maybe she wouldn't fire him. It might be more fun to keep him around and make his life miserable.

Oh, God, she thought. *I'm going to be a terrible boss.* But she didn't stop smiling.

She opened her drawer and took another look at the tile. It moved her, still, with the same fresh strength as the first time, when Kumiko had handed it to her in the park as a most impossible gift.

Kumiko, she thought, and put her hand on her stomach. Her still flat stomach. Her non-pregnant stomach.

Because of all the important things that could have been discussed, *that* had been the first thing Kumiko had said to her in the midst of the inferno.

The smoke, when Amanda entered George's house, was a monster. It was like drowning, if the water you were drowning in was not just boiling hot, but also alive and aggressive and angry, water that wanted to murder you, water that was, in fact, smoke from a raging fire and like nothing but itself.

'GEORGE!' she had cried, but didn't get much past the first G before the coughing took over. Two steps beyond the front door and she was choking, a third and a fourth and she was as good as blind. And now that she was inside the house, she didn't know what to do. This was all ridiculously heroic, but she was scared out of her mind, not only for her father and Kumiko, but for JP, back there without her. She couldn't leave him, but she couldn't leave her father either, not to die like this, not to burn up in agony. The indecision was paralysing and was seconds away from being deadly.

And then the ceiling caved in.

A beam struck her on the head and knocked her to the ground. The world disappeared into blackness.

Some time later, a time which would forever be a hole in her life, she felt a hand take hers to get her to rise. It was gentle but firm, and there was no resisting it. She rose unsteadily, her head hurting, her body covered in soot and smoke but, remarkably, without burns, despite the fire raging around her.

She looked up into Kumiko's eyes.

They were golden. And sad beyond the birth of the world itself.

Kumiko reached out and touched Amanda's stomach. 'You are not,' she said. 'I am sorry.'

'I know,' Amanda replied, surprised. 'I took a test.'

The fire and smoke roared, but seemed to do so slowly now, in a way that allowed them this pocket within the maelstrom.

'You thought it would give you a connection,' Kumiko said.

'I did,' Amanda said, simply, sadly. 'I really did.'

'You already have connections. So many.'

'Not so many.'

'But enough.'

Kumiko turned to the body on the floor. Amanda looked with her, knowing who it was, who it must be, but feeling for a moment that it was maybe not so important. The fire still raged but was receding somehow, blurring into a slow smear.

Kumiko reached a finger over to Amanda's chest and

drew a line down the jumper she'd thrown on. The fabric parted, as did Amanda's skin and tissue beneath it. Her heart was exposed to the light.

It was no longer beating.

'Oh,' Amanda said. 'Damn.'

Kumiko didn't respond, just reached in and grasped it, holding it in her palm.

'This is a ritual of forgiveness,' she said, closing her fingers over Amanda's heart. A light came from behind them, and when she opened her hand again the heart was gone. 'And so is this.' Kumiko made the same line on her own chest, her flesh opening to reveal her beating, shining, golden heart. She reached in and removed it, bringing it slowly towards the darkened opening on Amanda's chest.

Amanda caught her by the wrist. 'I can't. *You* can't.'

'And yet we will. Take my heart. Forgive it. By doing so, you forgive us both. And there is nothing more that either of us needs.'

She moved her hand again, Amanda no longer resisting. Kumiko placed her heart in Amanda's chest, its golden light shining even through the scar as Kumiko closed the wound.

'But you,' Amanda said, looking into Kumiko's eyes.

'It is done,' Kumiko said. 'At last. I am free.'

They left the body on the hallway floor, but it was different now. Different, finally and forever. Kumiko guided Amanda through the flames, through the blazing walls of the sitting room and into the kitchen, though nothing seemed to burn them and the smoke was only the remotest concern.

They reached the edge of the fire, where a door opened, out into the world beyond.

'You need only step through,' Kumiko said in her ear. 'You need only say yes.'

Amanda took a Kleenex from the box on her desk and wiped her eyes.

She'd found herself, somehow, stumbling out the back door of the house, dirty but unscathed. She had been groggy, from whatever had happened with the falling ceiling and the impossible smoke that stuck to her insides, but then she'd seen JP and it was as if she'd woken up again. She'd seen her father laid out on the grass. She'd seen the still-inexplicable presence of Rachel. And she'd breathed in the brutally cold but welcomely clear air of the night.

The fire brigade reached them not too long after, and a fire chief told them with great dignity that a badly burnt body had been found on the floor of the hallway, killed by the collapsing ceiling or possibly thrown there from the room above.

Amanda and George wept together then. And had done so more than once since.

'Are you all right?' said a voice.

Amanda carefully closed the desk drawer and, through tears, smiled at Mei. 'Yeah. Just . . . memories, you know?'

Mei nodded gravely. 'How's the new office?'

'Quiet. Which I like. You'll have your own soon. Now that I'm having lunch with power once a week.'

Mei nodded again. 'Can tonight start an hour later than we'd planned? My babysitter has a clarinet lesson and I'm still not sure of my outfit.'

JP was in France with his father – even though the homesick Skype sessions had convinced Henri a week was long enough, JP was also simultaneously having the time of his life; a second visit was already planned for summer – so Amanda and Mei had decided to give clubbing a go. Neither of them was particularly enthusiastic, but if it ended early with wine and TV, what was the harm?

'Of course,' Amanda said, 'but no backing out. You still have to go.'

'So do you,' Mei said and took her leave. Amanda really did have work to do, after all, quite a lot of it in this new capacity. It turned out Rachel had been world-beatingly good at her job, and that was something Amanda was going to have to try to live up to.

But first, she took out her phone.

Though she'd shared the tile, she felt like she couldn't tell George about the hallucination in the fire, how she must have been knocked senseless by the collapsing ceiling, and how that strange vision, or whatever it was, had kept her walking through the flames and out the back of the house, saving her life in the most improbable fashion. But as she tapped the most called number in her directory, she put a hand to her chest.

No, there was no scar there. No, she didn't believe a golden heart was beating inside. And no, she didn't really believe the ghost of Kumiko had guided her to safety.

But maybe she did believe that when death had entered the room, her brain had conjured up Kumiko to calm her fears, to make everything all right, to allow her the chance to live.

Which was something. Which was more than something.

And so she wanted to speak to her father now, not about anything in particular, just hear his voice, sadder, older, even in these few weeks. She wanted to hear him say her name. She wanted to say *his*. And she wanted them both to say Kumiko's.

She listened as it rang and rang. With his still-recovering feet, he sometimes took a while to struggle his phone out of the desk or his bag or wherever he'd left it this time. She didn't mind. She would wait.

She wanted to speak to him, yet again, of love. And of forgiveness. And of hearts, broken and beating.

There was a click as the call connected.

'Sweetheart!' her father said, and the welcome in his voice was food to feed a thousand.

Realistically, he knew he'd never make another cutting. He hadn't tried yet, of course, it was too soon, *way* too soon. He couldn't even look at a second-hand book these days without feeling as if a hole had been punched through his heart. But even if that passed – and he knew, intellectually, that it would, but knowing a thing and feeling a thing were entirely different and probably the cause of all his species' problems – he couldn't picture himself ever again instinctively making a cut here, a cut there, unsure what the image was until it was made.

The cuttings had been nothing without her anyway, of course. Just silly little trifles that signified not much.

But with her. Oh, with her . . .

He sighed deeply.

And felt a gentle pat on his back. 'I know, George,' Mehmet said, passing him on the way to the front of the shop. 'Let it out.'

Mehmet was busy training his replacement, a tiny girl from Ghana called Nadine, just about to start university.

In drama. Mehmet had hired her. George couldn't find it in himself to mind.

The shop was back to its previous unspectacular-but-decent business, though there was still the occasional desperate drop-in, coming in with hope on their faces and sometimes tears in their eyes. They left disappointed, but only partially, as George always let them look at what the world thought was the last unsold tile, the dragon and the crane, still watching over him from the wall above his desk, even though it was now worth considerably more than the shop itself.

After the funeral, Amanda had told him of the tile Kumiko had given her, the peaceful, strangely quiet, strangely *final* one that seemed the end of a story just as the dragon and the crane seemed the start of one. In a back room of Clare's home, away from the few other mourners at the wake, she had shown it to him and he understood everything. He accepted no apologies from her for keeping it secret because none were needed. He would have done the same and agreed readily that the secret remain, for now, something they could share together, just the two of them.

'I love you,' he'd told her, 'so much my heart breaks. So much that the thought of you having any unhappiness–'

'I know, Dad,' she'd said. 'And knowing helps. It really does.'

The wake had turned out to be an afternoon of revelation, as Mehmet had also pulled him aside and confessed, honestly distraught, to being a better actor than George had ever given him credit for. Mehmet, of course, had been the one who helped early word along, starting rumours, secretly sending details to the right sites, even inviting most of the awful people who'd come to the party, hoping to turn it all into a runaway phenomenon.

'*Someone* had to, George,' he'd cried. 'You just *won't* take care of yourself. And aren't you glad you have that money now?'

George hadn't even been angry. Mehmet, in his own way, had done it all out of love, and there was no way George was ever going to reject anything done out of love for him from now on. He'd even allowed Mehmet to open an official site about the tiles, despite there being nothing left to sell, because at least it was a kind of memorial to her.

He looked up at the dragon and crane now. Like his daughter, he kept his tile as close to him as he dared, bringing it with him every morning and taking it away every night, not just for safety but because he wasn't ready to be parted from it just yet, even for a day.

Because she was gone, and this was all he had left.

He'd been unable to return the confession to Amanda and tell her what had happened – or what he *thought* had happened – in the back garden. The way Kumiko had asked him to remove her heart, the way she had blurred, the way she had kissed him before vanishing. Indeed, it seemed, the way she hadn't been there at all. JP could only remember Rachel bringing him around the house to where his *grand-père* was lying alone on the grass.

What JP hadn't seen was Kumiko.

Because Kumiko, of course, had died in the fire, a fire the investigators seemed to think was 'probably' caused by an unattended candle, a fire he and his daughter had only survived by some miracle.

Some miracle, he thought, tapping his fingers on the cutting pad on his desk. If Kumiko hadn't brought him to the frost-covered grass, how had he got there? Some miracle, indeed.

He still dreamed, but they were different from before, heavily featuring Amanda's tile. They were dreams of a quiet, sleeping mountain and the constellation that flew over it in the shape of a great bird. They were dreams where he couldn't touch her, couldn't speak to her, only see her cast against the sky, eternal and out of reach. They were dreams of the end of the story.

But they weren't exactly unhappy either. There was grief, of course, he often woke from them weeping, but he felt a sense of peace there, too, as if a battle longer than time had finally ended. There was calm. There was release. And if that release didn't involve George, then at least it involved Kumiko. As the days stretched on from her actual death, he became more and more a remote observer in the dreams, too. An observer in a story that was turning into a history with every passing day.

He looked up.

An observer. An observer who told a different version of the story. An observer who would tell the story differently than *she* might. Not in any adversarial way, just someone who might tell it in his own words . . .

'Mr Duncan?' a high, melodically accented voice asked him, breaking in on his train of thought. A train he would come back to. Oh, yes.

'What can I do for you, Nadine?'

'I was wondering,' she said bashfully, 'if I could maybe come in late on Thursday?'

'How late?'

She winced. 'Four hours?'

298

George saw Mehmet swinging back and forth on the stool at the front counter. 'Is it for an audition?'

Nadine looked amazed. 'Wow! How'd you guess?'

'Intuition.'

'Oh, let her go, George,' Mehmet said. 'You should hear her sing. The voice of a dazed trumpet.'

'And that's good?'

'Like you wouldn't believe.'

'I could sing for you,' Nadine volunteered.

'Not right now,' George said. 'And yes, you can come in late.'

'Thank you, Mr Duncan.' There was some whispered gesturing from Mehmet. 'Oh,' she said, 'we found this. Mehmet said to give it to you.'

She held out her really quite astonishingly tiny hand – George had a sudden vision of her having huge success in a racial- and gender-blind cast of *Oliver!* – and handed George what, at first, looked like a small slip of paper.

He took it from her.

And nearly tumbled from his chair.

'It had fallen behind your work desk there,' Mehmet said. 'It's so small, it probably just got blown there by a puff of air.'

'We wouldn't have found it at all if I hadn't dropped that box of paperclips, remember?' Nadine said.

George nodded slowly. It had been a big industrial box containing ten thousand, ordered by mistake and dropped in spectacular fashion by the tiny hands of Nadine, spreading them to every corner of the shop. George expected to be finding paperclips until his retirement.

But these were just passing thoughts, floating idly by as he stared at what they'd given him.

It was a crane, cut from a single piece of paper, just

like the one he'd cut on that very first day, the one now stuck to the tile above his head.

But that was impossible.

'That's impossible,' he said.

'Not impossible,' Nadine said. 'Just a mess.'

'No, no,' George said. 'I only made one. Kumiko took it. She used it in a tile. *That* tile. Up there.'

'I've seen you doing those cuttings,' Mehmet said. 'You make about a million of each until you get one right.' He shrugged. 'I don't really think that's how *artists* do it, but it seemed to work for you.'

'I didn't with this one, though,' George whispered, his eyes still on it. He really didn't. He was sure of it. Especially because this one looked *nothing* like a goose.

He began to cry again, softly but beyond his control. Nadine, used to it after working here a week, put a reassuring hand on his shoulder. 'My father died when I was twelve,' she said. 'It doesn't really get better. But it changes.'

'I know,' George said, nodding, still holding the crane, so small, so perfect. It was cut from a wordless page, the stretch of it pure and white.

A wordless page, George thought.

'We were right to give it to you, yes?' Mehmet said, coming over. 'We found it, and I know that since you lost pretty much everything in the fire . . .'

This was only inaccurate in that *pretty much* didn't quite cover it. He hadn't even had any clothes left, having escaped not wearing a single stitch. Worse was that he'd lost his old phone, too, which contained every picture he had of her. And there was nothing left in *her* flat because she had only, that very day, moved the last of her belongings into his house.

There had been nothing but her body, which they had buried, a practice the undertaker had gently tried to dissuade him as American and impractical, but having found no family of Kumiko's to contradict him, he'd bought her a new dress, a new overcoat and the closest thing he could find to the suitcase she always carried to bury alongside her, though her burns were so bad he hadn't been allowed to see her body. He had no idea if the clothes were even used.

He hadn't even been able to kiss her goodbye.

Except, of course, he had.

'I'll say it again, George,' Mehmet said, as George continued to quietly cry. 'Take more time off. We can run this place while your feet heal properly and you look for a new house and you know, whatever, *grieve.*'

George considered this for a moment. There was wisdom in it. Clare and Hank had, with unhesitating kindness, picked him up from the hospital and deposited him immediately into a far-too-swanky room in Hank's hotel. Though George had an embarrassing pot of money in the bank from all the tile sales, they had refused to entertain a penny of it, seeming genuine when they told him to stay as long as he needed. He assumed they wanted to keep an eye on him, and for once he found he didn't really mind that they did.

The nights had been hard, of course, but the days even harder until he started coming back to the shop, limping in on his crutches, much to Mehmet's scandalised surprise. Mehmet, despite his moaning, had done extremely well on his own, and George had no doubt he could keep it up until things became easier, particularly as Mehmet didn't actually seem in that much of a hurry to leave.

But no.

'No,' George said now, wiping his eyes. 'I need to do something. I can't just sit around all day. I need to keep busy.'

The bell on the door chimed and a customer came in.

'Go help him,' George said. 'I'll be fine.'

Mehmet and Nadine watched him a moment more, then left to deal with what looked like another order for stag-night t-shirts. George could already hear Mehmet setting a terrible customer-service example for Nadine, but he let it slide.

Because he was staring at the crane again.

It was impossible. He had never cut this. Had he? No. It was too *skilled*, for one thing. Too sharp, too tight, too much of a crane. It was impossible that it was his. It was impossible that it was *here*.

But a live crane in his back garden with an arrow through its wing was also impossible. So, too, was the almost accidental creation of the tiles and their inexplicable success. In fact, Kumiko in her every particular was frankly impossible.

Did he really believe she was the crane? Did he really believe she had come to him and brought him happiness until he grew too greedy to know more of her? Did he really believe what happened in the garden after the fire? That *that* was the way their story ended?

If any story even had an ending. If every ending wasn't just someone else's beginning.

But no, of course, he didn't believe it.

And yes, beyond anything he'd ever felt, he knew it to be true.

A crane, made of paper. Made of *blank* paper.

If this was a message, he thought he knew what that message might be.

*   *   *

He placed the crane down carefully, making sure not to crimp it. He'd put it under glass later, protect it with the utmost care, but for now an urgency had taken over. He would no longer make cuttings, no, that was clear, but this crane, however it had arrived, had been cut from a page without words. A page without a story on it.

A page waiting to be filled.

He grabbed the first pad of paper to hand. It was a freebie from a supplier and had their name and details across the top of each leaf. He threw it out. He kept looking, opening drawers, rolling his chair to the supply cupboards. There was an unimaginable stock of paper in this shop, from ultra-cheap scrap to stuff you could probably sleep on, but to his increasing disbelief, no proper notebooks, not even lined ones like students used in class. Actually, he thought, did they even still do that or did they just take in laptops or smartphones and record everything?

'Mehmet!' he barked, surprising them and the customer. 'Where the hell are all the notebooks?'

'I have one,' Nadine said. She pulled her rucksack from a cupboard under the counter, took out a green notebook and handed it to him. 'I was going to use it for class.'

'A-ha!' George said, triumphantly. 'You *do* still do that!'

'What are you going on about?' Mehmet said, a little alarmed, as if he'd been waiting for George to crack and was less prepared than he'd hoped to be now that the moment had finally arrived.

'Nothing, nothing,' George said, opening to the fresh front page. Nadine hadn't even started using it yet. No matter, he'd buy her a new one. 'Thank you,' he said to her and 'Sorry' to the customer and used his body language to indicate he was to be left alone now.

He took out a pen, held his hand over the page and hesitated a moment.

He wrote, *In her dreams, she flies.*

He felt his heart surge, as if a golden light was flowing from it.

There was a distant sound from somewhere, and a less occupied part of his mind told him a phone was ringing. He ignored it.

Because this was it. Yes. He knew it somehow, knew it as he'd known every right thing about her. *This* is where he would remember her. *This* is where she would live. He would tell her story. Not her whole story, of course, but the story of him and her, the story *he* knew, which were the only stories anyone could ever really tell. It would be only a glimpse, from one set of eyes.

But that would be why it was right, too.

In her dreams, she flies, he read again.

And he smiled. Yes, that was the beginning. *A* beginning, rather, but one that would do just fine.

He brought down his pen to write some more.

'George, *seriously*,' Mehmet said, holding out the loudly ringing phone to him.

George blinked uncomprehendingly for a moment. But of course the phone was *his*. The new one from the phone company after the fire. No frills, a ringtone he didn't recognise, and carrying all of three contacts. His daughter, his ex-wife and his shop's main assistant.

Amanda, the small screen read.

'Thank you,' he said, taking it.

His daughter was calling him, as she had at least twice a day since the fire. But yes, this was right, too. He was eager to talk to her. More than eager, *excited,* excited to speak again of Kumiko, excited to talk about the book he had realised, just this moment, he was going to write.

More than anything, he was excited to speak of the time that had just passed. The time of his life he would look back at with pain, yes, but also with amazement. Amanda was the only one who would understand, and though he could never tell her the whole truth, maybe he could write it in a book.

And maybe that way the Kumiko he knew would live on and on and on.

Yes, he thought, tears in his eyes again.

Yes.

He answered the phone to his daughter with a broken but joyous heart, ready to speak with her of astonishment and wonder.

Notes & Acknowledgements

The original story of the crane wife – which is not at all, by the way, the story Kumiko tells with her 32 tiles – is a Japanese folk tale I've known my whole life, having first heard it as a wee blond five-year-old from my kindergarten teacher in Hawaii. She was called Mrs Nishimoto, and I loved her with the deranged abandon that only a five-year-old can achieve. A wonderful person and teacher, she told stories in a way that lingered, like the one of a certain crane rescued from injury.

I'm not the only one who's been inspired by it. The greatest band in the world, The Decemberists, use it on a brilliant album also called *The Crane Wife*. The epigraph to this novel is taken from the song 'The Crane Wife 1&2', written by Colin Meloy. If you haven't yet bought music by The Decemberists, I worry for you.

Shortly after giving George his pastime of cutting shapes from books, I was directed (by a perfectly innocent party) to the extraordinary work of Su Blackwell (www.sublackwell.co.uk). To compare what George does to what Su does is to compare fingerpaints to

Kandinsky. No overlap is intended, but seriously, check her out.

My thanks to Francis Bickmore, Jamie Byng and all the rather excellent folk at Canongate. Thanks to my agent, Michelle Kass, who doesn't blink no matter what left-field project I turn in. Also to Andrew Mills, Alex Holley and Denise Johnstone-Burt.

A Note on the Type

Sabon was designed by the typographer Jan Tschichold (1902–1974) in the 1960s. It embodies Tschichold's return to classical, serif typefaces, and is based on type designed by Claude Garamond in the fifteenth century.

Created in 1996 by Zuzana Licko, the much loved Mrs Eaves is a revival of the English typeface Baskerville, designed in 1757 by John Baskerville, and named after Sarah Eaves, Baskerville's wife. Friendly, elegant and with an updated twist, in Licko's own words Mrs Eaves 'makes the reader slow down a bit and contemplate the message'.